Officer Needs Assistance . . . Again

OFFICER NEEDS
ASSISTANCE
....AGAIN

DON PARKER

CAROLDON BOOKS
PENSACOLA, FLORIDA

Other Books By Don Parker

YOU'RE UNDER ARREST - I'M NOT KIDDING
The Trials and Tribulations Of A Reluctant Cop

Caroldon Books
1075 Farmington Road
Pensacola, Florida 32504

ISBN 0-9620073-2-3

ACKOWLEDGEMENTS

I am grateful to the many folks who helped make this book possible. Carolyn Cooper, again, came through like the true professional she is and handled all the complex production details I am incapable of doing myself. Frances Dunham did a beautiful job on the cover and with the overall design of the book. If anyone needs a great print broker and a wonderfully-talented artist, give me a call. I highly recommend both.

Working with Joy and Linda at Type Designs is one of life's great pleasures and the photograph by John Blackie is one reason the cover turned out so nice. His work made Frances' job easier when it came time to do the watercolor.

No matter how well a book is written, it is only as good as the people who print it and R.R. Donnelley & Sons have been superb. Although I am one of the world's smallest publishers, they have always treated me like I am one of the biggest.

I also aknowledge the tremendous contribution made by the readers of my books. The support and encouragement, the letters, cards and phone calls (and, of course, the book orders), have convinced me I am on the right track. As long as you keep buying, I will keep writing.

And to my wife, Carol, I owe a tremendous debt of gratitude. Her optimism, her determination and her love are what really make my books possible.

DEDICATION

This book is dedicated to those men and women who are out there, right now; enforcing the law, doing their jobs, preserving the peace. Unsung heroes who will get little recognition and not much glory, but still do what has to be done.

I did that job for 18 years. I'm glad I just write about it now.

CONTENTS

INTRODUCTION

In the course of my wanderings around the country, giving speeches, doing talk shows and promoting my books, I meet dozens of interesting people. Depending on where I am at the time (airplane, banquet hall or restroom) my identity as a retired cop usually becomes known. When we have gotten past the fact I spent 18 years wearing a badge and gun, I frequently hear something like, "I wouldn't do your job for a million dollars!"

Sometimes I try to convince them the job is not all high-speed chases and shootouts, but I rarely succeed. Unless they have been in the biz themselves, they tend to believe what they see on television or in the movies.

Once I spent several hours on an airplane, sitting next to a retired military test pilot. When I told him I had been a cop, he, too, came out with the old, "I'd never do your job for a million bucks," line.

"But why?" I asked. "The benefits are nice, the work is usually not strenuous and the endless variety certainly keep things interesting."

When I finished he just shook his head and said flatly, "Your job is too dangerous."

Dangerous? This was a man who had risked his life flying some of the most perilous airplanes to ever get off the ground. As he freely acknowledged, he had lost plenty of friends in fatal air crashes, and yet, he thought my job was too dangerous. Amazing.

Now, I don't for one minute, deny that law enforcement does entail a certain amount of risk. I have been injured several times, I have been shot at, I have lost good friends, killed in the line of duty, and I was involved in a fatal shooting of my own in 1977 (an escaping prisoner tried to shoot me, but I shot him first).

But it's not dangerous all the time. Sometimes it gets boring. Very boring. Once, I was part of a team that staked out a drug store because we had information; good, solid information, that it would be burglarized. We knew who was going to do it, we knew what they were driving, we knew what they planned to steal; we just didn't know when. For eight nights, from midnight until daylight, we sat and sweated in the humid darkness, waiting and watching. Nothing ever happened.

But that's the way it goes, sometimes. It's an unpredictable business, enforcing the law. Many of our decorated heroes were simply in the right place at the right time, doing what they were paid to do. And it's certainly not for everyone. Although it can be pretty monotonous at times, there is always that constant note of tension, droning away in the recesses of our minds. We know the next car we stop may contain only a snotty teenager... or a heavily-armed, psycho-killer. We know it, but we prefer not to dwell on it.

Sometimes, though, that droning note of tension begins to increase in volume and may even make it impossible for a law enforcement officer to continue doing his or her job. For whatever reason, memories of near misses and close calls combine with fears of what might be, and some find they can't take it any longer. If they are lucky, they simply choose another career. But some try to keep on keeping on, attempting to bury the growing fear, or blot it out. When the blotting out involves the overuse of alcohol or other chemicals; broken marriages, wrecked careers, and even death, may be the result.

I have seen friends die from the effects of unrelieved job-related stress, and they died in the line of duty just as surely as if they had been cut down by a bullet.

So, it's not all fun and games and I want to make sure that you, the reader, understands this distinction. In this book, I am not seeking to portray law enforcement as some sort of wacky, fun-filled, laugh-a-minute, type of life. But neither is it all whining bullets and screeching tires.

What I write about are the day-to-day incidents that happen to all cops. I get letters from officers all over the country, thanking me for trying to show this side of the profession, and assuring me that my stories remind them of incidents they have experienced.

Talk show hosts often ask, perhaps with just a touch of skepticism, if my stories are REALLY true. Interestingly enough, other cops never ask that question. They know the stories are true because many have been through incidents that equal or surpass mine. They also know there is no need to invent stories; this is one job in which fact is often stranger than fiction.

In the course of this book, I have certainly altered a few facts and changed a few names, usually because I wanted to protect someone's privacy. For instance, all the names of bad guys have been changed and I deliberately disguised their identities.

In a few places, I made it difficult to recognize some of the law enforcement officers who appear in a less than flattering light because I could see no good reason to embarrass them all over again, about incidents that occurred 10 or 15 years ago. Besides, they will recognize themselves instantly.

But keep this in mind: the person who appears in the least flattering light of all, is me. Not that I set out to be anything other than Supercop, you understand, it just turned out that way.

Of course I feel compelled to share these stories with you, even if my actions were less than heroic. All I can do is tell you what happened. Perhaps it has something to do with my view of life. I am constantly bemused by the humor that surrounds me. The late Pat Lloyd, a newspaper columnist, once told me, "Don, you think funny."

She may be right, but I certainly don't do it on purpose. I don't even think of myself as a writer, I'm just a story-teller, using the medium of print to chronicle the human experience. I also don't think of myself as a humorist. The people and the incidents I write about supply the humor, I just put it down on paper.

Like the two old drunks who engaged in a lengthy, but non-fatal shootout... with single-shot shotguns. Or "Bad Luck Brown," a small-time crook who must have stayed up nights thinking of new ways to get himself arrested. Or the dope dealers who managed to lose six pounds of cocaine, but arranged to buy it back for only $10,000, a real bargain... except the "sellers" were undercover cops.

Stories like these don't have to be improved; they almost tell themselves.

1

Just Doing My Job

It had been busy for a weekday afternoon, and I had already answered five calls, none of them particularly interesting. Now I was sitting at the far edge of the shopping center's parking lot, finishing up the report about a theft of a tape player from a car belonging to a very upset teenager. I glanced at my watch. It was almost 7:30 P.M. I decided to go ahead and buy the cat food now, while I was still checked out on the call, rather than wait until later. It might get so busy I'd forget about it, and I didn't relish the idea of explaining to my wife I had forgotten. Again.

The parking lot was crowded, so I left my marked cruiser car where it was, parked on the side of the building, in the loading zone, right in front of the "no parking" sign.

The pet food was at the end of aisle 14, in the far corner of the store. I didn't bother with a shopping cart, since I was only going to get half a dozen cans. Just as I reached for the tuna surprise, a voice hissed in my ear, "My god, you've got to do something!"

I whirled, badly startled. A store clerk in a bright green smock was standing beside me. "I beg your pardon?" I said.

"There's two men up front," she whispered, pointing with a shaking finger. "They have guns. I think they're robbers."

1

"Robbers?" I said stupidly, not truly registering the meaning of her words.

She nodded, her eyes round with terror.

Robbers. With guns. And I was a cop. With a gun. I finally got the old brain in gear. "Can you get to a phone without their seeing you?" I asked her. This was back in the days before we had portable radios, so I couldn't call for help myself.

"I... I think so," she gulped, "There's a phone in the produce office."

I handed her one of my business cards. "Call the sheriff's department," I said quietly. "Tell them I'm in the store and to send help." I put my hand on her shoulder. "Can you remember that?"

She nodded and scuttled off.

Now it was time to earn my pay. I slipped along the aisle, pulling my .38, crouching for a quick peek. I saw a skinny, pimply-faced guy in a long raincoat about 30 feet away. He was holding a sawed-off shotgun on the manager, who was on his knees, frantically spinning the dial on the safe.

Further to the left was another man, short and stocky, pulling handfuls of bills from a cash register, a revolver in one hand. Here and there, frightened customers were frozen in place, not daring to move. I sat back.

What should I do? Probably the best choice was to wait for help, but that might take some time. I had the element of surprise and if there were only two of them, I had a chance. Undoubtedly there was a getaway car and driver outside, but that shouldn't be a factor.

But before I did anything, I needed to be sure there were really only two men in the store. I leaned forward again. The scene was essentially unchanged, except the manager had the safe open and was filling a shopping bag with cash. I leaned a little more, looking for more bad guys.

"CRASH!" A large jar of pickles, dislodged by my arm, smashed on the floor.

2

The guy with the shotgun whirled, looking straight at me. "Cops, Robbie!" he yelled, and fired. There was a tremendous blast, something hot burned into my right arm, and I was pelted with fragments of glass and bits of pulverized pickles. Shoppers screamed and ducked for cover.

Although stunned by the noise, I got my gun up and snapped off a quick shot. Quick but lucky. It caught him just above the eye. There was a spray of blood and brains, and he went down in his tracks.

The entire sequence, from the time the pickle jar broke to the death of the robber, could not have taken three seconds. I was so intent on this first guy, I momentarily ignored his buddy. "BLAM!" A bullet whined by my ear, thumping into a plastic tub of mustard. I looked up and saw the guy with the revolver preparing to shoot again. I headed for the floor as a second shot ripped through the thin shelves above me. The gunman ducked behind the check-out counter.

I stayed low, breathing hard, considering the situation. He couldn't get out the front door, because I would have a clear shot at him. His only hope was to run for the back, which meant he would have to cross the open space between the check-out counters and the shelves.

My right arm was killing me. I looked down and was amazed to see the sleeve soaked with blood. Two small holes told me I had stopped some shotgun pellets.

But I'm left-handed, and I could still shoot. "There's no place to go, buddy," I yelled. "Half the sheriff's department will be here in a minute; why don't you give it up?"

There was a muffled curse, then, "BLAM-BLAM," as he fired at the sound of my voice. More jars of condiments bit the dust. Some poor clerk was going to have quite a mess to clean up. Finally, there came the sound I had been waiting for, sirens in the distance. "Here they come," I shouted. "It's all over now." I got ready, sighting toward the open space, using a roll of paper towels as a gun rest.

Right on schedule, the guy scrambled to his feet, getting off another quick shot, but I ignored it. I led him slightly and squeezed the trigger. The .38 bucked in my hand, and the shot caught him square in the chest, spinning him around. Desperately, he tried to bring his gun up, but I shot him again, and he collapsed, the revolver skidding across the floor. I waited a few seconds, then walked over and kicked the gun further down the aisle, but I could tell he wouldn't be using it again. Whimpers and sobs were coming from the still terrified customers as they began to get up off the floor, but it didn't look as though anyone else was hurt.

There was still the possibility a getaway vehicle was waiting, so I ran out the door, a little awkwardly, dizzy from the pain. Sprinting down the sidewalk, I tried to think where the car could be. I hadn't seen any suspicious vehicles on the side where I was parked or in front of the store. It had to be toward the other end.

And there it was. A rusted van, facing me, parked in the fire lane about 25 yards from the store. All I could see of the driver was shaggy hair and dark sunglasses, but I just knew he was the one. And he knew that I knew, because as I approached, he slammed the van in gear and accelerated, right at me.

For some reason, I wasn't concerned. I had three bullets left, and I was determined to stop this guy. I aimed at his torso, clearly visible through the large windshield, slowly squeezing the trigger...

"Tiffany!" a woman screamed. I glanced to the right. A toddler had broken away from her mother; laughing and giggling, oblivious to the peril, she was now directly in front of the onrushing van. Even if I blew the driver's head right off his body, the speeding vehicle would still hit the kid.

I was beside the child in two steps, snatching her out of the way while trying to line up on the driver again, but the vehicle was too close. I threw myself to the side, shooting blindly toward the van, trying to get out of the way. I didn't make it.

4

Suddenly, I was airborne. Although I felt no pain, I knew the van had hit me, and I had to be hurt bad. Time seemed to slow, and I floated through the air, distinctly hearing the wind whistling past my ears. I expected the landing was going to be a lot rougher than the takeoff, but I never landed. The blackness closed in on me before I hit the ground, and sound faded away.

I woke two days later in the intensive care ward. Although unable to move because of the various splints, casts, and bandages, I had survived. As it turned out, my last shot had punctured one of the tires on the van, causing it to crash into a line of shopping carts, and my buddies quickly captured the remaining bad guy.

They made quite a fuss over me there in the hospital, lots of TV, radio, and newspaper interviews. Even the governor got into the act, flying in to help the sheriff award me the department's medal of valor, the medal of courage with oak leaves, and the gold life saving award. Additionally, he gave me the first ever "Governor's Award," a special medal the state legislature came up with as a result of my actions at the supermarket.

In my weakened condition I was exhausted by the ceremony but I still loved it when little Tiffany gave me a kiss in front of all the cameras. I soon drifted off to sleep, happy I had saved her life.

I hope you enjoyed this story, but there's something you should know: It never happened. I made the whole thing up. Every word of it. The entire tale is pure fabrication. There was no supermarket robbery, no shootout, no van, no Tiffany, and no medals.

I know, I know, you're irritated because I misled you, but wasn't it exciting? Didn't it set your heart to pounding as you imagined yourself in my shoes, facing death but emerging triumphant? I felt the same way as I was writing it.

But, why would I do such a thing? Several reasons. I figure you probably wanted to hear about dramatic shootouts and bodies falling like bowling pins, and I hate to disappoint. Also, I always thought that someday, I'd actually be a mega-hero, but I never was. Oh, I had my share of close calls, but nothing like this.

And so it is with most cops. We go through our careers ready, even willing, to be heroes, but it doesn't happen. In fact, there are plenty of cops who retire without ever firing their guns.

The stories I tell are stories you will probably never see on television or in the movies. I didn't plan it that way. When I first became a cop, I always knew I'd eventually write a book about my exploits, and I planned to fill it with heroic tales, much like what you just read. Unfortunately, none of my exploits measured up to my expectations. But you can still learn a lot about what it's really like to be a cop. My stories may not have been as exciting as I'd hoped, and I may never have won any medals, but I think they'll give you a look at our profession you wouldn't get any other way...unless you have been a cop yourself.

2

Hysterical Woman

I couldn't take my eyes off her hands. They seemed to be disconnected from her body, fluttering and flapping like injured birds, first one in the air than the other. "I was so scared," she said with a nervous laugh, "but I felt like he wouldn't hurt me if I did what he said, so I gave him the money." A flittering hand made a vague gesture toward the check-out counter. "I doubt if there was $35 dollars in the register." She sighed, "He was just a kid."

"Can you describe the gun?" I asked.

She nodded vigorously. "Oh, yes. I'll never forget it." She made a circle with her thumb and index finger. "The end of it was this big."

I suppressed a smile. Hysterical exaggeration was common with crime victims, and this was the first time this convenience store clerk had ever been robbed. "Do you know anything about guns, ma'am?"

"No, but my husband has a .22 he keeps in his truck. She shuddered as her hands darted, fingers twisting and flexing. "I'm terrified of guns."

"Did this gun look like your husband's .22?"

"Oh, no. The end was much bigger."

This time I did smile. "Ma'am, it's easy to make a mistake

and exaggerate when you're scared.''

"I'm not exaggerating,'' she said with some heat. ''I know what I saw. You could have dropped a silver dollar in the end of that gun.''

I took the rest of the information I needed, thanked her for her cooperation and left the store. Except for the fluttering hands, she seemed relatively calm, and the description she gave of the robber had been quite detailed. It would all be useful, except for the part about the gun. I chuckled: boy, that was something. I had heard about robbery victims saying guns looked as big as cannons, but this was the first time I had actually talked with one.

I met the lieutenant later and gave him the report. I related the story of the robber's gun, and we both had a good laugh. "I don't know, Parker. You might have said the same thing if someone had stuck a gun in your face.''

"Aw, come on, boss, I'd never say that, even if it was against my nose. That was just a typical hysterical woman, going to pieces because someone pointed a gun at her.'' I went back to work, hoping I might spot our young robber, but I didn't.

The next night a citizen reported someone acting suspicious around another convenience store and called the cops. One of our investigators drove by and spotted the suspect lurking in the shadows. He took up a concealed position and directed several other deputies into the area. When everyone was set, they moved in and captured the guy.

He turned out to be a 16 year-old with a gun in his pocket, preparing to rob the store. He was no hard case, and after being assured he would spend the rest of his natural life in prison unless he cooperated, quickly admitted what he was planning. Not only that, he copped out to the armed robbery I had worked the night before, as well.

The weapon was interesting. The kid said he took it from his father's gun collection. It was an old flare pistol from World War II. It was unloaded, which was just as well. The flare might have killed someone if it had hit them at close range.

The end of the barrel was huge. It must have been an inch-and-a-half across. It was so big you could have dropped a silver dollar in it...just as the woman had told me.

3

Easy Come, Easy Go

The door opened even before I knocked, and I beheld a very angry homeowner. "I'll tell you one damn thing," he said, "if I coulda got to my gun, you wouldn't need to look for no prowler."

"I take it you're the one who called?"

"Yeah, I called." He stepped outside and closed the door. He was shirtless and barefooted and still zipping his pants. "I don't want to upset my wife any more than I have to." He shook his head, "It like to scared her plumb to death."

"Tell me what happened," I said, opening my notebook.

"Well, we was in the bed, uh...watching television, and I heard a noise outside the window."

I made some notes. "What kind of noise?"

He thought for a moment, rubbing his chin. "It was kind of a scratching noise." He turned and pointed to a window. "Right there it was, at that window."

"What did you do?"

"I didn't do nothing at first. I figured it was a cat or something," he said, "but my wife, she said she seen a face."

"Did you see it, too?"

"Not right then, but she was undernea...I mean, she was looking at the window, and she kept whispering to me someone was out there, so I jumped up and opened the blinds." His voice rose. "I come face-to-face with a goddamn peeping tom, right outside my window."

"Can you describe him?"

"Yeah, he was a young kid." He concentrated. "As I recollect, he had brown hair." He looked at me. "That help?"

It certainly wasn't going to win any awards for thorough descriptions, but it would have to do. "All right. I'm going to drive around the neighborhood and see if I can find him."

He pounded a fist into his hand. "Damn! I wish I coulda got to my gun."

As I stepped off the porch, I noticed a woolly little dog of uncertain lineage, bouncing around in front of the man's pickup. The animal had been there when I pulled up and, although doing plenty of yapping, didn't seem aggressive. Still, I gave him a wide berth, not wanting to put him to the test.

As I walked to my car, he charged at my heels, barking, barking, barking, then danced back toward the truck, sniffing busily. "Your dog seems pretty excited," I said to the guy.

"Hell, it ain't my dog." He followed me down the driveway, and the dog left the side of the truck, yapping at his feet. "Get away from me, you little shit-ass!" he yelled, kicking at him.

The yapping fur-ball scrambled back to the truck.

I laughed. "He acts like he lives here."

"He don't live here," the man said, scowling. "I never seen him before."

The dog's behavior was strange. I'm no expert, but this particular dog seemed to have laid claim to the pickup. I got into my cruiser and cranked up. "I'll be back in a few minutes," I said, turning on the headlights. The dog was now lying down as close to the pickup as he could get, squinting from the lights. I wondered what the attraction was. I put the car in gear, started backwards...and then I spotted him.

With the headlights shining on the driveway, I could see a tousled head of brown hair by the left rear wheel. Someone was

11

under the truck! I slammed the car into park and jumped out. "Someone's under your truck," I yelled at the complainant, who came running. "Watch the other side." I bent down and grabbed a handful of hair and shirt and pulled.

Out popped a very scared young boy, perhaps 12 or 13. His little dog capered around us, yelping with joy, unaware he had tipped me off. "All right, kid," I said sternly, "what were you doing under the truck?"

"Let me at him!" the homeowner, bellowed, trying to get past me. "I'll teach him to peep in on folks."

I pushed him back while maintaining a grip on the kid. "Just calm down, I've got him now." We started toward my cruiser car. "I'll turn him over to juvenile authorities," I told him.

We reached the back door of my cruiser, and it was then I made a tiny error, one of those little mistakes that seem inconsequential at the time but actually have long-term effects. I had a grip on the kid with my right hand and my flashlight was in my left, but that made it a little difficult to open the door. I probably should have let the irate complainant handle the door, but I didn't really want him that close to the boy. He was still steaming, and I was afraid he would smack him if he got the chance.

So I opened the door. With my right hand. Letting go of the kid to do so. The creak of the door hinge was accompanied by the sound of running sneakered feet, fading rapidly.

"He's getting away!" the man shouted. And so he was. By the time I turned to look, the boy was a block ahead of me and accelerating, the little dog yapping like mad and matching him step for step. I took off after the fleeing kid, feeling like I was running in slow motion, handcuffs and extra bullets rattling and clinking, holster flapping against my leg, my heavy military style shoes thudding on the pavement,

I quickly discovered a terrified adolescent was capable of speeds that could have put him in the Olympics. I chugged along behind, chest heaving, lungs burning, trying to keep him in sight.

12

The lad crossed a yard, and sailed over several fences. I made it over the first one but not the second, falling heavily. I staggered to my feet and resumed the chase, crashing into garbage cans, dodging clotheslines, hoping I wouldn't meet any large, unfriendly dogs.

We were back on the street now, and I was only seconds away from a fatal heart attack. I tried a last-ditch bluff. "You better...stop, or I'll....shoot." I croaked. From somewhere far ahead, a high-pitched juvenile voice floated back to me, "Don't shoot," it said faintly.

I was done. I could go no farther. I leaned against a tree, retching and blowing, convinced my heart was going to explode. Around me were the sounds of the night, the wind sighing softly through the pine trees, crickets chirping, the distant sound of traffic out on the highway. There were, however, no sounds of running steps or the barking of the little dog.

The kid was gone.

I tottered back to my car, surprised to see how far I had run. It took a long time to make the trip, but of course, I was walking very slowly. The homeowner was waiting. "Did you catch him?"

I shook my head, wondering if he thought I had him in my shirt pocket. "No, he got away."

"Couldn't get a shot at him?"

"I was just trying to bluff him," I said. The guy looked disappointed. I drove around for a while, hoping to spot the boy, but I never saw him again.

It was the only time I ever lost a prisoner.

4

Aren't They Wonderful?

One of the more endearing traits of children is their tendency to say what's on their mind, regardless of the impact it may have on their listeners. Never forget it was a child who told the emperor he had no clothes. Like all parents, I have been victimized by the statements of my children, but rarely has it occurred in so public a manner as the day I met my wife and son for lunch in a local restaurant.

The place was crowded when I arrived, and I had trouble finding a parking place. I finally spotted one and waited patiently for an elderly woman to back out of the space. She was doing fine until she realized the vehicle waiting for her was a police car and she stopped abruptly, halfway out of the parking space, effectively blocking the entire lane. I motioned for her to continue moving, trying to make her realize I was just a motorist attempting to park and not on an emergency call. She stared at me anxiously, twisting her hands on the steering wheel, totally intimidated by my looming presence. Finally, she understood she was holding me up and resumed backing, quickly. Too quickly. She accelerated and the car stalled. Panicky, she jammed it in park, the car jolting to a stop. For long seconds the starter ground away until, at last, the engine caught. Moving more cautiously now, she headed out of the parking lot, no doubt weak with relief.

I parked and went inside. I am used to this type of reaction, particularly from true law-abiding citizens, and I was also used to the reaction I got when I stepped into the restaurant. Just about every head in the place turned toward me, my green and gray uniform standing out like a beacon. Just as quickly, they all turned away, embarrassed by their reaction. Two heads didn't turn away, my wife and son. "Over here, Daddy," Christopher yelled, waving frantically, his piercing five-year-old voice slicing through the restaurant chatter.

I slid into the booth, "How ya doing, big boy?".

"Oh, fine. Daddy, can I have a large order of French fries?"

I was ready for that one. "If you eat all your fries, we'll get you some more, okay?" I glanced at my wife, and she nodded approvingly. This parenting stuff was a snap.

"Busy today?" she asked.

"Oh, not too bad. The lieutenant approved my vacation request."

She started to speak, but Christopher interrupted. "Daddy, can I...."

"Son, it's rude to interrupt. Your mother was trying to say something."

"I'm sorry." He lowered his head.

"I started to say that we could leave town a day early if I you want," she said. "I'm taking the whole week off."

That was good news. "Yeah, let's do that. That way we can beat some of the crowds." We were going to Disney World, and the middle of the week was supposed to be less crowded. I turned back to Christopher, who had been fidgeting impatiently. "Now, what do you want?"

"Can I go to the bathroom?"

"Of course. You know where it is?"

"Uh huh." He was already sliding out of his seat.

"And wash your hands," his mother said.

"Okay," he said over his shoulder, heading for the restrooms.

15

The waitress brought me coffee and took our orders.

We discussed the upcoming vacation and possible side trips, trying to estimate expenses. I had just taken a sip of coffee when Christopher emerged from the bathroom. "DADDY!" he yelled, the obvious urgency in his voice instantly stilling all conversation in the restaurant. "Yes, son?" I said calmly, as all eyes shifted to me.

He held up his hands. "There's no paper towels," he shrieked, "and I peed on my hands." In the instant of stunned silence, several things happened. My wife covered her face, mine flamed scarlet, and a wave of laughter washed over me as I left the booth and crossed the floor to assist this little boy with the big mouth.

I helped him wash his hands, and as we left the bathroom, the still chuckling patrons burst into applause.

5

Slow-Motion Shootout

The two old men had been living on the same street for years and had been enemies most of that time. The original argument began when one accused the other of stealing his woman. This was essentially true, but the lady in question soon discovered she had traded one abusive drunk for another and moved in with someone else. There had been bad blood between the two ever since, and they were constantly fighting. While this didn't resolve anything, it did keep the neighbors entertained.

This particular day they started out early, cursing each other when they passed on the street. Although it was barely ten in the morning, they both were staggering from wine. The dispute turned into a shoving match. The loser, who ended up on the ground, beaned the winner with a rock, and that really did it.

Bellowing with rage, the wounded man lurched into his house and emerged with a shotgun. His opponent, realizing his peril, ran for his own shotgun, and now both men were armed. A crescendo of threats and curses erupted, and finally, one of them pulled the trigger. The resulting explosion sent the neighbors running for cover and peppered the nearby houses with pellets.

This first shot missed its intended victim, and he fired back. His aim was better, and the first gunman yelped as several pellets penetrated his leg. At this point, the shooting stopped because both men were using single-shot weapons and they had to reload. One had an ancient bolt action 20 gauge and the other, a little .410. Both were using light loads, so the lethal range was necessarily limited.

It must have been an amusing sight as the two drunks fumbled with their guns, dropping shells in the street, trying to get reloaded. Gunman number two won the contest and snapped off a quick shot, neatly removing the left earlobe of his opponent. With blood streaming down his neck, the wounded man retaliated, peppering his adversary's backside, exposed as he turned to reload.

And so it went for the next 15 minutes. Both men roaring with rage and pain, leaking blood from dozens of minor wounds, stumbling and ducking, reloading and firing. Slowly. At one point, witnesses said, one of the shooters went back inside for a fresh supply of ammunition, while the other waited in the street, shouting curses.

Of course, the neighbors called the cops, and we hurried to the scene. And what a scene it was. Both men were down now, covered with blood, still trying to reload so they could shoot again. We took their weapons, loaded both victims into the same ambulance and sent them to the county hospital. The paramedics told us later they had their hands full trying to keep the two old warriors from duking it out in the ambulance.

I checked on them after they had been undressed and cleaned up, and it looked as though someone had worked them over with ice picks. X-rays revealed dozens of tiny pellets in each of them, but none of the wounds were serious. One man did catch a pellet in the eye, but it missed the cornea and was safely removed. This same guy also had a pellet in his tongue. Evidently, he had his mouth open when he was hit. When we shook out their clothing, shotgun pellets rolled all over the floor.

Neither one wanted to press charges, insisting it was a personal matter, but since we were dealing with reasonably serious felonies, we arrested them. They both pled guilty and received probation. Both recovered from their various wounds, and as far as I know, they are still feuding, but without their shotguns. We confiscated those.

6

First Ticket

"Parker, see me in my office before you leave."

I felt a prickle of apprehension. "Okay, Lieutenant," I said, ignoring the catcalls, jeers, and dire warnings from my fellow deputies. I couldn't help wondering what this was about. With less than six weeks under my belt, I was still a rookie, and little talks with the shift commander were common. So far, they had been more educational than correctional. I hoped this would prove to be the case today.

A few minutes later I stepped into his office. He smiled. That was a good sign. "Come in, and close the door." That was a bad sign. "Have a seat." I did. "Well, how's everything going?"

"Oh, pretty good. I'm still learning and the other guys have really helped me."

"You've done well so far, and I think you're going to be a fine deputy sheriff."

"Thanks." When would he get to the point?

He leaned back in his chair. "There is one thing, though."
Uh-oh.

He pulled a monthly activity report from the pile of papers on his desk and handed it to me. It was my own. "I want you to look at your activity report." I studied it carefully, already familiar with the data since I had just turned it in a week ago.

I had worked over a hundred calls during the month, made eight felony arrests and 21 misdemeanor arrests, recovered two stolen vehicles, and taken one day of compensatory time. It was a pretty active month. "See anything unusual?" he asked. I shook my head.

His finger traced a column titled 'Traffic Citations'. "What do you see here?"

The column was empty. While all the other columns were filled with numbers, this one was a pristine white track, splitting the page from top to bottom like a smooth highway through a tangled wood. "Uh, I see nothing."

"Right. Why is that?"

"I didn't write any tickets last month."

"And how many tickets have you written since you finished your field training?" he asked patiently.

"You mean all together?"

He nodded.

I gulped, "Actually, none."

He let this admission hover in the air for a few moments. Then he said, "You didn't have any trouble writing tickets when you were in training; what's the problem now?"

"I just get busy, I guess. I forget to write them."

He consulted a small notebook. "You certainly haven't forgotten how to make traffic stops, though. Let's see...on Tuesday you made six stops, on Wednesday you made eight, on Thursday four, and tonight you made five." He closed the book and looked at me. "23 traffic stops this week and not one ticket. How come?"

I licked my lips and tried for a small joke, "Just lazy, I guess."

He wasn't having any of that. "You're not lazy. You work as hard as anyone on the shift, and you answered the second highest number of calls last month."

"I'll try to do better."

"I hope so. Traffic enforcement is an important part of our job. You can't drive around out there for eight hours without

21

a traffic violator damn near running over you, even if you are in a marked cruiser car. If you're having a problem, just let me know.''

''No problem. I just have to remember to write tickets, that's all.'' That concluded our discussion, and I left.

But there was a problem. I was afraid to write tickets. It was that simple. It was one thing to write tickets under the watchful eye of an experienced field training officer who told me what to write on each line, but it was quite another to do it myself. It was an unreasoning fear. Traffic citation phobia. I was probably the only cop in the entire world who was afraid to write tickets.

It was of course, a self-created syndrome. Even with assistance, I was constantly making mistakes. Little things, like forgetting to write the driver's license number, or the nature of the violation, or the address of the violator. Once I failed to write in the court information and let the guy drive off. My training officer made me call the man at home and give him the necessary facts over the phone. I thought I would die from embarrassment.

Is it any wonder I didn't like to write tickets?

But that was going to change. I resolved to do better, starting tomorrow. The first driver who committed a traffic violation in my presence was going to get a ticket, and that was that.

The next day I spent a few minutes studying the traffic citations. I looked at each line, mentally filling them in. I could feel little pangs of nervousness in my stomach, but I ignored them. Fear of failure, that's all this phobia was. Giving it a name made me feel better. Two hours into the shift, I got my opportunity. Proceeding north on a four-lane highway, I approached a traffic signal which was red. I slowed, but the light turned green. As I accelerated, a car heading east ran the red light, right in front of me, and turned south. I made a U-turn and flipped on the blue lights. The driver, a young woman, obediently pulled to the side of the road.

I got out and approached the car. ''May I see your driver's license, please?''

She fumbled in her purse with shaking hands. "What did I do, officer?"

I pointed toward the traffic signal behind us. "You ran that red light."

Her lower lip began to quiver, and a tear trickled down one cheek. "But I didn't mean to." She handed me her license.

I studied her name and checked the expiration date, feeling the old nervousness beginning to grow, toying with the idea of letting her go with just a warning. She was only 19, she hadn't given me any trouble; maybe I'd write the next violator. I was about to give her license back when the lieutenant pulled up behind my car. "Wait here," I said.

"Yes, sir," she said piteously. I walked back to see what my boss wanted, ostentatiously holding my citation book.

"Everything all right?" he asked.

"Oh, yeah. Fine." I nodded toward the woman, "She ran the red light right in front of me. She's lucky she didn't cause a wreck."

He laughed. "I told you they'd run over you if you didn't watch out."

I held up my citation book. "I was just about to write her up."

He nodded. "That's what you get paid for." He drove off, and I returned to the car, steeling myself for the upcoming ordeal.

"Ma'am, I'm going to have to write you a ticket for running that red light."

Her eyes widened, "Oh, God. I was afraid you'd say that." She was really crying now. "My father will kill me."

I pretended I was not affected, but her loud wails were distracting. I opened my citation book and began to copy the information off her license. It was slow going. Not only were the lines very close together, but I am left-handed. Because I turn my hand almost all the way around when I write, I kept bumping into the metal clamp at the top of the book, which slowed my progress even more.

The sobbing woman got out of the car and paced up and down

beside me, wringing her hands, saying, "What am I going to do?" over and over. Too inexperienced to truly take charge of the situation, I let this bizarre scene continue, grinding away at the citation, ignoring the curious stares of passing motorists.

I was using the hood of her car, and her license was on the fender next to my ticket book. In those days, Florida driver's licenses were flimsy pieces of paper and not the heavily laminated little cards they are today. The car was still running, and the air conditioner was on. The compressor kicked in, the engine revved up, and the paper driver's license suddenly disappeared, sucked under the hood.

One second it was there and the next, gone, pulled into the space between the fender and hood. Shocked, I looked at the spot where the license had been. It was definitely gone. The woman noticed my consternation. "What's wrong?"

I pointed helplessly, "The car ate your license."

She burst into even louder sobs. "Now what am I going to do?" she cried, lifting her arms toward the sky.

I ran to the front of the car, fumbled with the release, then raised the hood. The roar of the engine was much louder, and a wave of heat washed over me. The engine was leaking oil, and the woman's license was plastered to the side of the block. I carefully peeled it off. It was soaked through.

I closed the hood and turned to her. She had watched my every move, bawling loudly, tears streaming from her eyes. I handed her the oily remains. "Thank you," she said between sobs, making me feel like a total jerk.

I finally completed writing the citation, had her sign it, explained how to pay the fine, and left. She never stopped crying.

It was two weeks before I worked up the courage to write another ticket.

7

And Justice For All

Working in the booking area of the county jail will never be considered fun. Listening to the screaming and yelling, enduring the constant abuse, and wrestling with violent drunks does not make for a pleasant job.

This particular night was a busy one, and the city police had endeared themselves to the correction officers by bringing them a particularly obnoxious drunk. A chunky, disheveled blond with eye-watering body odor, Sandra had been making everyone miserable since her arrival.

The holding cells were well-populated this night, the smooth concrete floors and walls perfect resonators for the shouting, cursing, babbling, sobbing occupants. As the young officer removed the cuffs, Sandra added to the din. "I'M GOING TO SUE," she shrieked. "YOU HAD NO RIGHT TO HANDCUFF ME!"

A female correction officer intervened, "Let's go, sweetie," she said, taking her by the arm.

"Don't touch me, you bitch!" Sandra snarled, jerking away. That was a mistake. The victor of thousands of bouts with unruly drunks, the correction officer pulled her off balance and expertly spun her arm behind her back, raising her up on her toes. Sandra's howls echoed from the walls, and the CO marched her down the hall. A moment later she was locked inside a cell, free to curse and scream as much as she wanted.

And this she proceeded to do. For the next two hours. Not content to just yell, she found she could make a really satisfying noise by shaking the door to her cell, and soon the entire booking area reverberated from the monotonous crashing. Finally, the sergeant had had enough. She walked back to the cell and glared at the still raging Sandra. "If you don't leave that cell door alone," she said, "we'll put you in a straitjacket, and you won't be able to move at all."

Sandra saw the iron determination in the eyes of the sergeant and wisely decided to give the door a rest. Truth to tell, she was a little tired. It had been a long and exhausting night, and she must have put away at least three six-packs. She yawned hugely and curled up on the bench. Maybe she would rest for just a little while.

Now, correction officers are not by nature cruel people, but these correction officers had just been through a harrowing night, made doubly unpleasant by the non-stop noise of Miss Sandra. These factors might help explain the sergeant's reaction when she was informed their tormentor was now, finally, fast asleep.

"Asleep?" the sergeant shouted. She walked briskly to the cell and gazed upon the horizontal form with a grim expression. Grabbing the barred door, she shook it violently.

The horrible, clattering crashing brought Sandra bolt upright, eyes round with terror, heart hammering. "Are you all right, dear?" the sergeant asked sweetly. Sandra nodded dumbly, her pulse still racing. "Okay, honey, you call me if you need anything." Sandra lay down again, quivering from the fright, but there was still enough alcohol left in her bloodstream to propel her into quick unconsciousness once more.

She had hardly drifted off when the same hellish clatter jolted her awake again. This time it was a male officer. "The sergeant wants to know if you're all right."

"Fine, fine," she mumbled, lying down again.

A few minutes later, the cycle repeated itself as yet a third officer brought her back to painful consciousness. By this time, she was a wreck, her whole body desperately yearning for sleep.

It was not to be. For the rest of the shift, the officers took turns rattling that cell door, gleefully inflicting a tiny bit of retribution.

It probably wasn't right, but it was justice.

8

Raffle Tickets - Part 1

I slid into my chair just as Lieutenant Swinney started to read the day's announcements. "Glad you could make it, Deputy Parker."

"Sorry, Boss. The President called again. I couldn't get him off the phone. Another mission to save the free world, but I told him I had to work."

"Don't you hate it when he begs?" Charlie Suarez said.

"I don't mind the begging as much as the sobbing and the weeping."

"Why don't you become a communist, Parker?" my buddy David Hightower asked. "That would give us the best chance of winning the cold war."

I was going to reply when Lieutenant Swinney rudely interrupted our amusing banter. "You clowns can jack your jaws on your own time. Right now I've got work to do."

"You tell him, Daddy," Lee Wasdin said from the back of the room.

"That includes you, Wasdin."

"Yes, sir."

Swinney finished making the work assignments, and we trooped outside to our cars. Hightower sidled up to me and said quietly, "Watch it, Rush is selling raffle tickets again."

I felt a chill. I was bound to be his target, since I was coming back to work after two days off on compensatory time. "Did you buy any?" I asked. Hightower fumbled in his shirt pocket and extracted two light-blue ticket stubs.

Suarez overheard the conversation. "Everyone buys raffle tickets from Rush." He patted his own shirt pocket for emphasis.

But I had made up my mind. "I don't." They both stopped and stared at me. I kept walking.

"Everyone buys raffle tickets from Rush," Suarez repeated.

"Not me," I said over my shoulder.

"Everyone!"

I shook my head and got into my cruiser car. Suarez started in on me again from across the parking lot. "Everyone buys raffle tickets...." I closed the door, ending the conversation. I spent a moment arranging my stuff on the front seat, checking the radio and the emergency equipment, and locking the shotgun in the vertical dash mount. A horn beeped behind me, and I glanced in the mirror. Hightower was pointing toward the administration building. The portly figure of Deputy Sheriff Don Rush was hurrying in my direction, and he was clutching a book of light-blue raffle tickets. There was no time to waste. I started the car and quickly backed the length of the parking lot, leaving the panting Rush behind. I made a quick turn and hurtled out the gate. Safe. At least for now.

My precipitous retreat hadn't been without incident, however. In my haste, I hadn't closed my briefcase and reports, paper clips, sunglasses, and extra pens were scattered across the floorboards and seat. I pulled into a parking lot to clean up the mess. I was working busily and did not notice the other cruiser car until it came up beside me. I caught my breath, but it was only Hightower, waving his ticket stubs at me, grinning evilly. I sped off, more determined than ever not to succumb.

I knew I would have my work cut out for me. Deputy Don Rush was the best seller of raffle tickets I had ever known. His dogged persistence and single-minded determination were nothing short of amazing. He was a member of the Fraternal Order of Eagles and constantly winning sales awards and contests. The local chapter had recently constructed a new building, financed, no doubt, with the proceeds of Rush's raffle ticket sales.

It's been said that the only real secret to success in sales is to talk to lots of people, and Don did just this. He was totally unselfconscious and would try to sell a ticket to anyone: other deputies, waitresses, people he met on calls, people he had arrested, even the sheriff.

I had bought my share of tickets over the years, and although I didn't like it, I grudgingly admitted that he was fair. He never tried to sell anyone more than two tickets, and he was always unfailingly polite. He was not an articulate person but, like all good sales people, believed passionately in his product. It also didn't matter if the prize was half a frozen cow, a new shotgun, a riding lawn mower, a kid's bike, or a weekend trip to New Orleans; Rush went into raptures over each one, and there wasn't an objection he couldn't handle.

"This bike is perfect for any kid," he'd say enthusiastically. "I even brought some tickets for my own grandbabies."

"Is it a boy's bike or a girl's bike?"

"It's either. Old Jake over at Cycle World is a friend of mine, and he said we could have whatever we wanted."

"Well, we don't have any kids of our own."

"No problem. Jake'll let you have an adult bike so you can give it to your wife as a surprise gift. She'll love it!'

"But Don, we're thinking about getting a divorce, and I'd hate to have a nice bike like that tied up in a messy property fight."

"That's all right. Jake'll give you a gift certificate, and you can pick it up after the divorce is final."

"Actually, I'm dying of a dread disease. The doctor says I've only got a few months left, and if I ride a bike it'll cut my remaining time in half."

"That's too bad. At least, you can have the satisfaction of knowing you donated the bike to one of the needy kids we help

30

at Christmas.''

There was no way to beat him.

Of course, part of it was Rush's irritating tendency to act as if the sale of the tickets was an understood thing. The only question in his mind, was how many did you want. He never said, ''Do you want to buy a raffle ticket?''; it was always, ''I've got your tickets,'' or ''The tickets just came in,'' or ''I've got change of a five if you need it.'' All the sheep would then go bleating to the slaughter, pulling out their money, buying their tickets, placidly accepting their fate.

Well, not me. At least, not anymore. This was one time I was absolutely and positively not going to buy a ticket. I said it out loud: ''I'm not going to buy a raffle ticket.'' I felt much better.

It was a busy shift, and I spent the time jumping from call to call. Some hours later, I was standing at the booking counter in the jail, completing the paperwork on a drunk driver, when someone plucked at my sleeve. It was Rush. ''I've got your tickets for you,'' he said. ''You can win a side of beef.''

I shook my head. ''I don't want to buy any raffle tickets.''

He nodded agreeably, extending two pale blue slips of paper, ''They're only a dollar.''

I folded my arms, refusing the proffered tickets. ''No, thanks, Don, I really don't want any.''

''The money goes to benefit the building fund.''

I turned back to my paperwork, ''I'm not going to buy any tickets.''

Rush fell silent, but I could hear his adenoidal breathing behind me. ''Wheeze-wheeze, wheeze-wheeze.''

I started on the probable cause statement, explaining my reasons for stopping this particular drunk.

''Wheeze-wheeze, wheeze-wheeze.''

I completed the probable cause and started in on the breathalyzer forms. The man had run a healthy .16, way over the legal limit of .10. It was a solid case.

''Wheeze-wheeze, wheeze-wheeze.''

31

The radio room called. "How much longer are you going to be tied up, 109?" the dispatcher asked.

"About ten minutes."

"10-4, I'm holding a report of a theft," she said.

"I'll be out of here as quick as I can."

"Wheeze-wheeze, wheeze-wheeze."

I finally finished and started paper-clipping the reports together.

"Wheeze-wheeze, wheeze-wheeze."

It was driving me crazy! I whirled around. "Look, Don, I don't want to buy any raffle tickets. That's my decision, and I'm not going to change my mind."

He nodded solemnly, "You don't have to pay me now."

"You think I can't afford it?" I said hotly, pulling out a wad of bills. "I've got the money; I just don't feel like spending it on stupid raffle tickets."

"The drawing is this Saturday."

I threw the reports in the proper baskets, gathered up my notebook, and headed for my car. Rush was right beside me. I waited for the correction officer at the control panel to open the heavy, barred door. We stood in silence, and I refused to look at him.

"Wheeze-wheeze, wheeze-wheeze."

The outer door opened, and I strode across the parking lot, Rush almost trotting to keep up. I got in my cruiser car as he stood beside the front fender, not saying anything. By now, I was beginning to feel a little guilty. But only a little. "Look, Don, I said. I know the Eagles do a lot of good in our community, but this is still a free country, and I have the right not to buy raffle tickets if I don't want to, and right now, I don't want to."

Rush stood quietly, listening intently, nodding, always nodding, clutching the tickets. "You know, that beef comes already cut and wrapped."

That did it. "I DON'T CARE ABOUT THE BEEF," I shouted. "I AM NOT GOING TO BUY THOSE DAMN TICKETS, NOW OR EVER. I DON'T WANT THE TICKETS,

32

I DON'T WANT THE BEEF, AND FRANKLY, I DON'T
CARE IF THE ENTIRE FRATERNAL ORDER OF EAGLES
ORGANIZATION GOES BANKRUPT BECAUSE I
REFUSED TO BUY ANY RAFFLE TICKETS, AND I DO
REFUSE. DO YOU UNDERSTAND?''

He patted me on the arm and said, "Look, if this is a bad
time, I'll get with you later.'' With that, he turned and trudged
back across the parking lot, carefully putting the two tickets in
his shirt pocket.

9

How To Impress The Ladies

I knocked on the door of the apartment again. "Who's there?" a muffled female voice asked from inside.

"Sheriff's department," I said loudly.

There was a rattle as a chain was removed, and the door opened. "Come in."

I stepped inside, and she closed the door behind me. "Heather McNamara?" I asked.

She nodded, smiling with perfect teeth. I was looking at a very pretty face. Curly brown hair falling softly to her shoulders helped accent her large blue eyes. She had a very nice shape to go along with the pretty face, and I could see quite a lot of it, since she was wearing only a light pullover and shorts. She was barefooted, and I found myself following two long legs all the way down to crimson toenails. It was a pleasant journey. "Did they tell you why I called?"

I shifted my attention from her feet to her face. "Something about a vandalism."

"Yes. Some scrounge messed up my car." A door opened, and two more young women joined us, both blond, one tall, the other short. They, too, were quite attractive. "These are my roommates," Heather said.

As I looked at them, I realized they were checking me out

as well. At the risk of being immodest, I must say I wear a uniform rather well. I am almost six feet tall, and while I am certainly not muscular, I have managed to keep my waist around 34 inches. Standing there in the small apartment, wearing my straw Stetson, mirror sunglasses, dark green uniform, and all that creaking leather, I suspect I must have been a pretty imposing figure.

"And who is this?" the taller one asked.

I extended my hand, and she took it, her fingers soft and cool. "I'm Don Parker."

She smiled, "Hi, Don Parker; I'm Jennifer, and this is Holly."

Holly gave me a big smile, and I felt a little dizzy from all this femininity. I sucked in my stomach and straightened up a little. It suddenly seemed a little warm. "Well, let's take a look at this vandalism."

Heather and I went outside and inspected her car. Someone had run a sharp instrument along most of the driver's side, inflicting a major scratch. Her radio antenna had been bent into an interesting geometric shape and the outside mirror broken.

After examining the damage, I made an educated guess. "It looks like you're having problems with somebody's girlfriend."

Her eyes widened. "How did you know?"

"This is girl vandalism. A man would have sliced up your tires, smashed the windshield, or thrown paint remover on the finish. I think you must be dating her boyfriend." I smiled, "I can't say I blame the guy."

She blushed. "Well, I think I know who might have done it, but I don't have any proof. My insurance agent said I had to make a police report before they would pay the claim."

We went back inside. Jennifer and Holly were waiting. "He's amazing!" Heather said. "He took one look and knew Amanda did it."

Her roommates were obviously impressed. I was impressed to see they had both applied makeup and fixed their hair while I was outside. The uniform gets them every time. "Well, let me write this report for you, Miss McNamara.''

She smiled fetchingly, ''Oh, please call me Heather.'' All three women watched as I opened my notebook and prepared to write. It was a little dim inside the house, so I removed my prescription sunglasses and replaced them with my regular glasses. It was also a little warm, so I took my hat off.

There was an instant of stunned silence, then I heard a muffled noise behind me. I looked up and saw Holly quickly put her hand over her mouth. Jennifer's mouth was twitching strangely. ''Is anything wrong?'' I asked.

Her mouth continued to twitch, and suddenly she blurted, ''You don't have any hair!'' This announcement was certainly no surprise to me, not having had much hair since my early twenties but apparently, it was quite a revelation to my three admirers. I turned to Heather and saw her staring at my shiny dome, mouth slightly ajar. She didn't seem as amused as her friends, and I thought her to be more mature than her two friends. Surely she wasn't going to judge me on such superficial grounds. ''How old are you?'' she asked. So much for that idea. I told her my age, and she said, ''No, really.''

Needless to say, things went downhill fast after that. I completed the report and gave her the complaint number. Holly and Jennifer had long since left the room, so Heather walked me to the door. I lingered a moment, standing outside, hoping to recapture the mood that had existed just fifteen short minutes ago, but it was too late.

''Now you be sure to call me if you have any more problems.''

''I sure will, and thanks so much, Ron.''

''No,'' I said, ''it's Don....'' but she had already shut the door.

10

The Case Of The Missing Tire

I heard the car before I saw it, but I didn't know it was a car at first. The high-pitched squealing carried well in the still night air, and the vehicle must have been half-a-mile away when I first heard the noise. The light turned green, but I remained sitting at the intersection, waiting to see what was causing the commotion. Since mine was the only car moving at that time of night, I wasn't exactly holding up traffic.

The noise was getting closer, coming up the hill to my left. Now I could hear a steady rumbling in addition to the squealing. I got my first view of the car as it topped the hill, and what a view it was. Listing to the right, the vehicle approached, moving rapidly. A stream of fire seemed to be shooting from the right front wheel, lighting up the whole side of the car, reflecting off the store windows, illuminating the street.

The driver had the green light and turned left, ignoring my stationary cruiser car. But I couldn't ignore him. What I thought was fire was actually sparks coming from the wheel rim. The tire was long gone; the guy must have been driving on it for some time. The car straightened out and continued down the street. Amazing.

I blinked and came back to reality. It was also illegal, since one is not supposed to drive a car without tires on the wheels.

Not only can it damage the road, it tends to make the vehicle a little difficult to control, although this guy certainly wasn't having any trouble. I flipped on the blue lights and set off in pursuit.

He pulled over immediately, probably expecting to be stopped, and I saw there were two people in the car. I walked up to the driver's window. "May I see your driver's license, please?" I said.

The man was staring straight ahead, jaw muscles working, both hands clamped on the steering wheel. He jerked the license from his wallet and handed it to me, his eyes smoldering. This was one very mad driver. I looked inside and saw the passenger was a thin, middle-aged woman. She was watching me with wide eyes. A quick glance revealed no beer cans or whiskey bottles, and there was no odor of alcohol. Very strange. I had the guy pegged as a drunk.

"Mr. Whitehurst," I said, reading off the license, "step out of the car, please."

He muttered a low curse and stepped out quickly, slamming the door so hard the car rocked. He clenched his fists and stood glaring at me, nostrils flaring. He was a big man, tall and rangy. I could see by the size of his arms and the width of his shoulders he was very strong. I certainly hoped we could resolve our differences peacefully.

"Mr. Whitehurst, don't you know your right front tire is gone?"

"Yeah, I know it," he snapped. "So what?"

"So what? Well, I'll tell you 'so what.'" He was starting to make me angry. "It's a violation of the law to drive on the rim."

He continued to glare, breathing hard. "Okay, it's a violation of the law. So I'm sorry."

He sure didn't sound sorry, but I let that pass. Nothing says you can't get mad at a cop, provided, of course, you don't do anything more than get mad. Naturally, this is not the smartest thing to do, but by itself, it certainly isn't illegal. Of course, cops are human, too, and since we are the ones with the badges and the guns and the power of arrest, it's usually not wise to see how far you can push us.

Many cops, myself included, tend to start looking for violations when we are confronted with someone who is really nasty, and it's surprising how many tickets can be written for just one traffic stop. What's not surprising is the direct correlation between the number of tickets written and how high the cop's blood pressure was elevated.

I remember as a rookie booking someone in the jail, when one of the veterans brought in a really mouthy drunk. The guy was so loud and obnoxious, he was immediately placed in a cell to let him cool down for a while. "Whatta ya got him for?" one of the correction officers inquired of the veteran.

The deputy was already filling out the arrest report. "P.M.O." he replied laconically, not even looking up. The correction officer nodded and walked off, evidently satisfied.

But I was confused. This was an abbreviation I had never heard before. I was familiar with D.U.I. (Driving Under the Influence), C.C.W. (Carrying a Concealed Weapon), AKA (Also Known As), C.I. (Confidential Informant), and G.T.A. (Grand Theft Auto). I had never heard of P.M.O.

I was a little hesitant to openly display my ignorance, particularly to a veteran officer, but how else is one to learn? "Uh, excuse me, Jack." He looked up. "Could I ask you a question?" He nodded. "What does 'P.M.O.' mean?"

He smiled. "Hell, boy, that's what you charge someone with when you can't think of anything else." He leaned closer. "It stands for 'Pissin' Me Off.' "

Of course, he really wasn't going to charge him with a nonexistent violation; he was just telling me the guy got himself arrested because of his mouth. Once he got him to jail, he'd come up with the necessary statute to make it legal.

So the driver of the car with the missing tire was not doing himself any favors by giving me a hard time. "Who is that in the car?'' I asked.

He looked away. "My wife."

She got out, and I obtained some ID. She was indeed his wife and also seemed sober, but very frightened. We walked to the front of their car so I could talk to her privately. "What's the problem with your husband?"

She ducked her head, and I saw a tear start down one cheek. "He gets so mad sometimes," she said.

"Did you two have a fight?"

"Yes," she whispered. "It was my fault."

"Will you be all right?"

She sniffled. "I'll be fine." She wiped her nose. "I just want to go home."

Satisfied there was nothing else going on here except a marital dispute, I walked back to the driver. "Mr. Whitehurst, you have a choice," I said. "Either park the car or change the tire. It's up to you."

He started to say something but thought better of it. Snatching the keys from the ignition, he strode to the trunk, opened it, and removed the jack and the spare. He loosened the lug nuts on the ruined wheel, put the jack under the bumper and started cranking.

But something was wrong. "Mr. Whitehurst, what about the jack plate?" I said, pointing. The thin shaft of the jack was balanced precariously on the concrete road.

He turned, still in a crouch. "Ain't got one," he said shortly.

"But that's dangerous."

He snorted and went back to work, ignoring me. The car rose quickly, swinging back and forth on the flimsy jack. What little hair I had was beginning to stand on end. If the car shifted a few inches more, and it was rocking most alarmingly, that jack would likely shoot out like the bolt from a crossbow. I stepped back.

Whitehurst was oblivious to the danger. Roughly he jerked the ruined wheel off the car. I held my breath when he slammed the spare into place, expecting him to be impaled any second.

When he began tightening the lug nuts, I almost couldn't look. Each time he leaned on the tire tool, the car swayed, but somehow the jack stayed upright, and soon he was lowering it again. I had hardly dared to breathe throughout this ordeal, and it was a relief to watch him angrily throwing the tools in the trunk.

He drove off, still mad, and I was so impressed with his reckless courage I didn't give him a ticket.

11

The Last Act

Dawn was just breaking when I arrived at the scene, a house in a shabby residential neighborhood which had definitely seen better days. A motorist on his way to work had spotted the old man and thought something didn't look right. So he called the cops. It was dispatched to me as an "Unknown Assistance" call, one of those catch-all phrases used when the dispatchers really don't know what's going on. This is not to be confused with "Unknown Disturbance" calls, which are usually generated from screams or gunshots or other incidents of potential violence.

I pulled up in front of the house and saw immediately why the motorist thought something was amiss. There was someone lying on the sidewalk, covered with a blanket, a shotgun lying on top of him. I walked carefully to the body, looking for any evidence. An empty whiskey bottle was at the head, a note propped against it. "To Who It May Concern," was written on the outside of the envelope.

Close up, I could see it was an older man, and he was wrapped in a sleeping bag. Beneath the sleeping bag was a plastic shower curtain. The man's head was resting on a pillow, his eyes half open and filmed over, a gray stubble of beard on his sunken cheeks. Both hands gripped the shotgun, and his right thumb was on the trigger. I knelt down and checked for a pulse. His arm was stiff and cool. He had been dead for quite some time. There was a hole the size of a quarter in the outside of the sleeping bag, just about the center of his chest, but there was very little blood. The ragged edges of the hole were scorched from the powder. From all outward appearances, it looked like a suicide.

I called for the lieutenant, an investigator and the crime scene technicians. I wondered what was in the note, but I didn't touch it. While I was waiting, I knocked on the door of the house, but no one answered, and the door was locked.

Within a few minutes, the scene was bustling with activity. Crime scene technicians were taking photographs and collecting evidence, the investigator was waking people in the nearby houses to find out what they knew, and I was taking notes for the report.

According to the neighbors, the man lived alone, had a serious drinking problem, and was in poor health. He lived on Social Security and a small disability pension, but no one knew if he had any family in town. As the crime scene technicians finished doing their jobs, one of them opened the note with a surgical-gloved hand. The man had written that he couldn't go on any longer, that he was tired of being sick, ashamed he couldn't stop drinking, and sorry for any trouble he might have caused anyone. He included the name and address of a daughter in Ohio, said he was leaving everything to her, told us where to find an insurance policy, and said his keys were in his right front pants pocket.

The last paragraph was interesting: "I have therefore decided I cannot any longer go on living so I am choosing to take my own life. I have tried not to make a mess."

As the body was removed from the sleeping bag, we saw to what lengths he had gone. He had placed a towel over his chest before pulling the trigger, and this had soaked up much of the blood. Just to be safe, though, he spread the plastic shower curtain beneath the sleeping bag to prevent any blood from staining the sidewalk.

All of us were very pleased with the overall neatness of the scene. There now was no doubt it was a suicide, we had the name of the next-of-kin, and the keys to the house. There were no loose ends to tie up, and best of all, he had not killed himself inside the house, where he could easily have lain for days, unnoticed until the neighbors called to report what the newspapers euphemistically refer to as "an objectionable odor."

Yes, it was very neat, but it was a sad end to an obviously sad life. As I drove away, I hoped the guy knew that, although it was the last thing he did, we appreciated his efforts.

12

Attack Of The Balloons

As you may suspect, practical jokes are frequently used to relieve stress, raise spirits, and generally amuse everyone concerned, except the victim. While I have enjoyed some of the pranks pulled on my fellow deputies, I generally prefer jokes with a little originality. I mean, how often can you laugh at a dead fish hidden under the seat of a cruiser car?

While never a master of the practical joke myself, I did have my triumphs, and I would put my "Balloon Attack" up against the best of them. Of course, if the judges were other cops, I would surely lose because no one was maimed, no marriages broke up, and no one had their career irreparably damaged.

Personally, I don't believe practical jokes should be life-threatening, because the unexpected death of the jokee can diminish the humor. As for putting marriages in jeopardy, even the most hilarious practical joke doesn't seem nearly as funny when explained under oath in divorce court. And while it can be amusing to retell the story of how one of your former buddies, sole support for an invalid wife and four kids, was fired because of the repercussions of a practical joke, it's probably best to avoid jokes of this type.

So the "Balloon Attack" would be judged hopelessly wimpy by the majority of my peers. But it was funny. My only regret was that I didn't get to see the reaction of the victim. Luckily, there were plenty of witnesses, so I got it secondhand, which was almost as good as being there.

The joke took place in the men's locker room of the county jail, which is where we macho crime fighters changed into appropriate athletic attire before going to the gym and torturing ourselves in the name of physical fitness. A surprise birthday party had been held that morning for one of the secretaries, and for some reason, I had picked up a package of unused balloons.

I was sitting on the bench after my workout and shower, waiting for my buddies to dress, idly contemplating the balloons, trying to think of a use for these multi-colored bits of latex. At that precise instant, the entire practical joke flashed through my mind. I saw it all: the setup, the reaction of my victim, the reaction of the witnesses, and the retelling of the story for years to come.

I felt as a clairvoyant must, when he or she has a vision of the future. I knew exactly how everything was going to go. It was eerie, but it did not distress me. I now had a mission and I had to get to it. My friends were out of the shower, getting dressed, talking, laughing; I paid them no heed.

Opening the package of balloons I selected a red one. Turning to the locker belonging to Deputy Roger Tyree, a friendly, trusting man, and, therefore, a perfect target, I carefully inserted the balloon into the ventilation slot at the top of the locker door, leaving the open end hanging out. Then, applying my lips to the balloon, I inflated same, knotted the end, and pushed it the rest of the way into the locker.

Presto! A fully inflated balloon was now inside a securely locked locker.

My companions had long since ceased their conversations and were staring, slack-jawed, as I worked on the balloon. When it disappeared into the locker, they burst into laughter, finally understanding what I was doing. Young Deputy Tyree normally worked out in the morning, a time of day I tried to avoid, and one of my buddies said he preferred mornings as well and would report back to us.

The next day, Tyree opened his locker to prepare for his workout and was amazed, my friend reported, to find a large, red balloon inside. His padlock seemed secure, the balloon had certainly not been in the locker when he left, so it was something of a mystery. He showed the balloon to the other guys, but none of them, including my lying buddy, had any idea how it could have gotten in the locker.

Shrugging it off, Tyree disposed of the balloon, changed his clothes, and headed for the gym.

The next day I put a yellow balloon in the locker and eagerly waited for my informant to report back. He said Tyree was even more perplexed and not a little concerned. After all, if some rascal was breaching the security of his locker the contents could well be at risk. He thoroughly checked the entire bank of lockers, thinking someone might have entered from behind, but they were securely bolted to the concrete wall.

He also went over the inside of his locker to determine if someone could have gained entry from an adjacent locker, but the metal was solidly welded. The sight of the suspicious Tyree tapping on the sides and floor of his locker was almost too much for my spy, who said he had to laugh into a towel.

I was off for a few days, and when I returned, a shiny new combination lock had replaced the supposedly compromised padlock. I put two balloons inside this time.

The informant said Tyree was nearly beside himself at this obvious mockery. He went through the entire locker again, inch by inch, trying to find some way the balloons could have gotten inside. He was, of course, unsuccessful, but his confidence in his present locker was shattered, so he moved all his stuff to another one. I gave him three balloons to christen the new locker.

My agent said for a while he feared for the boy's sanity. When Tyree opened the door, the poor guy collapsed on the bench, staring at the three balloons bulging from the small compartment at the top of his locker, shaking his head, completely demoralized. By this time almost everyone was in on the joke, so when the distraught Tyree asked them if they had any idea how the balloons kept mysteriously appearing inside his locker, they solemnly assured him they did not.

Although disheartened by his failure to keep the pesky balloons out of his locker, Tyree was consoled by the knowledge that at least so far, nothing had been taken. Finally admitting defeat, he chose to ignore the balloons and continued his workouts. Each day, muttering and cursing, he would open his locker, savagely rip out the gaily colored balloon bobbing around therein, explode it with a violent thrust of his pen, and dress for his workout.

This daily ritual continued until I finally ran out of balloons and at last brought peace to the oft-harassed Deputy Tyree. It was one of my better efforts.

13

Raffle Tickets - Part 2

I waited until the last minute to sneak into the muster room. I wanted to make sure Don Rush was already seated so I wouldn't have to talk to him. I was still grimly determined to avoid buying a raffle ticket. Unfortunately, all the seats close to the door were taken, and Rush was in the next row. As soon as he saw me, a big smile lit up his face, and he gave me a friendly little wave, two raffle tickets visible in his hand. I nodded at him and slipped into my seat.

Hightower leaned toward me. "Did you buy your tickets?" he whispered.

"Hell, no!" I whispered back, feeling superior.

He just smiled. "Everyone buys a ticket from Rush," he said.

"Not me."

The lieutenant began calling out the district assignments and giving us the hot tag numbers of the day's vehicle thefts. I copied the information, but I was thinking about what to do when muster broke up. Rush was only three seats away, and he was sure to buttonhole me about the tickets before I got out the door. Even if I bolted for the car, he was bound to follow, and I really didn't want to listen to his pitch. I finally came up with a plan which seemed workable if a little simple-minded.

As soon as muster was over, I ran for the bathroom. It only

had a toilet and sink in it, and I intended to stand around until Rush was in his car. Since we worked at opposite ends of the county, I was pretty sure I wouldn't have to deal with him again until muster the next day. That meant he had only one more chance. Tomorrow was Friday, and the drawing was Saturday.

I locked the door and flipped on the light. The ventilation fan came on, its irritating roar filling the tiny room. I sat on the toilet seat lid, leafing through an old police magazine.

A moment later, someone knocked. "Yeah?" I hollered.

"It's me, Rush. I've got your raffle tickets."

Damn! He never gave up. "Uh, I can't hear you; the fan is too loud."

"I've got your tickets," he said again.

I flushed the toilet, trying to increase the noise level. "Is that you, Lieutenant?"

"No, it's Rush. I'll wait for you. I've got your tickets."

"I'll be in here a while," I yelled. "Sorry, must be a stomach virus." I flushed the toilet again, prepared to wait him out. A movement caught my eye, and I looked down. An envelope was being pushed under the door. It had my name on it. I didn't touch it.

Five minutes later, I cracked the door and peeped out. The room was empty. I picked up the envelope. Of course, it contained two tickets along with a brief note: "Don, here are your raffle tickets. Please pay me tomorrow."

I had to give him credit, he was certainly persistent. But I was more persistent. I crossed off my name, substituted Rush's, and slid the envelope under the door of the lieutenant's office. He was bound to come back to the office before the shift ended to do paperwork. He would see the envelope and put it in Rush's mailbox. I congratulated myself on my shrewdness.

Three hours later, the lieutenant called me to meet him in a parking lot. I pulled up beside him. "What's up?"

He handed me the envelope. "I found this on the floor of my office. It had Rush's name on it, so I brought it to him. He says there's been some mistake. Those are your raffle tickets.''

"Thanks,'' I said weakly. The lieutenant drove off, while I sat there for a while, staring at the envelope.

For the rest of the shift, I thought about what to do. I finally decided the only thing I could do was insist Rush take the tickets back.

At the end of the night, I waited until he was gassing his car. He turned as I walked up, a smile of genuine pleasure on his face. "How's it going?''

I didn't return the smile. This was serious business. "Do you remember the conversation we had last night about these tickets?'' I asked.

He frowned, trying to think back. "Do you mean when we talked outside the jail?''

"Yes. Outside the jail. I told you I didn't want the tickets, didn't I?''

He was puzzled, "But the drawing is the day after tomorrow.''

"I don't care if it's in five minutes, I don't want the tickets.''

"Did I mention the beef is all cut and wrapped?''

"Yes, you mentioned it, and no, I don't care. I do not want the tickets. No tickets. Nada, nein, no, n-o, no!''

"They're only a dollar.''

"I don't care if they're free. I don't care if you pay me to take them. I DO NOT WANT THE TICKETS!'' I placed the envelope on the hood of his car. "There are the tickets.'' I started backing away. "I refuse to take further responsibility for them. They are now your tickets.'' I walked off.

"Don,'' he said quietly. Against my better judgment, I stopped and turned. He had the tickets, and he looked around to make sure no one could hear our conversation. "Listen, if you're in a bind, I can wait until payday.''

I stifled the urge to scream and bolted for my car.

As I headed home, I began to calm down. Only one more day to go, and I still hadn't bought any tickets yet. He was good, but I was better.

14

Fringe Benefits

It was just getting dark when I pulled in behind the big Oldsmobile, which headed for the curb as soon as I touched the siren. Having clocked the driver doing 62 in a 45, I was inclined to write him a ticket, but first I would listen to the explanation.

I walked up to the car and discovered he was a she, a woman, probably in her late thirties, quite attractive, really: long dark hair, nice make-up, and well dressed. I could even detect a hint of her perfume through the open window. "May I see your driver's license, please?"

She smiled nervously, digging it out of her purse. "Why are you stopping me, officer?" she said, handing me the license.

I checked the expiration date. It was current. "Ma'am, you were doing 62 miles an hour. The speed limit is 45."

"I'm so sorry, I certainly didn't mean to; I was just in a hurry." I noticed the bright yellow dress she was wearing was rather low-cut, and showing a significant amount of cleavage. The woman had a very impressive chest. I forced my eyes back to her face, and she smiled. I had been caught.

"Yes, well, you should be more careful," I said, cheeks burning. "You could cause an accident."

She continued to smile. "You are so right, it was a stupid thing to do, but I hope you won't give me a ticket." The woman had beautiful teeth.

"You were driving very fast, ma'am, almost 20 miles above the speed limit and..."

"Oh," she said in a husky voice, "I'd do anything to avoid getting a ticket."

I was beginning to feel warm. "Well, I can understand how you feel, but it's really...."

She interrupted me again. "Do you understand? I'd do anything." She sort of shrugged, and the right shoulder strap of the dress slid down her arm, exposing most of one breast. She stared at me, no longer smiling.

My whole body felt flushed. "Ma'am, are you trying to bribe me?"

She ran her tongue across her lips. "Not with money."

I was truly shocked. I had heard tales of women offering themselves to cops to get out of tickets, but I never believed them. The lurid stories of back seat encounters told by my buddies were, in my estimation, mostly wishful thinking, but I was always happy to listen.

It was amazing how similar the stories were. They all seemed to involve a gorgeous, over-sexed woman, who, when stopped for a traffic infraction, offered horizontal ecstasy instead of a ticket. The story teller invariably took her up on the offer, brought the woman to a multi-orgasmic frenzy, and never saw her again.

There were never any complications like jealous husbands, supervisors who came along at the wrong moment, or having to explain to a suspicious wife why SHE had to take medication for HIS bladder infection. Just the lack of complications alone made me skeptical. I always enjoyed the stories, although I never expected to find myself actually being propositioned. But I was, and right now, too. I found myself in a quandary. While I was undeniably attracted to the lady, I was fearful of the possible consequences. Not only could I place my marriage in jeopardy, I would also be taking a chance with my job. It was a contest between lust and logic, and I could almost feel the ethical tug of war within me.

"So you'd do anything to get out of a ticket?" I said, stalling.

She smiled, more confident now. "That's right. We could have a nice party."

Alarm bells went off in my head. A party? That wasn't what I had in mind at all. "Ma'am, I wouldn't feel very comfortable at a party."

She laughed delightedly. "Silly. I don't mean a real party. I mean just you and me. We'll make our own party."

"Oh, sure, I know what you mean." I felt like a rube.

"And stop calling me, 'ma'am'; you make me feel old. My name is Lydia."

"Okay, uh, Lydia." I took a deep breath, realizing I was surrendering to lust and not caring, "What did you have in mind?"

Naming a motel a few miles away, she said would meet me in the back parking lot as soon as I got off, and we would spend a few hours in one of the rooms discussing her driving and how it could be improved. She winked as she drove off. "I'll be waiting."

I returned to duty in a turmoil, repulsed by this obvious weakness in my moral fiber but looking forward to the encounter, too.

The rest of the shift passed slowly, and I kept thinking about what I had done, or, rather, what I was going to do. The whole situation was unreal. Beautiful, over-sexed women just didn't proposition strange men, even if they were cops, unless they weren't normal. Maybe that was it. Maybe she was a psycho. Maybe she would get me alone, pull out a straight razor, and carve me to ribbons. I had seen a movie about one such woman, and the bloody scenes left little to the imagination. I shuddered, imagining my frail carcass, drained of blood and missing various parts.

I breathed deeply, trying to get a grip on my galloping imagination. While I was pretty sure she wasn't a crazed killer,

I still wondered about her. Suddenly a paralyzing thought seized me. What if she was just setting me up! Maybe she was working for internal affairs, attempting to lure deputies to commit themselves to moral turpitude. If that was her game, I was already dead meat. She had probably recorded our entire conversation. I wiped my face with a shaky hand. Why, oh, why, hadn't I been more careful?

I could just see the screaming headlines: "SEX-CRAZED COP ARRESTED" - "OPERATION PLUNGING NECKLINE NETS HORNY DEPUTY" - "DISGRACED OFFICER FIRED, 'HE'S NO SON OF MINE,' SAYS MOTHER" My God! What could I do?

After thinking it over, I decided I would talk with the veteran deputy who had been my training officer. I called him on the radio and asked him to meet me in a nearby parking lot.

He pulled up a few minutes later. "What's wrong, Don? You look awful."

"I need some advice." I swallowed hard. "I think I might have messed up bad."

"What the hell did you do, shoot the lieutenant?"

I shook my head. "No, worse than that." I related my encounter with the flirtatious driver. His eyes grew wide as I finished my sad tale.

"And you said you were going to meet her at the motel?" he asked.

I nodded miserably, sensing his disapproval.

"But now you don't want to meet her?"

I shook my head, knowing he had lost all respect for me.

"Hmmmm," he said, rubbing his chin, "this is a serious problem."

"Look, I know what you must think of me, but I promise I'll never do something like this again." I really admired this guy, and I didn't want him to be disappointed in me. "I just hope it's not too late to..."

"And you're sure you're not going to meet her when you get

off?''

"I'm sure," I said. "I'm going straight home as soon as I sign out, and I..."

"Then you won't mind if I give it a try."

"How's that again?''

He smiled, "No sense in both of us missing out just because you got cold feet.''

I couldn't believe what I was hearing. "You're going to go out there?''

"Sure. I hate to think of that woman all by herself in that lonely old motel room." He chuckled, "I'll tell her you assigned me the case.''

"But what about internal affairs?''

He laughed. "I'll take my chances," he said, starting his car. "You said her name was Lydia, right?''

I nodded, "But she might have been using a fake Driver's License and....'' He was already driving off.

I completed the shift in a trance. Not only had I been propositioned, something I regarded as a once-in-a-lifetime event, I had managed to talk myself out of it. Now my buddy was going to reap the benefits of my moral failing. It was irritating in the extreme.

The next day I grabbed him as soon as he came into the muster room. "Well?" I demanded. "How did it go?''

He gave me a disgusted look. "There wasn't no Oldsmobile, there wasn't no Lydia, and the desk clerk didn't know who I was talking about. I stayed in the bar until they closed, checked the parking lot more times than the security guard, and didn't get home until four." He glared at me with bloodshot eyes, "I think you made the whole thing up.''

"It was all true, I swear.''

He brushed by me. "That's the last time I'll ever listen to you.''

I went on to muster, but I was feeling strangely pleased. I was glad he didn't meet Lydia, and I was almost glad she conned me out of a traffic ticket. I decided I had enjoyed being propositioned by an attractive woman, even if nothing came of it. And it wasn't a total loss; at least now I had my own story to tell.

15

The Born-Again Alligator

We were sitting around a coffee shop one night after finishing a brutal evening shift, half-a-dozen weary deputies, too keyed up to go home just yet. Naturally, we were telling war stories, and someone asked Doug to tell us about the Born-Again Alligator. He was happy to oblige.

He didn't catch the alligator himself, his father did, after spotting the creature sunning himself alongside a rural highway. A relatively small 'gator, perhaps four feet, he still put up a spirited fight before being subdued and loaded in the trunk. Doug laughed at the thought of his 70 year-old father wrestling with an alligator. "He took the 'gator home, tied a rope around his neck, and put him in the backyard;" he said, "then he calls me up, all excited, and tells me to come over and see his new pet."

"Did he tell you what it was?" I asked.

"No, but I knew it had to be something unusual. Pop wouldn't have called me if it was only a stray kitten. Well, it took me a little while. I was getting ready to go to work, so I had to eat, get cleaned up, and put on my uniform."

When he got to his father's house, he found that tragedy had struck. The alligator had crawled up on a wood pile and fallen off. The rope caught and the poor 'gator hung himself. It was a cold winter night, and the late alligator was now as stiff as a board, twisting slowly in the chill wind, still hanging by the rope.

"I asked Dad if I could have him, and he said sure. I think he just wanted to get out of having to dig a grave for the thing." They cut him down, and Doug, about to start a midnight shift, took the alligator to work with him.

Deciding they had to put the gator to good use, Doug enlisted several of his buddies. Their first victim was a fellow deputy, a tall, gentle soul named Lewis. After some discussion about the best way to achieve the maximum amount of terror, they devised a plan. They removed the bulb from the ceiling light inside his cruiser car so it wouldn't come on when the door was opened. Propping the dead 'gator's jaws open with a stick, they placed him carefully on the front seat.

When muster was over, Doug asked the boy to drive him to the far end of the parking lot. Kindly soul that he is, Lewis agreed. He got in his car and leaned across the seat to unlock the door so Doug could enter. In so doing he came face-to-face with this cold, leathery thing full of teeth. Lewis left the car much faster than he entered it. "You should have seen him run!" Doug laughed, wiping the tears from his eyes, "I didn't know old Lewis could move that fast."

When he slowed down a little and heard the shrieks of laughter, Lewis realized he had been bamboozled. He was less than pleased, and now it was the turn of the conspirators to run. His rage soon dissipated, however, and he was persuaded to join the alligator squad.

"We put the dead 'gator on the steps outside the muster room," Doug said, "and called Lieutenant Swinney on the radio and asked him to come outside. He was right in the middle of some paperwork and didn't really want to break free, but we told him it was important." He started to laugh again, "Oh, it was great. When he started down the steps, we all screamed, 'Watch Out!'"

The lieutenant looked down, saw the gaping jaws of the 'gator, and 260 pounds of shift commander leaped gracefully to the hood

59

of a nearby cruiser, shivering and shaking while his subordinates howled with glee.

"Didn't he get mad?" I asked.

"Yeah, he was a little pissed," Doug conceded, "but what could he do? Half the shift was standing around laughing at him."

"He could have shot you," someone suggested.

"Nah, he wouldn't have done that. We were too short of personnel as it was."

Doug loaded the alligator into his cruiser. He had a partner that night and the two of them hit the streets, taking the dead 'gator with them on calls. Of course they were hoping they'd be able to arrest someone so they could put him in the back with their passenger. Unfortunately, it was a quiet night, and they were unsuccessful.

But all was not lost. They decided to stop at their favorite barbecue restaurant. "So I tied a rope around the 'gator's neck," Doug continued, "and we dragged him inside." He shook his head, "Boy, did we empty that place out in a hurry." They proceeded to terrorize the cook by putting the 'gator on the counter, demanding he barbecue it. Back in the car they discussed their next move. They considered going to one of the all-night bottle clubs and tossing the alligator onto the crowded dance floor, figuring this might provoke an amusing reaction from the drunks gathered therein.

"We were laughing about that when I felt something bump me under the seat," Doug said. "Well, I figured it was David messing with me, so I told him to quit it, but he said he wasn't doing anything. A few minutes later, I felt it again. I was just about to cuss him out, when we both hear this loud hissing sound from the back. I thought a tire had sprung a leak."

Before they could get out of the car to check, there came a crunching and crackling from the back seat. It sounded exactly as if a small stick were being chewed to pieces. They turned on the inside light and discovered, to their horror, the supposedly dead alligator was now very much alive and had just made a meal of the stick in his mouth.

"Of course, we figured out later he had not really hung himself at all, he had just gone into hibernation or something because of the low temperature."

Once inside the warm cruiser car, however, he had come back to a full and vigorous life. Obviously, they had a problem. There was more crunching, and they discovered their guest was now dining on one of the door handles. They had to do something fast.

"So, what did you do?"

"We drove to a nearby lake that had a boat ramp. I opened the back door and jumped out of the way, but nothing happened." He chuckled. "I think Mr. Alligator liked being in our warm car. Every time we got close to the door, he'd start hissing and snapping his jaws. Finally, I got David to distract him, and I grabbed the rope and jerked him out of the car. He hit the water and disappeared."

They weren't sorry to see the 'gator depart, and both agreed they liked him a lot better when he was dead. "There's only one thing I regret," Doug said.

"What's that?"

"I really wish we had thrown him onto the dance floor at the bottle club. Man, that would have been something."

16

How's That Again?

It was a quiet weekend, and I was sitting in the muster room getting caught up on some paperwork and performing guard duty at the same time. A group of juveniles on a court-ordered work detail were picking up trash around the building, and the lieutenant told me to stay inside until they finished. It was not unheard-of for office equipment and other small items to disappear when these little hoodlums were around. Once a phone vanished, right off the shift commander's desk. Another time, the candy machine was burgled.

One of the girls was cleaning our small bathroom. Tall and slim with long brown hair, she had been working steadily for an hour and had not spoken three words to me. Not that I cared, mind you, but I couldn't get it out of my mind that I had seen her before.

She finished mopping and stepped into my office, which held the only a vacant chair. She sat and stared at the floor, waiting for the counselor to come and get her. Her glacial silence was distracting, and I finally closed the file I was working on and looked at her. "Don't I know you?"

She turned and stared at me. She really was a pretty girl. Large brown eyes framed by long lashes and just the right amount of eye makeup. "Yeah, you know me," she said bitterly, "and you know my boyfriend, too."

This was interesting. "What's your name?" She told me, and I recognized the last name. "Don't I know your brother and your father?" She nodded. "Is your brother still in prison?"

"Yeah, he's in prison, but he'll be out in seven months."

"So, who's your boyfriend?"

When she said his name, the light finally dawned. Now I remembered her. "I arrested him last year, didn't I?"

"Yes, you arrested him last year," she repeated sarcastically, "and he's still in jail, thanks to you."

I remembered the case well. An alert was broadcast for a car seen leaving a burglary of a residence. I thought I knew who owned the car and soon located it, parked at a sleazy bar. I found her and her boyfriend inside, trying to sell a portable TV to the bartender. The boy offered no resistance, but his girlfriend, the bathroom cleaner, fought like a tiger. It took three of us to get her in my car. Now she was working her sentence off cleaning toilets. Small world. "You really gave us a battle," I chuckled.

"It's not funny. My boyfriend's still in jail because of you."

"I think you've got that wrong. He's in jail because of himself."

"But you arrested him," she said furiously. "Because of you he lost his job and got a year in jail."

"Look, he did the crime, now he does the time. It's that simple."

"You could have given him a break."

"As I recall," I said, "it wasn't the first time he was arrested for burglary. He's lucky he didn't get five years."

She glared at me. "How can you just arrest people like that? Don't you feel guilty?"

This reasoning was so bizarre, I could only stare at her, completely dumbfounded. "Let me see if I have this right. You think I should feel guilty for arresting your boyfriend?" She nodded. "Well, what about the people he stole from? Should they feel guilty, too? After all, they did call the cops."

"He had to steal that stuff; he has a drug habit."

I was talking to an idiot.

She left, still defiant, still maintaining it was my fault, and I know I didn't change her thinking one iota. Of course, she didn't change mine, either, and I must confess; I have never felt a second's guilt for arresting her boyfriend because he burglarized houses to support his drug habit.

I guess I'm just unreasonable.

17

I'd Rather Do It Myself

I handed the clerk the faucet set. "Will there be anything else, sir?"

I shook my head as I wrote the check. "No, that'll do it."

"Going to do a little plumbing, eh?"

"Yeah, the old fixture has just about had it."

"Well, this here faucet's a good un'. It'll do the job for you."

"Yes, I'm sure it will," I said, feeling a little uneasy. I'm always intimidated by hardware people. They are usually leathery old guys like this one, who know everything about building or repairing things. They can talk plumbing or woodworking, roofing or gardening. They might as well be speaking Arabic, as far as I'm concerned.

"I'll be here when you come back," he said."

"When I come back?"

He laughed. "You know what they say: you have to make at least three trips to the hardware store to fix anything."

"I won't be coming back," I said. "I've got what I need."

He tapped his name tag. "Name's Gus. Just ask for me."

I took the package and walked back to my car. Why are hardware store clerks always named Gus or Mort or Hank? Why can't they have names like Lance or Pierre or Alphonse?

The kitchen faucet was badly in need of replacing, and it was high time I got to it. It was so old, the finish was almost completely worn off and water spurted out of the base whenever it was turned on. Of course, the whole house was old. Built in the 1940's, its wiring and plumbing were barely adequate. When we put in a window air conditioner, the electrician had to wire it separately so it wouldn't burn the place down.

The faucet problem was just another thorn in my side because I am not what one would call domestic. I hate yard work, hate making repairs, hate anything which interrupts my attention to whatever I am doing at the time. Part of this dislike for things domestic springs from my inability to repair anything. Naturally, I am cursed with a father who can build an entire house in a weekend and two brothers who are constantly doing their own brake jobs, repairing malfunctioning appliances, or steam cleaning their own carpets. I feel like making a news release when I successfully reset a tripped circuit breaker.

But I'm not totally inept. I can change light bulbs, gas up my own car, and once I even straightened a bent blade to stop the clatter in a window fan. I am also pretty good at assembling toys, barbecue grills, and tricycles. But these skills only go so far. One time, because of the needling of my brothers, I decided to change the oil in my car. It was a disaster.

I followed the advice of a friend and took the car to a wooded area. It was a simple process, he said, to dig a hole in the sand, drive the car over the hole, and drain the oil (The possible effects on the environment were not considered in those less enlightened times). I did as instructed, digging the hole and pulling the car over it. After much searching, I finally located the drain plug in the oil pan. He hadn't warned me that the engine would still be hot, but I managed to keep from suffering any really serious burns. I loosened the plug with a crescent wrench, scraping my knuckles painfully in the process. I let the old oil drain into the hole, refilled the car with five quarts of new oil, and started the engine, thinking I ought to let the oil circulate a moment before I drove it. The oil light came on almost immediately. I figured it was only a temporary glitch, but it stayed on.

I finally shut the car off, trying to figure out what was wrong. It was pretty simply, really. When I looked underneath the car for a possible cause, I found the drain plug still on the ground. I had run all five quarts of the new oil right through the engine. It was a long walk to a pay phone, and my wife made sure everyone in the southeast knew I had almost destroyed the car while just changing the oil.

This kitchen faucet thing was beginning to get on my nerves. She kept insisting I do something about it before the counter was ruined from the water. I was loath to hire a plumber, knowing how much that would cost, but I wasn't confident I could do it myself. "Why don't you call your father to help you?" she asked.

"I don't need to call my father," I huffed. "I'm quite capable of replacing a faucet."

"Well, do it," she shouted, "or I'll call a plumber myself."

She was really upset, but that gave me a good excuse to talk the lieutenant into giving me a day off. I figured I'd replace the faucet in an hour and have the rest of the day to loaf. The first step was to turn off the water. Amazingly enough, there were no shutoff valves under the sink. In fact, there were no pipes at all. How could this be? I looked again. The pipes were inside the wall. Very strange. I guess indoor plumbing was such a novelty when the house was built, no one could imagine ever wanting to turn off the water. That meant I would have to turn it off at the street.

This was actually not a problem. Somewhere along the way, I had picked up a tool used by the utility companies to shut off water at the meter. It came in handy when pipes froze in empty houses during the winter, and I had used it several times. I shut the water off quickly, proud of my efficiency. Back to the faucet.

I applied a wrench to the cold water side. It took some effort, but finally the rusty nut loosened, groaning and creaking. The hot water side did not require much effort at all. I put the wrench on the nut, applied some pressure, and it snapped off cleanly, the old faucet clattering into the sink. I stared at it with a sense of rising panic. The pipe had broken even with the wall. I examined the hole, running my finger inside. The edges of the pipe crumbled away, almost totally rusted.

Now what? There was no way to get to the pipe except by going through the outside wall. I would have to cut a hole and replace the eight inches of pipe leading to the faucet. This was serious. It took me about an hour to rent an electric saber saw, drill a starter hole in the siding below the kitchen window, and cut through the side of the house.

Finally, I had a clear view of the broken pipe. Unfortunately, my crescent wrench couldn't grip the smooth surface, so I went back to the hardware store. I needed to buy a piece of pipe, anyway, and I might as well get a pipe wrench while I was there.

Gus gave me a big smile. "I figured you'd be back."

"Yeah, well I ran into a problem." I explained about the broken pipe.

"You really should get PVC pipe instead of metal," he said.

"What's PVC?"

"It's plastic." He showed me a sample. "You glue it together, and you can join it with existing metal pipe." That sounded good. No threading or soldering to worry about. He sold me the pipe, the necessary attachments, the glue, and the wrench. Adding the cost of the faucet and the rental of the saber saw, this was getting expensive. When I got home, I applied my new wrench to the damaged pipe. It snapped off cleanly, right at the elbow, the corroded threads still intact inside the fitting.

Back at the hardware store, Gus was waiting. "More problems?" he asked, smiling.

"I need another fitting," I told him through clenched teeth.

"That ain't no problem. We've got all you need."

I paid for the plastic elbow, returned to the house, and started to work once more. I tightened the wrench on the elbow and pulled. There was a snapping sound as it gave way. For a second

I thought it, too, had sheared off, and I was relieved to see it was turning on the pipe. At last. Now I was making progress. I kept unscrewing the elbow, thinking how pleased my wife would be when she came home and found the sparkling new faucet installed. Of course, she might not be quite as thrilled when she saw the hole in the side of the house, but I'd deal with that problem later.

The elbow seemed to be taking an awfully long time to unscrew. I looked more closely. The entire pipe was turning. For a second I was mystified, but then it hit me; the pipe had broken loose at the bottom. I pulled on it, and sure enough, it came free, all four feet of it, the threads snapped cleanly off.

I felt dizzy and I had to sit for a minute. This must be a dream. I was going to wake up soon, and everything was going to be all right. Now I was going to have to crawl under the house to complete the job.

Gus hardly smiled this time as I explained what happened. "You need to put another wrench on the pipe that has the fitting on it. You hold it with one hand to keep it from moving while you're unscrewing the fitting."

"I don't have another wrench."

He held one up. "We got plenty of em'. How many do you want?"

I left with another wrench, another elbow, and four feet of new pipe. Getting under the house was something of a problem. I had to pull a ventilation panel off the side. There was only a few feet of space, and I wormed my way across the dirt, hoping I wouldn't bump into any skeletons. I did what Gus advised, putting one wrench on the pipe and the other on the elbow. I twisted in opposite directions. There was a creaking sound, and the elbow moved a little. I twisted harder and it, too, broke off.

I could feel my eyes bugging out. I told myself to stay calm. I took off the extra wrench, and as I did, a trickle of water ran down my hand. I glanced at it and thought I was going to throw up. The pipe had split. It was so corroded inside, the pressure

69

of the wrench had opened it up like a can opener.

It was hopeless. I was doomed to spend the rest of my life trying to unscrew corroded pipes. I wondered if Gus was on commission. He was likely to be a rich man before I finished.

Despairingly, I examined the rest of the pipe. It seemed to stretch on forever, but then a ray of hope. About six feet from the fracture point, was a union. The pipe had been connected to a newer pipe which ran from the street. Maybe this new pipe was in better shape.

I broke off the old stuff, applied both wrenches, and, after a silent prayer, successfully removed the union without damaging the pipe.

Back at the hardware store, Gus was scratching his head. "You know, I think you might have set a record for the most visits in one day for one repair job."

"I don't care, just sell me more pipe."

Amazingly enough, everything went smoothly after that. Other than getting a little woozy from the pipe glue in the confined quarters under the house, I was finished in less than two hours. The new faucet worked fine, and after a shower, I felt much better. My wife was very impressed and didn't even get too excited about the hole in the side of the house. "Did you have any trouble?" she asked.

"Nah, it was just a routine repair job. Nothing to it."

18

Raffle Tickets - Part 3

Today was the last chance Rush would have to sell me a raffle ticket. I expected a climactic struggle to take place immediately following muster, and I had been mentally preparing for it. I decided my strategy would be brutally simple. I would refuse to talk to him. No matter what he said, no matter how persistent he was, I would simply fold my arms and shake my head. It was brilliant! If I refused to debate with him, he couldn't draw me into playing his game, and I wouldn't be worn down.

Suarez waited for me as I parked. We headed toward the muster room together. "Have you bought your tickets yet?"

"I have not, and I don't plan to."

"But everyone buys..."

"I know, I know, everyone buys their raffle tickets from Don Rush. Well, I'm not everyone."

Hightower caught up with us. "Sounds like the pressure's getting to him," he said to Suarez.

"He's definitely under a lot of strain," Suarez agreed.

"I'm not under any strain;" I said irritably, "we're just talking about raffle tickets, for God's sake."

"No," said Hightower, "we're talking about the irresistible force against the immovable object." Suarez laughed. "I think the object is beginning to move."

OFFICER NEEDS ASSISTANCE

Actually, I was a little tense, and Hightower was right: it was starting to get to me. I was happy to see that Rush was not in the muster room, and overjoyed when I learned he was in court giving a deposition and would be delayed. This was stunning news, since it meant he had only one chance left to try and get me to buy his tickets: at the end of the shift.

I was whistling as muster broke up. In a way I was almost disappointed. It didn't seem fair that I should win on a forfeit. But on the other hand, a win was still a win, no matter how it was accomplished.

The shift was an easy one, and I glided through with no problems. As 11 P.M. approached, I deliberately volunteered to stand by at a minor traffic accident until a state trooper arrived to investigate. That took almost 20 minutes. I heard Rush check off the air at 10:45, so he should be long gone by the time I got back to the office. It was almost midnight when I completed the last of my paperwork and headed out the door.

I had parked at the far end of the lot, and it took a few moments to walk across the deserted asphalt. I stood beside my car, enjoying the night air. I had won. I hadn't bought any raffle tickets, and I couldn't wait to see Hightower and Suarez. All it took was willpower, and I certainly had....

"Hey, Don! Wait a minute, will you?" I turned, looking across the parking lot. A pudgy figure was headed toward me, walking rapidly. It couldn't be.

But it was.

At three minutes past midnight, on his own time, well over an hour after he had signed out, Don Rush was waiting for me. "I didn't know where you parked," he puffed, wheezing from the effort, "so I checked the side lot." He leaned against the fender, trying to catch his breath.

I was in shock. What was he doing here? "I'm glad I caught you." He said. He fished the two battered raffle tickets out of his shirt pocket. "These are the last two I've got, and I've been saving them for you. The drawing is tomorrow, you know."

I nodded.

"We're giving away a side of beef, and it comes already cut and wrapped. The tickets are only a dollar each."

Numbly, I handed him the money, filled out the stubs, and he gave me the tickets. He walked back across the wide parking lot, humming.

I stood there for a long time, trying to comprehend what had happened. Finally, it hit me and I started to laugh. The outcome was inevitable. In fact, the whole scenario was entirely predictable. It was just as Suarez had said: everyone buys raffle tickets from Rush.

19

It Takes An Expert

According to the neighbors, the Great Dane had always been a mean dog whose thunderous barks and blood-chilling snarls had caused them all to give his yard a wide berth. But he had never actually bitten anyone. Until today.

The first victim was a teenager working on his car. For no discernible reason, the dog leaped over the fence and chased the kid back inside his house, putting a few tooth holes in one leg in the process. The kid was yelling and cursing, and his next-door neighbor, a retired man, came out to see what the commotion was about, and the dog promptly went after him. He drove him off with a rake but had his hand ripped open.

Needless to say, they called the cops. I was assigned the call, and Deputy Richard Lowery was my backup. We arrived simultaneously. "I couldn't believe it," the teenager told us. "I was just walking near the fence when that damn dog came after me."

I was taking notes as he talked, but Richard was swiveling his head like a fighter pilot. He wasn't about to let the dog sneak up on us. "Did you antagonize the dog in any way?" I asked.

"Are you nuts?" he said incredulously. "That thing is the size of my Volkswagen. I'm scared to death of him."

We went next door to talk to his neighbor. He had a bloody

handkerchief on his hand and was preparing to go to the emergency room to get stitched up. "I'll tell you one thing," he said. "If I could have gotten to my shotgun, you wouldn't have had to fool with that dog." He shook his head, "He got me too quick."

The house where the dog lived was in the next block, so we drove around the corner, watching for him. I figured he wouldn't be hard to spot. I was right.

As we pulled into the driveway, an enormous light-brown head rose above the long grass on the side of the house. The animal stood up slowly, an ominous rumble in his throat. It looked more like a pony than a dog. The Great Dane advanced toward us, massive lips curling in a snarl, exposing teeth a great white shark would have been proud to own. Sitting there in my car, I was quite disconcerted to realize we were eye-to-eye, which gave me the momentary impression the dog was bigger than my cruiser.

I blew the horn, and the animal hurled himself at the door, frothing with rage, trying his best to get at me. I could feel the car rocking from his frenzied assault. I kept rolling forward, which seemed to make him angrier, and he turned his attention to the front tire, biting at it savagely. I would not have been surprised if he had punctured it. But he didn't. I finally stopped the car, and the dog calmed down a little. Backing off, snarling and growling, he glared at me for a while, then finally lay down beside the fence again, watching us.

The owner wasn't home, so Richard requested an officer from the animal shelter to bring a tranquilizer gun. The dispatcher said it would be a while before the officer was available, so we settled down to wait, safe inside our cars. Every so often, Richard would amuse himself by shouting, "Here, kitty, kitty", over the outside speaker, which would send the huge animal into a bellowing fury again.

A little while later the shift commander called me, wanting more information, and I briefed him over the radio. "All right, it sounds like you're doing everything you can,'' he said. ''Just don't get out of your car until the animal shelter guy gets there.'' Richard and I looked at each other and laughed. I love it when supervisors use their superior intellect and years of experience to help you understand how to deal with a tough problem.

It was then Deputy Buz Ozburn came on the air and asked the lieutenant if he could assist. ''I used to be a dog handler when I was in the military,'' he said, ''and I think I can help.'' The lieutenant left it up to me, and I told Buz by all means to come on down.

He arrived within minutes. ''You guys afraid of a dog?'' he yelled out the window. Richard and I nodded vigorously. He laughed and shook his head. ''You have to show them who's boss,'' he said, ''dogs can sense fear.''

''This is no ordinary dog, Buz,'' I warned, ''this is a big dog. A very big dog.''

''He's also a very mean dog,'' Richard added. Buz ignored us, and we watched, fascinated, as he stepped carefully from his car.

The Great Dane was probably exhausted from trying to eat my car, because for the past ten minutes he had been lying quietly, apparently asleep. He raised his head when Buz drove up but didn't even stand. Tired or not, I was convinced he would be all over Buz in short order. I unsnapped my .38, prepared to shoot the dog while there was still enough left of Buz to leave the casket open.

Buz advanced slowly toward the big animal, and I was almost afraid to look. Amazingly enough, the dog made no hostile move. Buz walked closer and closer. Maybe he did know what he was doing. When he was about three feet away, he stopped. He and the dog eyed each other and there was a breathless moment of silence.

Then the hairs on the dog's back began to stand up, his lips curled into a snarl, and he gathered his legs under him, prepared to spring. ''NO!'' Buz shouted, raising his arm over his head.

Startled, the dog cringed.

For long minutes they stared at each other; then Buz started to lower his arm. Instantly, the dog began to snarl. Instantly Buz screamed, "NO!" and the dog flinched. So it went for the next ten minutes. Every time Buz started to relax, the dog looked as though he was about to eat him, and Buz would yell.

Richard and I soon grew bored with the stand-off, so we started yelling, "Sic him boy!" over the outside speakers. Each time we'd holler, the animal would growl, and Buz would hiss urgently, "Will you guys shut up!"

After what must have seemed like a month to poor Buz, the animal shelter officer arrived. "Having a little trouble?" he yelled.

Laughing, Richard pointed to the rigid Ozburn. "He is."

"Hurry up," Buz muttered through clenched teeth.

The man loaded a dart into the rifle and took careful aim. There was a "pop," and suddenly the dart was sticking out of the Great Dane's rump.

The dog yelped and went charging around the corner of the house. A few minutes later, we helped him load the unconscious animal into his truck. We weren't sorry to see him go.

Drenched with sweat, Buz tottered back to his car. "See," he said in a shaky voice, "you just gotta show em' who's boss."

We were very impressed.

20

Undercover

While I spent a good portion of my law enforcement career as a member of the uniform patrol division, I don't want you to think that's all I did. I've had plenty of other assignments, including working undercover. Once. It happened while I was still a lowly rookie assigned to the radio room.

It seemed one of the local bars had become quite a hangout for pool hustlers, and according to information we were getting from informants, heavy-duty gambling was going on. Several thousand dollars changed hands on some nights, and with that much money involved, other problems were occurring. There had been robberies in the parking lot, losers who failed to pay were ending up in the hospital, and prostitutes, able to sniff out a hundred dollar bill at five miles, were also beginning to congregate.

Finally, there were rumors of narcotics transactions. While such information may hardly seem like big news in the drug-saturated society we live in today, it was pretty hot stuff back in 1971. Not much was known about the drugs, but it was said employees were openly selling white pills in the bar. They were also selling some sort of black capsule, and the informant said customers would pay five or even ten dollars for one. No one was sure what the black capsule was, but we hoped to find out.

If gambling was going on and if the employees were dealing drugs, the state beverage department could move against their liquor license and shut the place down. Actually, "shut down" was not the most accurate term, since they could still operate; they just couldn't sell alcoholic beverages. But it would certainly have the same effect. I couldn't imagine a bunch of pool hustlers standing around swigging Cokes while betting a $100 a game. Nor could I envision one of the working girls sidling up to a john and saying, "Hey, big boy, buy me a 7-Up."

The complaints became so numerous it was decided to work a joint investigation with the beverage department. They would supply the money, and we would supply the undercover people. Our department would make the arrests and gather enough evidence to allow the beverage folks to bring administrative charges against the liquor license. That would make everyone happy. The sheriff could get the publicity and the beverage department the credit.

And that's where I came in. I was selected as one of the undercover officers. "We need someone not known in the streets," the beverage agent in charge of the operation told me, "and since you haven't worked outside yet, no one will know you."

True enough. In those days rookie deputies worked as communication dispatchers or jailers. Rookies we might be but we had full arrest powers, and since our faces were unknown, we were occasionally tapped for operations like this. Of course it was only a one-night stand, so to speak, but I hoped an outstanding showing on my part could lead to other such operations.

I was to accompany a veteran deputy named David Neal. We would look for gambling around the pool table and any narcotics violations. In order to blend in, we would, I was happy to discover, drink beer purchased with money supplied by the beverage department. It sounded great.

In preparation for the big night, I borrowed a shoulder holster from a friend of mine. It was a rather peculiar style in that the revolver was carried upside down, but he assured me, it was the ultimate in concealability.

"But how do you draw the gun?" I asked.

"It's simple," he said, strapping the holster on the outside of his shirt, the gun tucked under his arm. "You see this thumb release here?" I saw it. He flicked it with his thumb and the gun slid into his hand. "See, gravity does all the work."

When I tried my own gun, I found it was slightly smaller than his and was rather loose in the holster. If anything, this increased the speed of the draw, since my weapon literally fell out when I pushed the release. I decided this was probably a good thing. Of course, the speed of my draw was significantly reduced since I had to unbutton my shirt first.

David and I walked into the bar around 7:30 that night and took a seat in a booth. We were to spend two hours inside, watching the gamblers, looking for narcotics violations, and, I hoped, fighting off prostitutes. Outside, a joint force of deputies and beverage agents waited across the street. When we had gathered sufficient evidence, I would go outside and give the signal that would bring them running.

We were seated close to the pool tables, and we ordered two draft beers. When they arrived, I gulped mine down. "Hey, take it easy on that stuff," David said. "We're going to be here a while."

"Beer doesn't bother me," I said confidently, "I can drink this stuff all night." I hiccupped slightly and he smiled.

My gun in the borrowed holster bumped against my chest whenever I moved, and I decided I rather liked the sensation. It made me feel powerful, invincible, like I could handle anything. I hunched forward slightly, rocking a little. Bump-bump-bump went the holster.

"You all right?" David asked, concerned.

"Huh?...oh...sure." I flushed. "Just an old football injury." I straightened up, rubbing a shoulder. "It bothers me a little sometimes.''

He smiled. "You played football?"

"Well, not very long, actually: the injury and all that." I felt like an idiot.

Luckily, there was plenty of action going on at the pool tables. It took us a while to figure out what was happening. Money was not openly changing hands, but David soon spotted how they were paying off. At the end of the game, the loser would casually place a rolled up bill under the cushion as the balls were being racked. The winner would walk by, retrieve the money with a smooth and almost undetectable motion, and drop it in his pocket.

We started keeping notes on beer coasters, which blended in well with our environment. We identified the players as "black shirt," "tattoo," "tank top," etc. As each game ended, we made a mark to indicate who played and who won.

Meanwhile, the beer kept coming, and I kept drinking. David was just sipping his, so I was way ahead of him. My initial nervousness had long since been replaced by a wonderful feeling of confidence and exhilaration. This was great! Another beer arrived as I was telling David how much I loved being a deputy and what a thrill it was to be in law enforcement and how great it was to be involved in an undercover operation like this. In the middle of my speech the waitress reappeared, shaking a brown plastic pitcher. "You gentlemen care to try your luck?" she asked, extending the pitcher. I peered inside, and my heart raced. There were several dozen large white pills and, nestled right in the middle, a black one.

The black capsule!

It was true. They were selling dope right at the table. David didn't seem at all concerned. "How much?" he asked the waitress.

"Everyone else pays 25 cents," she said, shaking the pitcher, "but for you, honey, only a quarter." He laughed, gave her a coin, and drew out a white pill. I couldn't believe how calm he was.

She was talking to me. "I'm sorry," I said, "would you say that again?"

She smiled, "I asked if you wanted to give it a try." I didn't know what to say. Should I go ahead and buy a pill? If I did, should I actually swallow the thing? It might be LSD. I might start freaking out from a bad trip, shrieking and screaming and battling imaginary snakes.

I tried to get some idea from David as to what I should do, but he wasn't even looking at me, just humming along with the jukebox and watching the pool players. I decided I'd pretend to go along, so as not to blow my cover. I gave her a quarter and also drew a white pill. My heart was pounding; I resolved to pop the pill in my mouth but not swallow it. When she turned her back, and before the drugs could affect me, I'd spit it out.

As I opened my mouth, she gave me a funny look, snatched the pill from my hand, and moved to another table. David let out a whoop of laughter, scaring the hell out of me. Maybe he had swallowed his pill and was hallucinating. "Did you take the dope?" I whispered anxiously.

"That's not dope," he gasped, "I thought you knew. It's a jukebox pool." He fell back against the booth, shaking with laughter. "Those things are plastic. If you get the black pill, you win. You get to split the total with the jukebox." He wiped his eyes. "I thought sure you were going to swallow that thing."

I was burning with embarrassment. "Aw, I knew that."

Time passed. I had several more beers, although David had long since stopped drinking. He was totaling the notes he had made on the beer coasters, when he wasn't laughing at me. "Take these chaaaaaaains from my heart and set me freeee," I warbled along with Hank. "You've gone away and no longerrrr care for meee."

David laughed. "Do you have any idea how awful you sing?"

My head flopped toward him. I was having a hard time keeping it level. "I knooooow that you are gone..."

He waved a napkin. "All right, I give up. No more, please."

I decided I loved this man. I had never met a kinder, more understanding person or a better conversationalist. "David, you're great."

"And you're drunk."

I tried to look him in the eye to assure him he was mistaken, but at the moment he had four eyes, and they kept swimming in and out of focus. I finally picked out the two I thought belonged to him. "I'm not drunk," I said, and he howled. "Okay, sure, I've hadda few beers," I belched, "but I'm feeling perfatly...perfidly...I'm feeling fine." I raised my glass, slopping beer on the table. "This stuff here," I took a big swallow, "it don't 'fect me at all."

David was still laughing as he looked at his watch. "I hate to break the news, but it's time to give the signal."

What was he talking about? I tried to concentrate. "Whatta ya mean?"

"The signal. Remember why we're here?" he pointed toward the door. "All those guys out there are waiting for us to tell them it's time to come in and start arresting people."

"Oh, the signal!" I hiccupped. "Is it time?"

"It's time," he said.

I slid out of the booth. "It's time to give the signal, the signal, the signal," I sang, staggering toward the door. People were turning and smiling, watching my progress. "It's time to give...." I lurched to a stop. My god, I had forgotten what the signal was! I spun around, almost falling, and worked my way back to the table. "David," I hissed. He turned. "What was it again?"

"Just go outside and raise your right arm," he said, laughing. "Think you can remember that?"

I was highly insulted. "Course I can 'member." I headed for the door, but I wasn't taking any chances. I kept repeating, "Just go outside and raise your arm, just go outside and raise your arm, just go outside and..." I was concentrating so much on remembering how to give the signal I crashed into the jukebox, ending the record. Howls of protest rose around me. "Oops, sorry," I said. David put his face in his hands.

As I turned, something cold and sharp raked across my ribs.

"What th...?" I yelped, spinning around. No one was there, but then something bit into my elbow. I looked down and saw a strange bulge, which moved slightly. Something was inside my shirt! I seized it with both hands, somehow convinced it was a rat. It was small and hard with rounded edges. Luckily, just before I ripped my shirt off, I realized it was my revolver. I must have knocked it loose from the holster when I collided with the jukebox.

I stopped struggling and looked around. Everyone close by was staring at me. "Sorry," I said, heading toward the door again, "Vietnam veteran. Flashback."

I managed to make it out the door, but it was difficult. Before I gave the signal I decided I had better be prepared. I laboriously unbuttoned my shirt, snapped the gun back in the holster, and slowly rebuttoned the shirt. Now for the signal.

I came to attention, facing the parking lot across the street. Slowly I raised my right arm and stood there in silence, feeling like a Nazi. I was uncomfortable with the comparison, so I raised my left arm, too. Now I felt like a diver getting ready to do a two-and-a-half double twist. I put both arms straight up. Now I was Pretty Boy Floyd, surrendering to the G-men.

A crowd of deputies and beverage agents charged across the street, headed for the bar. "Don't shoot, coppers," I yelled, as they rushed past, "I give up."

In short order they had the place secured and the gamblers rounded up. David pointed out the ones to be arrested, and they were handcuffed and escorted outside. I helped load them into the waiting cruisers, giggling and laughing the whole time. David told me later he had never heard a cop give a prisoner his rights by singing them.

I thought it was the least I could do.

21

Never Mind

My buddy Gary was the first cop to arrive at the scene of the wreck, and it was a messy one. Witnesses said the car must have been doing close to 60 as it came down the exit ramp off the interstate. Where the ramp made a sharp bend, the speed limit was only 25. The heavy sedan left the road in the first part of the turn, sailed through the air for about 40 feet and landed nose first, flipping end over end. It finally came to rest upside down in the parking lot of a service station.

The driver, a man in his fifties, was not wearing a seat belt and was thrown out of the tumbling vehicle. He died instantly, crushed as the car rolled over him, his blood puddling on the asphalt. There was already a good-sized crowd on hand when Gary arrived. He moved the people back, called for an ambulance, and awaited the arrival of a state trooper who would handle the actual accident investigation.

As he was getting the names of witnesses, a car screeched to a stop behind him. "Daddy!" someone wailed. Through the crowd came an extremely distraught man in his early twenties, frantically pushing people out of the way. "Daddy!" he cried again as he saw the body of the driver, now covered with a sheet.

He took in the horrific scene, and went to his knees. "Oh, my God!" he screamed. "Daddy, please be alive, oh, Daddy."

Great wracking sobs burst from him, and he began pounding the pavement in a fury of grief. "It's my fault, it's my fault," he moaned.

Gary said the sudden appearance of the anguished young man caught everyone by surprise, but he quickly moved to help. "Come on," he said to the sobbing man, helping him to his feet. "There's nothing more you can do for him now."

The man flung himself on my friend, weeping as though his heart would break. "Please say he isn't dead!" he cried. "Please let him live!"

Gary began moving him away from the bloody scene, and several members of the crowd came over to offer condolences. The man was almost incoherent with grief but managed to choke out a sad story of a family fight that came to blows between father and son. Considerably stronger and significantly more sober, the younger man easily bested his drunken father.

Enraged and humiliated, the older man staggered from the house, jumped in his car, and tore off down the highway. Terrified, the mother implored her son to stop him before he killed himself or someone else. His dad had a good lead, but the son closed the gap steadily and was only a half mile or so behind him when he saw the car turn off the interstate. To his horror, he arrived only seconds after the catastrophic accident, too late to do anything.

"Don't you see?" he said to Gary. "I killed him!" He hugged the deputy, sobbing on his chest.

The troopers were soon on the scene, and Gary led the weeping man to one side, where he could have a little privacy and wait to give his statement to the investigating officer. They walked a few steps, and the man suddenly turned, stretching out both arms. "Oh, Daddy, I'm so sorry," he wept, "I never had the chance to tell you how much I loved you." He was rocking back and forth, facing the demolished vehicle, tears cascading down his face. My friend said it was a supremely emotional moment and he himself had tears in his eyes.

Suddenly the man stopped rocking and stared intently at the upside-down license plate. "Hey, wait a minute," he said, running over to the car. He twisted his head to read the numbers, then straightened up. "That's not my daddy's car!" He ran to the body of the driver and lifted the sheet. Bending down, he peered into the dead man's face for long moments. "That's not my daddy," he said, backing away. "My daddy has red hair." There wasn't a sound from the watching crowd. "That's not my daddy," he said again. He turned, ran to his car, and drove off.

They never did find out who he was.

22

Never When You Need Them

Have you ever asked yourself why cops are never around when you need them? If you haven't, believe me, you're in the minority. Most people, at one time or another, have wondered why it is that when you try to squeeze a yellow light, there will be a police car on every corner, but when some drunk runs you up on the sidewalk, the only cops you see are parked at donut shops.

I was talking to a civilian friend one day, and he mentioned he had lived on his street for ten years and had never seen a marked cruiser car pass his home. I was young and idealistic in those days and took such comments very seriously. "Come on, John," I told him, "deputies probably pass your house all the time."

"Nope." He was adamant. "I'm outside all weekend long, doing the yard or working in the garden, and I've never seen a cop."

"Well, that doesn't mean they aren't on your street occasionally."

"It does to me," he said. "Out of sight, out of mind. Makes me wonder where my tax dollars are going."

"This is a residential area, and there isn't that much activity around here."

"That's what you think. We've had plenty of break-ins and thefts." He pointed at the house across the street. "Someone stole my neighbor's trolling motor out of his garage just last week."

"But," I said, "there's no guarantee that simply having a car pass by would prevent crime. I remember a study done in Kansas City by the International Association of Chiefs of Police, and they found...."

He waved this off. "Oh, don't give me that academic crap. I'm not interested what happened in Kansas City. I'm just saying I've never seen a sheriff's department car on my street."

"And I'm saying it doesn't prove a thing. The deputies who work this district are frequently in this area and...."

"Where do you work?" he asked.

I flushed, "Well, actually, I...uh, work in this district."

"And how many times have you driven down my street?" he demanded, boring in relentlessly.

My face got warmer still. "I can't remember exactly how many times I've..."

"You see?" he crowed. "Even you admit you don't drive down this street."

I left, knowing I had emerged the loser in the argument and not liking it one bit. I was still not convinced that the mere sight of a cruiser car would deter crime over the long term, but from talking with my buddy, I realized it would provide some comfort for the average taxpayer. That meant there was probably significant PR value, a factor I was overlooking.

With that thought in mind, I decided I would make a diligent effort to drive down his street as often as possible in the coming month. And I did. While it was too busy on the evening shift to do much, I practically lived on the street during midnights and days. Of course, he was usually sleeping or at work during these times, but I was confident the law of averages was in my favor and, sooner or later, he was bound to see my marked car. All told, I must have made 50 trips down his street.

One Saturday I took a report of a stolen bike a few blocks from his house and decided to drive by and see if he was home. He was, and I came in for a cup of coffee.

"So, John," I said smugly, "Seen any cruiser cars lately?"

He poured my coffee and set the cup in front of me. "Like I said, I've been living on this street for ten years, and except for today," he said, pointing at my car, "I've never seen a cop car patrolling."

I was astonished. I told him of the dozens of trips I had made up and down his street at all hours of the day and night. He didn't believe a word of it. I grew shrill with righteous indignation but to no avail. I did my best to change his mind, but I didn't succeed. To come up against such a brick wall of non-belief was maddening, especially since I knew the truth. I felt like a missionary preaching to a heathen. I finally had to give up, and it was frustrating in the extreme to think I had made that effort for nothing.

Thinking about it later, I concluded that, while his perceptions did not agree with the facts, those perceptions did constitute his reality. If my friend had happened to look out the window at the right moment just three or four times, he would have been ecstatic. But he didn't.

Actually, the whole thing was yet another valuable lesson, because it showed me how easy it is to influence people's thinking on the basis of statistically insignificant occurrences. I later understood how three armed robberies could seem like a crime wave and three arrests like a major crack-down. That knowledge would serve me well when I found myself working as a media relations officer later in my career.

But I didn't know that then. All I knew was the frustration of trying to convince a skeptic that cops are, at least some of the time, around when you need them.

23

Talk Radio - Part 1

I had been a little nervous during my first few minutes on the radio, but I was starting to get the hang of it now. The program was "Pensacola Speaks," a nightly call-in show on WCOA Radio. The host, Dave Pavlock, invited me to come on and talk about law enforcement issues that might be of interest to the program's listeners.

I was excited but wary. There were procedures I would have to follow. "Dave, I'll have to get permission from the sheriff first."

He laughed, "He's the one who gave me your name."

Well, I guess that solved that problem. "Okay, what time should I be there?"

"Come about 15 minutes early. We go on the air right after the news." I was pretty impressed. I had never been on radio or television before, but I was looking forward to it.

So far, the show had gone well, but it had been a little disorienting at first. For some reason, I expected a spacious studio that looked like the bridge on the Starship Enterprise. I was certainly not prepared for the impossibly narrow little room that was smaller than my bathroom at home. Crammed with boxes of old promotional material, hurricane tracking maps, and coffee supplies, it was equipped with a small table, two microphones, and a couple of rickety, mismatched chairs.

The phone receiver rested next to a speaker, and a tangle of wires ran from the base of the phone into various control boxes. Pavlock wore a headset and was constantly fiddling with knobs and switches.

We spent a few minutes talking about law enforcement and some of the recent changes in the laws, then he opened the phone lines. I was nervous about the kinds of questions I might get, fearing someone would ask about an obscure point of law. I needn't have worried. No one asked about obscure points of law, they stayed on one theme the entire program: self-defense. All of them wanted to know when it was legally permissible to blow away one of their fellow citizens and what were the chances of being arrested if they did.

I was surprised, then dismayed. A more blood-thirsty group I had never been exposed to. It seemed everyone was prepared to shoot first and ask questions after the funeral. I tried to explain that while our laws certainly allowed citizens to defend themselves using any method up to and including deadly force, there were often less lethal alternatives.

They weren't interested.

One of the calls typified the attitude of the audience and came in toward the end of the show. Since the callers didn't have to identify themselves, I only knew it was an elderly woman.

"Is this Deputy Parker?"

"Yes, it is."

"I'm really enjoying the show tonight. You've given us a lot of useful information."

"Thank you very much."

"Well, I want some information, too."

I smiled. "I'll do what I can to help you, ma'am."

"I'm having a problem in my neighborhood, and I don't know what to do about it."

"What kind of problem?"

"It's these kids," she said.

"What are they doing?"

"What are they doing? Why they're pestering me to death!"

"What kind of pestering?"

She thought about this for a moment. "They keep asking me for money, and I don't think I should give them any."

"Are they panhandling?"

"Well, sometimes they are. Other times they say they're selling magazine subscriptions or raffle tickets."

"I guess that's pretty annoying." I had no idea where she was headed with her question.

"It sure is," she said, "and I need some advice."

"What sort of advice do you want?"

"I want to know if I can shoot them if they come around here bothering me."

"I'm sorry, ma'am, we must have a bad connection. I thought I heard you say you wanted to shoot those kids because they were annoying you."

"That's exactly what I said. I want you to give me permission to shoot them if they keep coming around." She chuckled, "I've got me a fine gun."

"Ma'am," I choked, "I can't give you permission to do something like that."

"Well, who can? The sheriff?"

"The sheriff can't give you permission, either."

"Well, who can I talk to?"

"You can't talk to anyone," I said. "I mean, there's no one who can give you permission to shoot someone."

"Not even if they're pestering me?"

"Not even then."

She mulled this over for a moment. "How about if I just shoot them in the leg?"

"No! Not even in the leg." I was beginning to perspire.

"Well, where can I shoot them; in the arm?"

I felt like I was caught in some sort of bizarre dream. "Ma'am, you can't shoot them in the leg, you can't shoot them in the arm, you can't shoot them anywhere."

"Not even if they keep pestering me?"

I was breathing hard. "The only time you can shoot someone is if they are actually threatening your life."

"Who says?"

"It's the law," I said, mopping my face.

"Does the law say anything about people who keep pestering folks?"

"Yes, it does. It's very specific. It says you positively cannot shoot someone for that."

She was silent for a few seconds. "Is this some of that gun control stuff I've been reading about?"

"No, it's just the law."

"Well," she said reluctantly, "if it's the law, I guess I'll have to obey it."

I started to breathe a little easier. "I'm glad you feel that way."

"I'm a law-abiding citizen," she said, "but I'll tell you one thing."

"What's that?"

"I think it's a pretty stupid law!"

"Yes, ma'am. Thanks for calling."

24

The School Of Hard Knocks

"All right. I'll answer one more question; then I have to go back to work."

"Okay, what's that, Uncle Don?"

I glanced down at my uniform shirt to see what my young nephew was pointing at. "This holds my whistle," I said, touching the shiny, brass lanyard that ran from my right shoulder down inside the shirt pocket.

"Can I see it?" His eyes were dancing with excitement as I pulled it free of my pocket flap. When the object attached to the end of the lanyard came into view his excitement changed to bewilderment. "That's not a whistle."

I fingered the large paper clip, smiling. "You're right. This is really just a big paper clip. See?" He examined it carefully, not understanding why a cop would have a paper clip where a whistle ought to be. "But where's your whistle?"

"I thought you'd never ask." I opened my handcuff case, removed the shiny, silver, "Thunderer" brand whistle and handed it to him. It went immediately to his mouth.

"Uh-uh," my sister-in-law said. He froze. "Not in the house."

"Can't I blow it just once?"

I pointed toward the door. "Why don't you go out on the front porch and try it." He tore out the door and woke up the neighborhood with several long blasts.

Back inside he handed the whistle to me reluctantly. "But Uncle Don, why do you keep it in your handcup case?"

"They're called hand-CUFFs, and I keep it there because it's got hard edges and it digs into my chest."

He understood. "But what about the paper thing?"

"Paper clip. That's just to keep the whistle cord from falling out of my pocket when I move. If I have to direct traffic I take the paper clip off, attach the whistle and go to work."

"Do you ever give whistles to little boys as presents?"

I patted him on the head. "Only when I don't like their parents."

Back in my cruiser car I adjusted the whistle cord and checked to make sure the flap on my cuff case was securely snapped shut. I smiled as I remembered my nephew's expression when he saw that paper clip. It didn't puzzle just children; it was a mystery to adults as well — until I told them the story behind my decision to stop carrying the whistle in my shirt pocket.

My fingers went automatically to the small lump on my rib cage that was still there after four years. It's said the mind tends to block out memories of physical pain but I could vividly remember every detail. Even now, I fancied I could still feel that sharp ache. I wondered if I hadn't actually cracked a rib. It stayed sore for so long and there was that lump, as from a healed fracture.

How well I recall the incident that caused all that pain. It occurred during the morning on a day shift that should have been quiet.

"109."

I keyed the microphone. "Go ahead."

"Got a disturbance at Millie's Place. An intoxicated woman refusing to leave."

"I'll be enroute." I was only a half-mile away.

"86," the dispatcher said, "back up 109."

"10-4 headquarters," Hightower said, "I'm right behind

him."

And so he was. I glanced in the mirror and saw his cruiser turn the corner two blocks back. We arrived together.

Millie's Place was just one of the many beer joints in the area. Catering to a rough class of hard drinkers, this was not your cozy little neighborhood bar. No football games shown on TV here, no button-down businessmen stopping in for a convivial libation on their way home, and no love-starved singles ever chose this place to play the mating game. The furniture was strictly heavy-duty and most of it bolted to the floor. Other than a permanently out-of-order pin ball machine, the only diversion for the patrons, besides drinking and fighting of course, was supplied by a battered pool table with faded green felt, the wood scorched by years of cigarette burns.

Entertainment came from an over-worked jukebox, completely enclosed in a heavy steel cage. This served two purposes. The cage protected the jukebox box from flying objects like beer bottles and bodies and also kept out the persistent burglars. The decor could be classed as "traditional redneck" and consisted of a half-dozen lighting fixtures advertising different beers, various plastic clocks also advertising beer, and a crudely lettered sign which read, "We reserve the rite to refuse service to enyone" along with a moth-eaten rebel flag behind the bar.

No one remembered who "Millie" was. The bar had changed hands a dozen times over the past ten years but the name remained the same. It was no better and no worse than the other cut-and-shoot clubs in the area and it was always good for two or three fights every weekend. But this was not the weekend. This was supposed to be a quiet Thursday morning.

As I stepped from my car I heard a shrill voice. "I ain't going no place, goddamnit, now leave me alone!"

We went inside and I was facing the back of a woman who overflowed the bar stool like a pile of laundry. She was well over three hundred pounds. Greasy brown hair straggled to her shoulders and her neck bulged from the collar of her tent-like striped dress.

She was arguing with the barmaid, a dissipated, gray-haired woman with prominent pouches under both eyes. "You ain't drinking for free, dearie," she said, "you either pay the bill or you leave."

"What's the problem?" I asked.

They both turned. "She owes me three dollars and eighty-six cents," the barmaid said.

The woman glared at me, tiny, hostile eyes barely visible in her puffy face. "This ain't none of your business." She waved a ponderous arm in the direction of the barmaid. "It's between me and her."

"It's my business now," I said. "If you owe the woman money I'd advise you to settle up."

"I ain't paying her a damn thing! My credit is good."

I turned to the barmaid. "You can always press charges against her if you want."

"No. It's not worth it. I just want her out."

I nodded and Hightower stepped forward and tapped the Incredible Bulk on the shoulder. "Let's go, lady. Time to leave."

"I ain't going no-wheres!" she screeched, shoving Hightower away.

That did it. "Ma'am, you're under arrest," I told her. I took one arm and Hightower the other. We managed to get her on her feet and turned around but then she started to actively resist.

"Get your hands off me."

"Come on lady," I said, "make it easy on yourself." She suddenly jerked her arm free and went after Hightower, punching and clawing. I grabbed her again but it was difficult to hold on. The spongy flesh kept slipping away from me and the woman was incredibly strong.

We wrestled back and forth without making much progress and at some point, two more deputies arrived. With the extra help we were beginning to make some headway and almost had her to the door. I was still occupied with that one massive arm, now sweat-slicked and harder than ever to grip. Still determined to deal with Hightower she broke away from me again. I leaned forward to grab her just as she drew back to punch him.

An elbow the size of a watermelon thudded into my chest, driving the whistle in my pocket deep into my rib cage. A spear of agony shot through my chest and my legs turned to rubber. I collapsed backwards against the wall, clutching my side, certain I had been shot or stabbed.

The other guys succeeded in getting the woman out the door but I was immobile, both hands pressed against my chest, convinced if I removed them a gout of blood and various internal parts would gush forth. I was having trouble catching my breath and took little sips of air, trying to get oxygen. I could not believe how much it hurt!

I finally mustered up enough courage to lift my shaking hands to examine what I thought must be a mortal wound. Nothing. I looked closer. No blood, no internal organs, not even a rip in my shirt. I probed the area and yelped in pain as my hard whistle once again made contact with my badly bruised ribs. I finally understood what had happened and realized I would very likely survive.

Hightower stepped inside, puffing and blowing. "You okay?"

"Yeah," I said weakly, "She gave me a pretty good lick though. I thought she broke a rib."

"We put her...in your car," he wheezed, "I think she's about...done in herself." He gasped for a few minutes. "I know I am."

I was beginning to feel better although my ribs were still on fire. "Yeah, thanks."

I wobbled outside and got in my car stiffly, favoring my injured side. My prisoner was in the cage, handcuffed and very unhappy. I reached to close the door and groaned. "What the hell's wrong with you?" she asked.

"You damn-near broke one of my ribs."

She leaned back in the seat. "Good. I hope you die."

Yes, that was a fun day and that's why I keep my whistle in my handcuff case and not on the end of the lanyard, inside my pocket like I used to. Before that fight at Millie's Place.

25

It Ain't Necessarily So

Law enforcement is an unpredictable job, which, for me, is part of its appeal. Each day presents an endless variety of problems to solve, and those problems don't end simply because a cop goes off duty. I have run into my share of off-duty problems, but most have been minor. Still, I'm always prepared to take action, like the night I stopped at a fast-food outlet to get a burger.

I placed my order, and as I waited in line, I noticed a woman in the driveway of the nearby office building. An attractive blond wearing a colorful pullover and jeans, she was standing directly in front of a white four-door Pontiac. I could see her clearly in the glare of the headlights, and she was not happy.

She was talking steadily to the driver, occasionally waving her arms, and she was growing increasingly angry, although I didn't know why. I was a little too far away to understand what she was saying. I thought it might be a couple of drunks involved in a lovers' quarrel.

With my law enforcement instincts fully alerted now, I kept a close eye on the scene. The car inched forward, stopped, then, ever so slowly, began backing up. Another stop, and the vehicle began moving forward again, the blond retreating a step at a time.

So far the driver had made no attempt to leave the car, nor

had the woman attempted to get in. Odd behavior, but I was used to odd behavior from drunks. The woman stopped moving, but the car continued to creep forward until the front bumper was almost touching her leg. She shouted and the car jerked to a stop, then began backing again. The driver was turning at the same time, and the front wheels rolled slowly up on the curb.

I thought the blond was going to have a stroke. She started jumping up and down and pounding on the hood. The car rolled back onto the pavement and stopped. There was a heated exchange between the driver and the woman; then the car began moving forward once more.

I had seen enough. Like most off-duty cops, I kept my radio, badge, and gun with me at all times. I grabbed the radio and called the dispatcher. My intention was to ask for an on-duty deputy to meet me at the restaurant. Currently attired in a ragged T-shirt and equally ragged jeans, I had no desire to try and convince these people I was really a cop. It was a busy night, and the dispatcher told me to standby.

My coffee arrived, and as I paid for it, I asked the girl what was going on over there.

"Over where?"

I pointed at the blond, still in front of the car.

She looked. "Oh, they're just practicing their parking."

"They're practicing what?"

She laughed, "Their parking. You know, for the driver's license test? That woman's been screaming at her kid for the last 30 minutes, it's really funny."

The radio suddenly came to life. "109, go ahead with your message."

"Uh, cancel that last transmission," I said into the microphone, feeling the color rise in my cheeks.

The girl was impressed. "Are you a cop?"

"No, no, I'm a plumber. I was just checking on a customer with a backed up septic tank."

"Oh, yuk."

102

"Yeah, well, someone has to do it," I said as I drove off. The last I saw of the blond lady, she was still standing in the driveway in front of the car, still yelling at her kid.

26

Ready On the Firing Line

I was almost finished with my presentation to the group of senior citizens. They had been an enthusiastic and attentive audience, really getting into my "Self-Protection" talk. I enjoyed making these talks, even if it was my own time. The pastor of this particular church was a friend and had asked me to talk to the group as a favor. After I responded to questions, we broke for refreshments.

A woman approached me as I was sipping my coffee. "Deputy Parker?" she asked rather timidly.

"Yes, ma'am."

"I really enjoyed your talk, especially the part about gun safety."

"Why, thank you very much. I certainly enjoyed talking to your group."

"I was wondering how much you know about guns."

I laughed, "I'm certainly no expert, but I'm familiar with most of them. Why do you ask?"

"Well, I have a handgun my late husband left me, and to tell you the truth, I don't really know that much about it." She laughed nervously, "If someone were to break in, I might end up shooting myself."

"What kind of gun is it?"

She thought a moment. "It's kind of dark-looking, and it has wood handles."

I sighed. "Ma'am, do you know if it's a revolver or an automatic?"

"No, I don't."

"Well, that's not so important. What do you want to know about it?"

"If it's loaded or not."

I stared at her. "Don't you know?"

"Well, no, and I was wondering if I could bring it to you at the sheriff's department."

This was worse than I thought. "Ma'am, I don't think that's such a good idea. Maybe I'd better come to you." The idea of this woman carrying around a handgun that might or might not be loaded was not reassuring.

She was enthusiastic. "Oh, could you? I'm scared to death of the thing. I haven't touched it since he gave it to me 11 years ago."

I took her name and address, and the next afternoon I drove to her home. "Come in, come in," she said. I stepped inside. "I keep the gun in my dresser." We walked into her bedroom, and she opened the top drawer. "There it is."

And it was, a .32 caliber Colt revolver, in the bottom of the drawer. It was an old gun and might even be worth something to a collector, but I didn't care about that; I only had eyes for the hammer. When she had opened the drawer, I had seen instantly that the hammer was all the way back, which meant it was cocked. The rims of the cartridge cases were plainly visible along the edge of the cylinder. So the gun was not only cocked, it was loaded, too. "Ma'am, have you handled the gun since your husband put it here?"

She shivered. "No, I haven't. Guns scare me."

I picked up the revolver gingerly. A thick layer of lint coated the interior parts. I could well believe it hadn't been touched in 11 years. "All you would have to do is pull the trigger and it would fire.''

She took a step back. ''Can't you put the safety on?''

''Revolvers don't have safeties, but I can make it safe by letting the hammer down.'' I took a firm grip on the hammer and pulled the trigger. It didn't budge. I pulled harder. Slowly the trigger moved, making little gritty noises. I felt the trigger sear disengage the hammer step, but the hammer barely twitched. The insides of the gun were so full of goop, it couldn't function. I actually had to force the hammer down. ''Well, it was safer than I thought. This thing wouldn't have fired if you had hit it with a sledgehammer.'' I looked down the barrel. It was completely plugged with lint. ''Even if it had fired, it might have blown up.''

''Blown up?'' she said faintly, taking another step back.

''It's okay now, believe me.'' I recommended she take it to a gunsmith for a thorough cleaning, then sign up for a gun safety course.

She agreed, and I left, feeling depressed. I was glad she had asked me for advice, even if it had taken her 11 years, but I wondered how many other people were out there with the same problem. It was not a comforting thought.

27

Jail Tour

The evening had gone well. My wife and I and another couple, had enjoyed a nice supper and then a movie. Susan and Ted were fun to be around, and I always got a kick out of Susan's naive enthusiasm. Although the only child of wealthy parents and the recipient of a rather sheltered upbringing, she was always eager to try something new. We took them on their first all-day canoe trip because she had never been in a canoe before. They overturned twice, she lost a pair of expensive prescription sunglasses, got water in her watch and a really impressive sunburn. She loved it. Their zig-zag navigation, down the river, crashing into the banks, bouncing off tree stumps and running aground, was one of the funniest comedy acts I have ever seen. One day, thinking she was out of touch with the way the rest of the world lived, she decided to ride the city bus. She climbed aboard and presented the amazed driver with a fifty dollar bill. When told it was exact change only, she asked, ''Do you take American Express?'' Needless to say, she quickly found herself back on the street.

Not at all discouraged, she obtained the proper change, got on the next bus and rode for three hours, getting transfers and changing buses. She was propositioned once, asked for money three times, and scolded by an old lady who told her a nice girl like her had no business walking the streets. She said the worst thing was the fact the bus wasn't air-conditioned.

We had to pass the county jail on the way home, and she stared at the fortress-like building and shivered. "That place looks so...mean."

I laughed. "The jail isn't mean, it's the people in it."

"Are there really a lot of murderers in there?"

"Yup," I said, "and rapists, child molesters, burglars, bad check writers; you name it, we got em'."

"Can people visit the jail?"

"No problem." I glanced at her, "You want to go tonight?"

"Tonight?"

"Sure. The lieutenant in charge is a friend of mine. He won't mind a bit."

She turned to her husband. "Oh, Ted, could we?"

"Honey, that's up to Don." He looked at his watch. "How long would it take?"

"I'd say about 15 minutes, and since this is Saturday, things will be really jumping."

Susan was eager. "Come on, Ted, let's do it."

He laughed, "Okay, if it will make you happy."

"Oh, goody. Let's go, Don."

I turned around, and we parked in a spot with a clergy sign.

My wife frowned, "You're not supposed to do that."

I shut the car off and opened the door. "It's all right. I'm feeling especially religious tonight."

My wife made no move to get out, which didn't surprise me.

"Aren't you coming?" Susan asked her.

"No, I've seen the booking area on a weekend. One time was enough."

"Was it awful?" Susan whispered, goggle-eyed.

"You'll find out," she said, smirking. "Have fun."

I stashed my gun in the trunk since firearms are not allowed inside the jail and we walked to the prisoner entrance. The correction officer on the control panel recognized me and punched a button. The heavy door rumbled open, we stepped inside and it closed behind us. The inner door opened, and we stepped inside. It closed behind us with a loud clank, and Susan jumped.

The booking area was seething with activity. Prisoners were being fingerprinted; deputies, city police officers and state troopers were booking suspects; and one man, spread-eagled against a wall, was being searched by a correction officer. A corner of the room was used as the holding area, heavy fencing running from floor to ceiling. Inside were three benches, currently occupied by a dozen male arrestees, most of whom were in various states of intoxication and disrepair.

Judging from the amount of blood dried on his shirt and still crusted his hair, one tall, skinny guy, had emerged the loser in a fight. Several men were snoring on the floor, and even as we watched, a thin, bearded creature, wearing an army fatigue jacket, woke up. He raised his head, vomited quietly, then collapsed once again in the fresh puddle.

Susan and Ted tried to comprehend it, but it was almost too much for the uninitiated to grasp. "Come on," I said, "I'll show you around."

My companions were right beside me, heads turning left and right, trying to see everything. The sounds were the usual Saturday night bedlam: cries, moans, curses, maniacal laughter, occasional screams, the constant crash of the cell doors being opened and closed, telephones ringing, and the steady buzz of dozens of loud conversations.

I had them follow the same path an arrested person would take, starting with the booking, then to the fingerprint room, past the holding area, and finally to the dressing-out rooms. Here, those who would not be able to make bond gave up their clothing, got a shower and a delousing spray, and were issued jail uniforms. As we walked past the holding cells, a woman's arm shot out suddenly, grabbing Susan's sleeve. "You have to help me!" the prisoner screamed. Susan snatched her arm away. "The devil is out there," the woman cried, "you have to help me."

"Better stay in the middle of the corridor like I do," I said. "That way no one can grab you." They both moved to the exact center, Susan breathing hard from the scare.

As we turned the corner, I saw a pile of clothes on the floor across from a cell at the end of the row. Two muddy socks were tossed from the cell. "Hold up a minute," I said. They stopped. A stream of urine arced through the bars, soaking the clothes and splattering on the tile floor. "I think we'll go back the other way."

As we turned, the stream stopped. and a hoarse voice yelled, "Come here, girlie, I got something for you."

Ted chuckled, "One of your old boyfriends, Susan?"

"Very funny," she hissed.

As we walked back to the booking area, there was a commotion. A prisoner being removed from the holding area suddenly jerked away from the correction officer. Instantly, two other CO's and a nearby deputy grabbed the guy, pinning his arms behind him. "Get your hands off me, you bastards!" he yelled. "You're not puttin' me in no cell."

"That's what you think," the deputy said as they hustled him past us.

The shift lieutenant was standing at the records desk and I took my friends over and introduced them. "Well, how do you like our jail?" he asked Susan.

"It's...unbelievable!"

"Is it like this every Saturday?" Ted asked.

He laughed, "No, sometimes it gets busy." They both stared at him, and he threw up his hands. "Hey, I'm kidding, I'm kidding."

We talked for a few more minutes, and I decided it was time to go. "Do you have any more questions?"

Susan nodded. "We've seen the holding cells, but I wanted to know where you put the prominent people?"

The lieutenant and I looked at each other, then back at Susan.

"The what?" he asked.

"You know, the prominent people," she said earnestly. "Like if you arrest a doctor or a lawyer for drunk driving. Where do they go?" She waited.

It took me a moment to fully grasp what she meant, but when I got it, I burst out laughing. "Oh, the PROMINENT people." She nodded, and Ted and the lieutenant started laughing too.

"Susan," Ted said gently, "there are no cells for prominent people. This is it."

"You mean they have to go in with all these other...people?"

"That's right, ma'am," the lieutenant said. "Right in with the rest of the garbage."

I was still laughing, but Susan was too shocked to feel embarrassed. She hugged her husband's arm. "Ted, we are never, ever, going to drink and drive again."

He chuckled, "I'll drink to that."

"Don't make jokes. Do you want to end up in here?"

I thanked the lieutenant for his time, and we headed for the car. Susan was pale as we emerged from the tumultuous clamor into the peaceful darkness. "I'm going to have nightmares for a week," she said as I opened the car door.

"Well, how was the tour?" my wife asked.

Susan shook her head. "I should have stayed with you."

28

Talk Radio - Part 2

The radio show had been going well tonight, and the callers had covered a wider range of topics than the last time I was on. During that show, all they wanted to talk about was how they could legally shoot an intruder. There had been a few calls along those lines, but for the past 20 minutes, traffic enforcement had been the main point of discussion.

The host punched in another call for me. "Is this Deputy Parker?" the female caller asked.

I leaned closer to the microphone. "Yes, it is."

"Well, I have a question for you, and I certainly hope you can answer it." She sounded angry.

"I'll do the best I can, ma'am."

She gave a short, sharp laugh. "Yes. I'm sure you will." I waited. "The sheriff's department is supposed to be short of personnel, isn't that right?"

"Yes, ma'am." I said. "We are considerably below recommended staffing levels."

"And I'm sure the sheriff wants his deputies to concentrate on serious problems, doesn't he?"

She was leading up to something here. "Of course."

She pounced. "Well, if the sheriff's department is so short-handed, how come deputies are writing tickets to residents who have lived in a neighborhood for ten years, instead of concentrating on real crime?''

Now I understood. "I take it you got a ticket."

"Yes, I did," she said with some heat, "and the deputy said I was doing 42 in a 25 mile-an-hour zone. Do you know how much that is going to cost me?''

I calculated rapidly. "84 dollars."

"That's right!" She was breathing hard. "I don't remember when they lowered the speed limit to 25. Was that something our wonderful county commission did?''

I had to smile. "Ma'am, it's always been 25 in residential neighborhoods.''

"Well, I certainly wasn't going 17 miles above the speed limit.''

I had a ready answer. "If you're not guilty, ask for a judge trial so you can tell your side in court.''

"Oh, sure," she said, sarcasm dripping from every word, "I just bet he'll take my word over the deputy's.''

"You have nothing to lose by trying.''

"Never mind about the ticket, that's not the real problem.''

"What is?" I could hardly wait to hear it.

"It's the drinking and the drugs and the loud music that goes on in the park down the street. Evidently, the sheriff's department would rather write traffic tickets than take care of crime.''

"Actually, we try to do both.''

"Well," she huffed, "you'll never prove it by me.''

She told me the area where she lived, and we talked for a few minutes longer, but I didn't make much progress with the woman. I finally suggested she call me after the show was over so I could do some further checking for her. She did, and I got her name and number and promised to call her back. I thought this extra effort on my part might mollify her, but it didn't have the slightest effect; she was still just as angry when she hung up.

The next day I went to the traffic section and asked the lieutenant if his troops had been working radar in that particular subdivision. He checked and confirmed they had, in response to numerous complaints from residents about speeders and reckless drivers. I thanked him but didn't mention the woman's call. There was no point.

It was a familiar scenario. So many times we get raked over the coals because of traffic problems caused by "outsiders." We respond with increased enforcement and guess what? 75 percent of the tickets go to residents. An immediate and prolonged howl goes up because we wrote the wrong people tickets. We didn't, of course. It's just that they never expected to discover the real cause of their traffic problems.

I remember writing a ticket to a resident of a subdivision after she had run a stop sign right in front of me. She was very upset. "I live here," she wailed. "No one stops for that stop sign."

In this present situation, I could do nothing about the woman's ticket, but I did place a watch order on the park. After a week or so I called back to check on the problem. She grudgingly admitted things had been more peaceful, but I could tell she was still mad about the ticket. "I decided just to pay the fine and not go to court, but you can believe one thing for sure."

"What's that ma'am?"

"That's the last time I'll ever call the sheriff's department about a traffic problem!"

29

Eye In The Sky

When Lieutenant Louie Davis asked me if I wanted to go on a marijuana-spotting flight with him on my day off, I jumped at the chance. I didn't have much contact with the narcotics guys, and this would be something different. A fine pilot himself, Louie would be the spotter on this flight and leave the flying to Deputy Bob McGinn, a former military pilot.

It was a blistering summer afternoon, and the little Cessna 172 was like an oven. I couldn't wait to get up where the air was cool. The two men conducted a quick preflight, and we were soon rolling down the runway.

Louie told me we were looking for a small patch of marijuana only a mile or so from the airport. While we had some information about the general location, narcotics agents on the ground had spent several fruitless days tramping through the woods, looking for the stuff. He felt we could spot it from the air rather quickly.

Only seconds after we were airborne, we started circling, Bob flying while Louie and I looked out the window. We were making steep left turns, very steep left hand turns, and I was a little nervous to discover we were only 500 feet off the ground. The lower, the better, Louie explained. "Besides," he yelled above the roar of the engine, "it gives the dopers on the ground a more sporting chance if they want to shoot at us." I was pretty sure he was kidding, but I pulled another seat cushion under me just in case he wasn't.

"Let's go down to 250 feet, Bob," Louie said, and down we went, a little faster than I would have preferred. I quickly discovered the temperature at 250 feet was not much different than at ground level, meaning the heat was oppressive. Bob steepened the turn, and after a few more circles, I felt myself getting dizzy. It was not a nice feeling. I stared intently at the ground, trying to spot the marijuana plants.

"There they are!" Louie shouted. "Just beyond that little shed." I saw the shed, but I didn't see any marijuana. The pilot looked and nodded agreement. "You see it, Don?," Louie asked.

"I think so," I said, "there, by that shed." I figured that was a safe answer. Actually, I hadn't seen a thing.

"How many plants do you see?"

My eyes bugged out. "Oh, gosh, there must be at least *mfgzkptd* plants," I said, slurring the word.

"How many?"

"Quite a few,"

"More than a hundred?"

Why didn't he give it a rest? "Yeah, probably." He and McGinn roared with laughter, having pinned me to the wall.

"There's 21," he said.

I was astounded. Even from 250 feet I had trouble picking out individual trees and he had spotted 21 tiny plants. As it turned out, it was not really as astounding as I first thought. The informant had told him exactly how many plants were there.

Louie got on the radio and directed waiting ground units to the scene. Throughout the time they were working their way through the woods, we were circling, circling, circling, always to the left. It was hot, stuffy, and noisy in the small back seat, and my stomach was telling me it was not enjoying the trip. I wanted very much to feel hard, unmoving ground under my feet again, and I wasn't sorry when we finally called it a day and landed.

On the way back to the office, Louie talked about marijuana spotting. "You know a lot of spotters get so airsick they can't do it anymore?"

I wiped the clammy sweat from my pale face. "No kidding;" I said in a shaky voice, "that's hard to believe."

Louie glanced at his watch. "Almost lunch. You want to stop and get a barbecued pork sandwich?"

My stomach lurched. "No, I really need to get on home."

"We're going up tomorrow. You want to go along?"

"Gosh," I said, trying not to shudder, "I'd sure like to, but I've got a million things to do." I gulped, "Besides, I think I've learned all I need to know about marijuana spotting."

30

Bad Luck Brown

We had been sitting in the dark woods for well over an hour, watching the front of the motel. We knew what type of car the armed robbers would be driving, we knew they preferred to hit around midnight, we even knew they were planning to rob this particular motel. We just didn't know if they would be hitting tonight. All this information came courtesy of an informant, a brother of one of the robbers, himself a convicted felon and now awaiting trial on burglary charges.

Like most crooks he was always looking out for number one. The fact he was trying to set up his own brother was not of the slightest concern to him. Blood was certainly not thicker than a possible ten-year sentence in the state prison.

The investigators came to the patrol division asking for volunteers to help with the stakeout. It could last a week, and they didn't have sufficient bodies. I jumped at the chance. It sounded like real police work for a change, and I had visions of commendations dancing in my head.

Now we were in position, waiting for something to happen. We had two men inside the motel, hidden in an office. Two deputies were in cars at either end of the parking lot, and four of us were in the woods facing the motel, swatting mosquitoes.

We talked quietly and kept in touch with the other guys by

radio. There had been occasional cars pulling up, late guests for the most part, and we watched everyone through binoculars. Just past midnight a ragged old station wagon with one headlight made a slow pass by the motel. As it drove by, I could see there was only one person in the car. The vehicle didn't fit the description of our robber's car, but you never knew about these things. They could have changed cars, or one of them might be checking things out before they did the robbery.

The car went up the road, turned around, and came back. Another pass, and he reversed course once more. "You think that might be one of our guys?" I asked the corporal in charge of our little group.

He watched the car as it came back a third time. "No, I don't think so. But he sure is interested in something."

The vehicle turned into the motel, driving right past the deputy slouched down in his car at the end of the parking lot, and stopped about 20 yards past the front door. There was no sign of movement from the car except the puffs of oily smoke coming from the tailpipe.

"All units standby," the corporal said into his radio, "We've got some activity out here, but I don't know what's going on."

The driver opened the door and got out, looking around. He was clearly silhouetted by the street lights behind him: a short, chunky man, wearing a ball cap.

"Okay," the corporal said quietly, "he's on the ground."

The guy walked around the front of his car, checking out the parking lot. I felt my stomach knotting, he was acting very suspicious.

"He's on the other side of his car," whispered the corporal. The man came out from behind the car and faced in our direction. The corporal watched him through his binoculars, the radio in his other hand pressed against his mouth. "Okay, I can see him now, and he's ....oh, for Christ's sake, it's Bad Luck Brown!" Low chuckles greeted this announcement.

So named because of his atrocious luck, Bad Luck Brown was

a small-time hoodlum who spent more time in jail than out. I knew him well, and never had I met anyone who could find more creative ways to get caught. One time he broke into a church, stole the Sunday morning collection, and dropped his wallet. Another time he decided to stick up a liquor store and wrote a note to the clerk informing her of this fact....on the back of a letter from his probation officer.

I had helped arrest him after a burglary of an auto parts store. We found him a block away, sitting in his car which refused to start. It had a dead battery. Now he had stumbled into our stakeout, and we waited to see what he was going to do.

Satisfied all was well, Bad Luck turned and started across the lawn. We had a clear view as he headed straight to a lawn mower belonging to the motel. Evidently it had been left outside when they finished cutting the grass. He pushed the mower to the back of the rusting station wagon, dropped the tailgate, and started loading it inside.

The corporal was laughing. "He's stealing a lawn mower," he said into the radio. "Wait until he's back in the car, then move in."

The two men down in the parking lot acknowledged as Bad Luck closed the tailgate and got into his car. Before he could put it in gear, the two unmarked cars blocked him front and back. Escape cut off, Brown didn't hesitate, he jumped out and took off on foot.

Naturally, he lived up to his name and headed directly toward us, no doubt thinking he would get away easily. When he was about ten feet away, the corporal stepped out from behind a tree. "Sheriff's department," he yelled. "Hold it right there!"

Unfortunately, we had misjudged the determination of the fleet-footed Mr. Brown. Not at all discouraged by the sight of four more cops, he zigged to the left, plunging into the woods. We galloped after him, but it was pitch black and we caromed off trees, crashed into each other, and stumbled into invisible gullies. Yells, curses, and the sounds of heavy breathing could be heard all around. I had no idea where he was, but I was getting damn tired of bouncing off trees, so I decided to try a bluff. "HALT OR I'LL SHOOT!" I bellowed and fired a shot into the ground.

This didn't have the effect I anticipated. As soon as I fired, all the cops instantly hit the ground. Brown, however really put it into high gear and would have gotten away clean, except for a terrible piece of luck. He tripped over one of the prone investigators, spraining his ankle, allowing us to capture him easily.

We never did see our armed robbers.

31

Infernal Internals

Except for the clergy and internal revenue auditors, I doubt if any group of people is lied to more than cops. This has a tendency to make us hard and cynical, and it is all too easy to fall into the trap of believing everyone is a lying piece of garbage. But that is a fallacy. Most of our daily contacts are not with criminals but with essentially law-abiding citizens. These are the people whose taxes pay our salaries, and that's something we have to remember. Of course, just because they are law-abiding, that doesn't mean they are easy to get along with.

When it comes to how their tax dollars are spent, everyone has an opinion, and everyone wants to make sure they get their money's worth. We want everyone to be happy, but it's inevitable we will make some people unhappy and some of these unhappy people will complain. Loudly.

Most of the time, the complaining citizen is just upset because he or she got a ticket; got arrested; had a friend, spouse, or child arrested; or just plain didn't like the cop.

I worked with a guy who had the worst luck imaginable when it came to citizen complaints. In fact, he was famous for them. He was one of those unfortunate individuals who could fall into a bed of roses and come up smelling like a cesspool. Although a great street cop and the bane of the local hoodlums, he was an utter failure when it came to exercising basic human relations skills. He had a brusque, hostile manner that worked fine when he was intimidating burglars but enraged many of our more upstanding citizens and he attracted complaints like a wool suit attracts lint.

Once he was almost suspended for doing nothing. It was a boiling hot summer day, and an elderly couple, out shopping, returned to their car to find someone had smashed the passenger side window and removed the packages they had purchased earlier. The stress of the break-in, combined with the heat, was too much for the woman, and she grew faint. Her husband took her inside a nearby store and called the sheriff's department.

He was informed by the dispatcher that a deputy would be sent straightaway. The elderly gentleman returned to his car to flag down the dozen cruiser cars he expected would arrive momentarily with sirens screaming. The man had never, not once in all his 73 years, had to call the cops before, so to him, this was a true emergency.

Meanwhile, the deputy assigned to the call was only two blocks away. Unfortunately, he was already on a call, taking a report of a vandalism at an ice cream shop. Since the car burglary was certainly not an emergency to the dispatcher, she told the deputy to take the call when he completed the vandalism report.

When the deputy finished, the owner of the shop offered him a free ice cream cone, but he refused. This particular deputy had a strong sense of ethics and did not believe in taking gratuities or "free stuff," as he put it. "I don't want no one holding nothing over me in case I have to arrest them." He was the only cop I ever knew who refused free coffee. "I tell all them waitresses that I leave 50 cents on the table. They can use it to pay for the coffee, or they can put it in their pocket, I don't care."

So when the offer of the free cone was made, he accepted, but dug a dollar out of his pocket to pay his way, as he always did. Stepping into the blazing sun, he radioed he was back in service. The dispatcher gave him the car burglary call and told him the complainant seemed a little put out.

Back in the baking parking lot, the complainant was more than a "little put out." He was furious. It had been 25 minutes since he first called, and he had called back twice, demanding to know when the deputy was going to arrive. It was an extremely busy day, and the dispatcher was a little short with him, which angered him even more. The hard luck kid got in his car, licking the rapidly melting ice cream cone, drove the two blocks to the scene, and pulled up beside the livid complainant. Still licking the cone, he rolled the window down, glared at the scowling car owner, and said, "What's your problem, bub?"

Needless to say, the man complained long and loud to the sheriff about the rude deputy who took 25 minutes to respond to an emergency, almost caused him to die of sunstroke, then showed up eating an ice cream cone.

I, too, have suffered my share of citizen complaints, most unjustified, but the first time it happened, I was a nervous wreck. I had arrested a young man for drunk driving. He was nasty, abusive, and uncooperative. "Do you know who my father is?" he kept yelling as I put him in my car.

"No, I don't, and furthermore, I don't care. Now, get in the car before I put you in it."

"You touch me, and my father will sue you!" he shouted. It turned out his father was a prominent doctor but it wasn't his father who complained, it was his mother.

A few days after the incident, I received a terse little memo from the sheriff instructing me to meet with him and the mother of the kid. I racked my brain, trying to remember anything untoward that had occurred during the arrest, but it had been routine as far as I was concerned. Oh, the kid got pretty mouthy, and I'm sure I replied in kind, but I used no force. He was clearly drunk, and I figured I hadn't done anything wrong.

But they were friends of the sheriff, the doctor had been a big campaign contributor, and I was a very junior employee and very scared. This was the first time I had to deal with an irate citizen, and I didn't know what to expect.

Luckily, Sheriff Untreiner was extremely fair in these cases, refusing even to talk to a complaining taxpayer until the complaint was put in writing and sent through the proper channels. Since many of the taxpayers most likely to complain were not exactly intellectual giants, this requirement was a difficult hurdle indeed.

Those complaints that were written out were frequently so inarticulate it was almost impossible to decipher the nature of the gripe. That meant a lot of complaints, perhaps even some legitimate ones, simply faded away before they actually got to the sheriff. He didn't care. He was an attorney by training and had retired after 30 years with the FBI. He was used to handling problems on paper, and if a problem couldn't be written out, it probably wasn't worth dealing with in the first place.

This wasn't as unfair as it appeared. The kinds of complaints that fit this category were generally just bad attitude complaints. Often they were simply the result of personality disputes between citizen and deputy, nothing really serious.

I liked the Sheriff's method. While it may have discouraged a few people with genuine complaints, it significantly reduced the number of walk-in loonies who had no justification for a protest. Since I had my own share of complainers, the fewer unhappy people who negotiated the bureaucratic maze, the better.

But, of course, the doctor's wife had no trouble putting her complaint in writing and, with her ties to the sheriff, no trouble getting him to agree to discuss the problem. We met in his office, and she was angry indeed. "Sheriff, I can't understand why one of your deputies would pick on poor Michael like this."

He consulted my report. "Well, Judith, Michael was driving with no headlights, going the wrong direction on a one-way street, and Deputy Parker found a half-empty vodka bottle in the car." He looked at her. "Those are pretty serious charges."

"Well, of course they are but he didn't have to arrest him. Do you know he spent four hours in the jail?"

"He wasn't actually 'in the jail,' Judith, he was just in the booking area."

"I don't care what you call it; he was exposed to murderers, and child molesters, and god knows what else. I'm surprised he didn't catch a disease."

I wanted to tell her that our prisoners usually didn't catch diseases in the holding cells. They caught them upstairs, in the cell blocks, when the guards weren't watching them, but I doubted if she would be receptive to this interesting bit of knowledge, so I kept quiet.

"Nothing happened to him while he was being held, Judith."

"How can you say that?" She was breathing hard, "Michael is a very sensitive child. He may have suffered deep psychological damage from this entire incident."

I considered myself fairly sensitive, and I wondered if I too had suffered deep psychological damage from the very sensitive Michael's spitting on the back of my neck all the way to the jail while he screamed obscenities at me.

I saw a smile tug at the corners of the sheriff's mouth. "I doubt if he will be permanently affected."

"But he might be, you just don't know."

Now that was true. I speculated what psychological damage I might have wrought if I had fed the kid my flashlight as I was sorely tempted to do.

"Michael is an adult," the Sheriff said. "He has to learn how to take responsibility for his own actions. He violated the law and he got caught. Now he'll have to pay the consequences."

"But this is so unfair," she was crying now, "he was just trying to get home."

The sheriff closed the file and stood up. "Well, he shouldn't have done it while he was driving drunk."

"Can't you do anything?"

He shook his head. "I'm sorry. If you think he's not guilty, have him go to court and request a jury trial."

"Court?" She was horrified. Visions of crowds of clamoring reporters danced through her head. For the prominent and the

126

well-heeled, lurid publicity was a fate worse than an IRS audit. "Isn't there some other way?"

"Sorry, it's out of my hands."

She left, still sniffling, and not once had she acknowledged my presence, but I didn't mind. The sheriff thanked me for coming in, and I departed, the victor in my very first citizen complaint encounter.

Looking back, I only wish they had all been that easy.

32

BB Guns

Kids and BB guns. Never has there been a more troublesome combination. I have probably responded to hundreds of calls about kids shooting BB guns, and not all of the complaints were neighborhood busybodies with a case of the jitters. Each year thousands of dollars worth of plate glass windows are perforated by vandals using BB guns, not to mention all the street lights, car windshields, and outside Christmas decorations. And don't forget the injuries, both accidental and deliberate.

The lure of the BB gun is, of course, irresistible to any young boy. I can still remember, the feeling of sheer, swaggering power that flooded me at the age of eleven, the first time Harold Eansor let me hold his Daisy BB gun. As I stroked the smooth plastic stock, I instantly became a big game hunter, cowboy, and fighting marine, all rolled into one.

Holding that marvelous implement of destruction, I was suddenly filled with a burning desire to own one. The feeling was so strong it made all previous desires seem like mere childish longings. I would not feel that way again until my first year of high school when I caught sight of Barbara Jean Kaltenborough adjusting a garter.

The thought of this BB gun being desecrated daily by Harold's grimy hands was enough to make me weep. I vowed if I ever did get one of my own, I would never, ever, shoot it in an unsafe manner and, further, I would never, ever, aim at anything I was not supposed to.

"Ya wanna shoot it?" Harold asked.

A few seconds later we were running for our lives, Mrs. Morjazie's cat yowling like an air raid siren and Mrs. Morjazie's cries of rage speeding us on our way. Somehow, unbelievable though it seems, I had managed to forget my solemn vow.

So it is with other young boys. They will promise their parents anything to get that BB gun. If telling lies will get one condemned to an eternity in the lake of fire, then Hades' fiery streets must be jammed with men who once swore upon their souls they would always shoot their BB guns in a responsible manner.

Many states make it illegal for anyone under 16 to shoot a BB gun without direct adult supervision. That means someone actually standing there, watching and supervising. But the law suffers from a fatal flaw. No parent is going to spend the day tagging along after their eleven year old, making sure the kid uses his BB gun properly. By the same token, no kid is going to tolerate the presence of a parent while he sets out on an imaginary safari to Africa, battles attacking commies, or saves the earth from invasion of the dreaded space dwarfs.

So parents tells their kids to take the BB gun to the woods and shoot it in a safe and responsible manner, promising severe punishment if he fails to comply. Naturally, the kid agrees to do exactly as told, then proceeds to shoot up the entire neighborhood. Inevitably, someone calls the cops. We catch the kid and notify the parents. Enraged and embarrassed, daddy nods solemnly as the cop recites the law, agrees to pay for any damage done, and vows to confiscate the gun until the kid turns 21. Two weeks later the cycle repeats itself.

What is the solution to the problem? Girls. Once they discover the fair sex, the boys instantly lose all interest in BB guns.

I once suffered a reasonably severe injury as a result of a BB gun encounter. Responding to a call of kids shooting street lights,

OFFICER NEEDS ASSISTANCE

I actually managed to catch one of the shooters, a feisty little ten year old who barely came up to my waist. When I tried to take the gun away from him, the little monster hit me with it, the front sight slicing open my head.

After I delivered him to the juvenile detention center, bloody handkerchief pressed to my leaking noggin, I reported to the emergency room to get the wound stitched. "What happened?" asked the admitting clerk.

I hesitated, finding myself on the horns of a painful dilemma. If I admitted a ten year old midget had clubbed me with his BB gun, I would be the laughingstock of the hospital. On the other hand, I had to tell as much of the truth as my pride would allow, since this was an on-duty injury, covered by worker's compensation.

I considered various answers, then came up with one I thought was eminently satisfactory. "An armed suspect hit me with his rifle," I said.

She was very impressed and on my chart wrote, "Patient states he was struck in head with rifle barrel." It really looked much better.

I can truthfully say I never got in trouble because of a BB gun. I wish it was because I was an exceptionally safe and obedient child, but such was not the case. It was simply due to the fact my mother never allowed me to own one, even though I made the usual extravagant promises.

Of course, as a cop, I had real guns, but you know what? About five years ago I bought a BB gun of my own which I occasionally shoot out in the garage. With the doors closed. So the neighbors can't see me. While I do enjoy playing with it, I also figure it's good insurance.

Who knows when the space dwarfs might attack.

33

Officer Needs Assistance....Again

The dispatcher had told me to meet a narcotics unit in the parking lot of a nearby shopping center, and I had acknowledged eagerly. I made a quick U-turn, excitement rising within me. The summons to meet a narcotics officer usually meant action, and at that stage of my career, it was what I craved most.

I pulled into the parking lot and saw headlights blink on and off at the far end. I pulled up beside the car. Two scraggly-haired, roughly dressed narcotics officers were slouched down in the front seat of a battered blue Ford that looked as though it had been stolen from a junk yard.

"Turn off your lights!" one of them hissed. Embarrassed, I complied, cursing myself for not having done it sooner.

The driver swiveled his head slowly, checking the parking lot. I did the same, although I had no idea what I was looking for. Evidently satisfied, he turned to me and said, "We want you to help us serve a search warrant. I've already cleared it with your lieutenant. You'll be tied up about an hour. You interested?"

I nodded enthusiastically, thrilled beyond measure to be chosen for such a prestigious job. This could be one of those career-enhancing opportunities that come along so rarely. At the very least, I was sure it indicated my supervisors total confidence in my skills as a crime fighter. The possibility I had been selected simply because I was the closest deputy never entered my mind.

The plan was simple: the target was a house only a mile away, the scene of several months of non-stop drug activity. The narcs had managed to get an undercover officer inside, and he had made a series of controlled buys. Using this as the probable cause, they had obtained a search warrant, and tonight was the night to raid the place. There was a strong possibility we might get several pounds of marijuana from the house, and that was considered a pretty good haul in those days. Since I was the only one wearing a uniform, I would get to kick down the door and go in first.

There was a good reason for using someone in uniform for this task. If the bearded, shaggy-headed cops went in first, there was the distinct possibility the bearded, shaggy-headed dope dealers inside might think they were being attacked by rival dealers, and the chances of gun play multiplied accordingly.

A short time later, we were in position, assisted by five other disreputable-looking cops, all of whom had badges pinned to their clothing. On the signal, I was to pound on the door, yell "Sheriff's office!", then immediately kick it open and charge in. I would be followed by the narcs, and we would quickly subdue everyone, then look for the drugs.

"One more thing, Don," the sergeant said. I turned. "We have information they may be armed, so be prepared for anything." I nodded grimly, suddenly aware how fast my heart was beating.

He made one last check of everyone's position, then motioned me forward. I eased up onto the porch and drew my .38. Taking a deep breath, I pounded on the door. "Sheriff's office!" I shrieked. "Open up!" I stepped back and kicked with all my might.

Now, I must admit, I had never kicked a door open before, but I had seen it done. In the movies. Of course, it never occurred to me that what I saw on the silver screen might not bear any connection to reality. All my thoughts were on the possibly armed suspects who waited inside. The door was thin wood, and I expected it to explode, just like in the movies, but it didn't. Instead, my foot punched a ragged hole, right in the center, and there it stopped, my leg pinned by the jagged splinters. The door was still securely locked, and I was trapped.

I stood there frozen in place, gun drawn, immobile. To move at all sent jolts of intense pain through my leg. From inside came the sounds of yelling, screaming, furniture crashing, and toilets flushing. On the porch there was pandemonium. The narcs at the front couldn't get in because I blocked the door. They finally rushed around back and went in that way.

I stood there for a long time, sweat running off me in sheets, my leg on fire, waiting to be shot. Finally, the door was unlocked, and I hopped slowly inside, looking like an armed kangaroo. I had to stand there a while longer, perishing with embarrassment, while they ripped the door apart and freed my leg.

Although badly scraped up, I didn't suffer any real injuries, other than serious ego wounds. I was fortunate the bad guys were not armed, since they had had every opportunity to use me for target practice.

We made some arrests of the people named in the warrants, but needless to say, the dope was gone, flushed away before we ever got in. I limped around for a while, apologizing continually, enduring the glares from the disappointed narcotics officers, almost wishing I had been shot. I was finally sent back to the jail with a load of prisoners, happy to leave the scene of my humiliation.

In the back seat, the suspects seemed to be in high spirits considering their situation. They laughed and chattered among themselves, discussing the night's activities. There seemed to be universal agreement that the stupid cops had really bungled the raid. "Who was that yo-yo who tried to kick in the door?" one asked.

There was a burst of laughter. "I don't know," someone else

said, "but it was incredible. His foot was actually sticking through the door."

More laughter, and I felt myself shriveling with embarrassment. "What an idiot," the first voice said. "It was like a comedy act."

"Yeah, can't you imagine him on the radio, 'Officer needs assistance; send help, quick!'" They all roared with laughter again.

"Hey, officer?"

I didn't turn around. "Yeah?"

"You got any idea who that jerk-off was that got his leg stuck in the door?"

"Uh, no," I said. "I sure don't. I think he left before I got there."

"Aw, too bad," he said. "You really missed a good show."

"Yeah, too bad." I gave a sickly laugh, "It's hard to believe someone could be that stupid."

34

A Mother's Love

I had been dispatched to the shopping center on a report of a baby left unattended in an automobile. I found the car but no baby. The only evidence to indicate recent occupancy by a baby was a blanket on the floor and a half-filled bottle on the seat. I was about to give up when the blanket moved. I looked closer and saw a tiny foot protruding from one corner.

Although the door was locked, the window had been left open a few inches. Possessing an exceptionally skinny arm, I was able to reach in far enough to unlock the door and retrieve the baby from the floorboards. Other than a soaking-wet diaper, he seemed fine.

I waited a few minutes, holding the baby gingerly, hoping the mama would show up. When she didn't, I left a note on the windshield with the phone number of the sheriff's department. I was only a few blocks from the Division of Youth Services, so I took the child there.

When I arrived, I was surprised to find the intake counselor kept a supply of disposable diapers in her desk. "We often have to make an emergency change around here," she said, expertly replacing the sodden diaper.

I gave her the facts as she worked. "So when the mother didn't show up," I concluded, "I came here."

"I wouldn't worry," she said, "we'll be hearing from mama soon, I guarantee it."

Before I could reply, the radio room called. "109?"

"Go ahead, I'm still at youth services."

"We just heard from the mother of that baby, she's on her way."

"10-4," I said, "thank you."

"109?"

"Go ahead."

The dispatcher chuckled. "She's pretty upset."

Two minutes later the mother burst through the door and charged across the floor, eyes blazing. "Why did you kidnap my baby?" she shrieked in my face. Perfectly coiffed hair, an expensive dress and several thousand dollars' worth of diamonds told me this was a woman of substantial means.

"Ma'am, I didn't..."

"My attorney is definitely going to hear about this!"

"Ma'am, you left the baby unattended in your car, and no one knew where you were."

"I was getting my hair brushed and combed; I wasn't gone fifteen minutes." She took a deep breath, fighting for control. "I left him asleep on the seat."

I tried to explain I had found the child on the floor, but she turned her back on me and marched over to the intake counselor. "I demand you give me my child immediately."

Totally unimpressed with these dramatics, the counselor explained the law, making it quite clear the baby would be returned only when she was satisfied it would be cared for properly. She fixed the woman with a steady gaze. "You see, ma'am, if I think there is a significant risk, I can have your child placed in foster care until we have a hearing before the judge."

The woman paled. "A judge?" she whispered. The counselor nodded. At this point, the woman's attitude began to improve. Rapidly. In a few moments she was sweetness personified, apologizing all over the place, and was soon reunited with her child.

We watched them leave. "Do you think the kid will be all right?" I asked the counselor.

She sighed, "I hope so, but there's no way of telling."

I returned to duty, pondering what I had witnessed. I was no stranger to child abuse cases, of course. All law enforcement officers have to deal with their share, but I wasn't used to seeing a woman of obvious affluence neglecting her baby like some alcoholic barfly. She was lucky it was a relatively cool day, otherwise I might have been working a death investigation. It had certainly happened before.

The case really brought home to me the fact that child abuse and neglect can cut across economic lines and it's not just the poor who mistreat their children. I've always remembered that baby, and sometimes I wonder how he turned out.

35

Dropped Charges

I contacted her in the emergency room of a local hospital where she had gone for x-rays. She was as mad as any woman I have ever seen, and as she described the beating her live-in boyfriend had given her, bitter tears of rage squeezed from her eyes and streaked her cheeks. The tears accented the angry bruise on her jaw. She extended her arms, turning them rapidly back and forth for my inspection, the dark imprints from her boyfriend's fingers clearly visible. There were more bruises on her neck and a pronounced lump on her head. He had really worked her over.

"What do you want to do about this?" I asked.

"I WANT HIM IN JAIL!" she shouted.

I nodded approvingly. I am a firm believer in taking direct action against men who batter women, but too many victims are reluctant to do anything, hoping the cops will somehow scare the man into behaving.

I completed the paperwork quickly and had her sign the warrant affidavit. "I'll take it to a judge myself," I told her. "We'll probably arrest him this evening."

"Can you let me know when he's in jail, so I can get my stuff out of the apartment?"

I could and I would. When I left she was still cursing the guy and said she looked forward to testifying against him in court.

If she was half as angry when the case came up, she should be a good witness.

An hour later I was discussing the case with one of the circuit court judges. He reviewed my paperwork, agreed the charge of battery was solid, and set the bond at $500. I took it directly to the warrant division, handing it to one of my buddies, who agreed to try and arrest the guy at work. I asked him to notify me as soon as the man was in jail.

Just before I got off, the radio room called and said the suspect was being booked. I called the victim, and she chuckled with satisfaction. Her parting words made it clear how she felt about her now ex-boyfriend, "I hope he rots!"

That happened in late December. Early in June I found an envelope from the state attorney's office in my mailbox. It contained the following form letter.

Dear DEPUTY PARKER:
I would like to personally express my appreciation and that of this office for the help and cooperation you gave us in the above-styled case. The defendant was charged with BATTERY. A Nolle Prosequi, which is a dismissal, was filed in this case. Enclosed you will find a copy of the dismissal stating the reasons.

The letter was signed by the assistant state attorney who handled the case. There were other remarks, assuring me that my role in the case was an important one and that, "With citizen participation and assistance such as yours, we can look forward to a safer society."

I turned to the reasons for the dismissal. There were five:
1. The victim requested that the state drop the charges.
2. The victim states she loves the defendant, and they are to be married.
3. The victim does not want to testify against the defendant.

139

4. The victim and the defendant have reconciled their differences.

5. The victim did not suffer any serious injury.

I laughed as I read the reasons she listed. The fact she wanted to drop the charges didn't bother me, but her naive belief that the problem had been solved did bother me. A lot. I shook my head as I tossed the letter in the trash and silently wished her luck. She was going to need it.

36

Bad Night At The Dixie

The Dixie Restaurant. Just hearing the name let you know what you would find there: breakfast, sandwiches, and a variety of dinners, mostly fried. In its heyday it was a popular place for many of our deputies because of one fact: after midnight, all sandwiches were free to cops in uniform. The deal didn't apply to the expensive stuff like the fisherman's platter or the fried chicken, but I never knew anyone brave enough to subject their coronary arteries to that much cholesterol at one sitting. Of course, the owner didn't give us the free food out of the goodness of his heart. His restaurant was right across the street from Sy's Place, a tough, redneck bar, and from midnight on, the drunks beat a steady path to the Dixie, staggering across the busy highway, yelling, arguing, singing, laughing, and occasionally fighting their way through their meals. Deputy sheriff uniforms tended to be a calming influence, and the cost of free food was more than made up in the savings of furniture and plates.

I rarely ate at the Dixie. I preferred a few moments of peace and relative quiet when I was taking a break. The honky-tonk, combat zone atmosphere of the Dixie tended to kill my appetite. But tonight I had an eager young trainee with me. Larry had been hired just two months ago and was currently attending rookie school. He went to school five hours a day, which left him 15 hours short of the required 40 for which he was being paid. To make up this deficit he, and all trainees, had to work in the patrol division several days a week, riding with a veteran deputy.

In a lot of ways, he reminded me of myself when I had been new and eager. But that had been a few years ago, and I was a little jaded and cynical now. Larry was full of enthusiastic questions and wasn't bad company, although his eagerness tended to get on the nerves of some of the older veterans.

We were working a midnight shift, and things were relatively calm tonight. We had just finished a call, and I figured it was a good time for supper. "Time to eat, Larry. Got any preference?"

"Yeah. I heard the Dixie gives out free food to deputies in uniform."

"Well, that's true, but the food isn't that good." I glanced at my watch. "Besides, the place is bound to be full of drunks this time of night. Why don't we try the Howard Johnson's?"

"Aw, man. How can you beat free food? We'll have to pay at HoJo's."

"That's true, but at least we'll be able to eat in peace."

"But I've never been to the Dixie before."

I sighed. "Okay, we'll try the Dixie, but don't say I didn't warn you."

Just as I feared, the place was packed, and we had to sit at the counter. The drunks were so loud, we had to shout so the waitress could take our order. Larry ordered the barbecue pork sandwich, but I stuck with a grilled cheese and bacon. While rather plain, there was little chance of being surprised by the contents.

We got coffee first, and just as it arrived, there was the sound of a glass breaking, followed by a burst of raucous laughter. A large group in the far corner was really whooping it up. The language was strong enough to turn the air blue around them, and I felt uneasy. The potential for trouble was definitely there.

The food was delivered, and I opened my sandwich, carefully inspecting the contents, moving the bacon around, checking the cheese. "What are you looking for?" my companion asked.

"I just want to be sure I didn't get anything I didn't pay for."

Before he could say anything else, I heard what I had been waiting for: the sound of chairs going over. When drunks fight in a restaurant they must, of necessity, stand up. After all, it's rather difficult to punch someone while sitting down. Larry may have been a trainee, but he recognized the sound, too. We were off our bar stools and moving toward the fight before they got more than two punches in. There was quite a little melee, with much yelling and cursing, tables going over, chairs spinning across the floor, and crockery smashing. It took us several moments and a few more punches before we got the two combatants separated.

Crying women followed us as we hustled the two men out the door. I got the first one cuffed and in the car without much difficulty, but his opponent was a different story. Larry had the guy pinned against the side of the car but couldn't get him loaded. The drunk swung at me, and the punch bounced off my shoulder. There was a cracking sound, and Larry grunted. He had taken the punch full in the nose. We finally got the guy in the car, but all three of us were liberally coated with blood from my companion's nose. At the jail I booked the two drunks while my battered trainee, his enthusiasm for the Dixie's free food considerably lessened, had his slightly bent nose repaired at the emergency room. I picked him up at the hospital at the end of the shift. The white tape on his nose contrasted strongly with the two black eyes he was now sporting. Although in some pain, he was still cheerful. As we were driving home we discussed the fight, and I told him he had handled himself well. He stared out the window in silence for a while, then said, "You know what really makes me mad?"

"What's that?"

"I didn't even get a chance to eat my sandwich."

37

The Broad Side of a Barn

I pulled into the middle of the intersection and stopped. As I scrambled from the car, I could already hear the wailing sirens in the distance, rapidly growing closer. I stepped out in front of my headlights, silhouetted in the glare. Now I could see the flash of the approaching blue lights. They must be doing 90. I took a deep breath and drew my .38. They would be on top of me in a few seconds.

It had been a busy midnight shift, and I had just finished a call when one of my buddies stopped a Pontiac TransAm. His sudden yell, "He's running, headquarters!" galvanized me into action. I knew where he stopped the car, so I turned around and headed for the next major intersection, siren screaming. I arrived in a few moments, informing the radio room of my location. "We're headed right for you, Don," one of the pursuing deputies shouted.

What to do? I couldn't very well block off the entire intersection with my one small cruiser. On the other hand, I wasn't about to try and ram the fleeing vehicle. Suicidal I was not. I finally decided to step into the middle of the street so he could see me and be frightened into stopping. Why I thought this would work is something I can't explain. I think it had to do with my incredibly naive faith in the power of my uniform.

The hurtling cars were almost upon me as I leveled my gun at the fleeing TransAm. I could not detect the slightest lessening of speed, and I became acutely aware that my 170 pounds of fragile flesh and bone were no match for 1800 pounds of speeding automobile.

At the last second, when it became obvious the driver had no respect for law and order, I decided a strategic withdrawal was in order. I jumped back and the car roared past. There was no doubt in my mind the guy had made a serious attempt to kill me, so I fired twice at the vehicle as it flashed by. I fired twice more as it disappeared into the distance, which required that I shoot over the roof of the pursuing cruiser car. As might be imagined, this did not sit too well with the occupant of that cruiser, who later expressed his displeasure in what I regarded as excessively strong language.

I got back into my car and joined the pursuit, convinced I had riddled the vehicle. The chase ended quickly. The car wrecked when the driver lost control in a curve.

As it turned out, the car was stolen, and the driver, a 15 year old boy, was unhurt but very scared. We inspected the wrecked vehicle minutely and did not find a single bullet hole. As might be expected, I suffered mightily at the hands of my co-workers because of my poor marksmanship, but I endured it gracefully, happy I had not shot the kid.

A year later while working a day shift, I was dispatched to a service station at the same intersection where I had expended my four bullets. The place was being remodeled, and the owner met me in the driveway. "We just pulled down the rain gutter," he said, pointing toward the roof, "and I think we found a bullet hole."

I climbed a ladder leaning against the side of the building and used my pocket knife to dig the slug out of the wall. He and I examined it together. "Looks like a .38," he said. "You reckon it's been there long?"

I thought about the night of the speeding TransAm. "I would

guess about a year or so,'' I said. I dropped the bullet into my pocket. "But I wouldn't worry about it. It was probably just some drunk celebrating New Year's Eve."

38

The Children's Hour

"And so," she concluded, "I was hoping you might be able to come and talk to my class about your job."

"What grade do you teach?"

"First-grade."

I flipped open my appointment book. "My next day off is Thursday," I said. "Could we do it then?"

"Oh, that would be perfect."

"All right," I told her, "I'll just have to check with the crime prevention officer to make sure it doesn't conflict with any of his programs." We made the final arrangements, and I hung up.

A quick phone call got me the expected approval of the crime prevention supervisor. He had his hands full trying to keep up with school requests and certainly didn't mind a freelancer volunteering to do a few programs on his own time.

I looked forward to the program. Little kids were always such fun to talk with. While I had never done the kind of presentation she wanted, I thought it would be a snap. For one thing, six-year-olds automatically adore all cops. In fact, they adore just about anyone in a uniform: cops, fire fighters, soldiers, sailors, exterminators, you name it. Of course, talking to small children is definitely an art. It takes skill and practice to be make educational presentations that will hold their interest. Luckily,

I had no idea what I was letting myself in for.

I borrowed an instructor's manual from the training library. It was full of information about the proper preparation of lesson plans, how to make up exams, and other technical aspects of teaching. None of it seemed to apply to my situation, but one passage did catch my eye. "The good instructor," it read, "will occasionally pause for questions which can serve as an indicator that he is covering the material adequately."

That seemed to make sense. I made a note on my outline to ask for questions. This was yet another measure of my inexperience. The manual was written for instructors who would be talking to adults, and the advice was wasted on first-graders. But I didn't know that.

I arrived at the school about fifteen minutes before I was to speak and checked in at the main office. "I'm here to talk to Mrs. Davis' class," I told the clerk.

She flipped a switch on the control board for the PA system. "Mrs. Davis?"

A tinny voice answered, "Yes?"

"Your speaker is here."

Mrs. Davis showed up in a moment and escorted me to her class. "What sort of introduction do you want?" she asked.

"Well, the crime prevention officer has a regular program called 'Officer Friendly,' so why don't you just call me that?"

That was agreeable with her, and as we approached the class, I could hear the buzz of many little voices. I followed Mrs. Davis into the room, and there was instant silence.

"Boys and girls, we have a very special guest today," she gushed, "Officer Friendly from the sheriff's department has joined us, and he has a very special message to share with us." Not a kid so much as twitched. "Now I want everyone to be very quiet and pay very close attention to what he tells you." She turned toward me with a big smile, "Officer Friendly, please begin. We are so looking forward to your very fine program."

I was a little distracted, never having heard anyone use the word "very" that often, but I laid my outline on her desk and smiled. "Kids, I've come here to tell you about my job, to talk about the equipment I use to do my job, and to answer any questions you might have." Immediately, five or six hands went up. A little confused, I pointed to a child in the front row. "Did you have a question?"

Looking scared, he pulled his hand down and shook his head. I pointed to another little boy. "My daddy has a real gun," he said proudly. I was even more confused, but Mrs. Davis rescued me. "Let's not ask Officer Friendly any questions right now," she said. Hands were still waving; were they deaf? Officer Friendly was starting to feel nervous. "Hands down," she said firmly, and they slowly dropped.

I began my presentation, talking about the difference between policemen and deputy sheriffs. I discussed the color of the uniforms and the shape of the badges and as I talked, I grew more relaxed and began to enjoy myself. Hands kept popping up from time to time, but I followed Mrs. Davis's lead and told them this was not the time.

When I started describing the equipment on my gunbelt, the excitement began to build. I worked my way through the gun, the bullets, and the portable radio, then pulled out the handcuffs. "Okay, boys and girls," I told them, "I need two volunteers to come up and help me demonstrate the handcuffs." There was instant pandemonium as half the class surged forward, catching me by surprise. I was ready to run for it, but Mrs. Davis took control again. "Everyone sit down," she shouted, and her tiny charges reluctantly retreated. When a semblance of order was restored, I quickly picked my two helpers.

I stood them next to each other, handcuffed right arm to left, then used the key to unlock the cuffs. Mrs. Davis took a picture with her Polaroid, and the two kids returned to their seats, heroes.

There was still great enthusiasm, and as I waited for them to calm down a little, I saw the note about asking questions. This certainly seemed like a good place to check my effectiveness as an instructor. "All right," I said, "are there any questions about handcuffs?"

Instantly, every hand in the room shot skyward, and a deafening cacophony of bleating, whimpering sounds issued from each mouth. In their eagerness, many jumped to their feet, hoping I'd choose them. Knowing how hard it usually is to get an audience to ask questions, I was pleased by this obvious confirmation of my teaching prowess. I finally pointed to one small boy, who proceeded to launch into a long and rambling discourse about a recent trip he and his uncle had made downtown. It was punctuated by frequent "you knows," a great many "and ums," and a variety of mumbles and stutters. Throughout his speech, he twisted from side to side, rocked back and forth, hugged himself, draped his arms around his head, and fidgeted. A lot. In the midst of this almost unintelligible babble of juvenile verbalization, it finally dawned on me the kid was not asking a question at all. He was telling me that he and his uncle had been downtown, had seen a policeman, and that the policeman had handcuffs, just like mine.

When I eventually realized he was simply relating a personal observation, I had to fight the urge to scream, "That's not a question kid; it's a statement!" This would have been grossly inappropriate behavior on the part of Officer Friendly, so I merely gritted my teeth and thanked him for that fascinating account.

Mrs. Davis told me later that children of this age don't really understand the concept of a question, and the child was demonstrating that he understood my message by relating it to a real-life experience of his own. All I could think about was the four-and-a-half minutes I had stood in front of the class, sweating, while the kid droned on about his trip downtown.

I asked if there were any more questions. Naturally, a waving forest of hands sprouted immediately, and I pointed to a solemn-faced lad in the second row. "Yes, son," I said, "what's your question?" He looked at me blankly, hand still in the air. "Do you have a question?'' I asked again. His eyes widened, and he looked over each shoulder then back at me. Officer Friendly's patience was ebbing fast. "Yes, you," I said, "in the blue and white striped shirt." The kid looked down at his shirt, then back at me.

Touching his chest he finally said, "Me?" I nodded. "My daddy got arrested last night," he said.

That threw me. "Oh, uh, well, I'm sorry to hear that." I didn't know what to say, but the other kids paid not the slightest attention. I tried the other side of the room. "Okay, you, in the orange shirt," I said, trying to avoid a repeat of the last question.

This was a little girl, "You look like a movie star," she said shyly.

A movie star? Me? Who could she mean: Tom Selleck? Clint Eastwood? I had to know. "Which movie star?" I asked.

"Kermit the Frog."

Kermit the Frog? That was a shock. What I should have done was to politely thank her and move on to someone else but I didn't. I had to find out why I reminded her of Kermit, thereby violating one of the cardinal rules for talking to little kids: Never ask a question unless you want an answer. "Why Kermit?"

"Because," she said, pointing at my forest green uniform, "Kermit is all green, and he doesn't have any hair, either."

Needless to say, that brought down the house, but I had to admit the comparison was an apt one.

"All right, boys and girls," Mrs. Davis said, taking over again, "Officer Friendly has to go now, let's all tell him, 'thank you.'"

"Thaaank yoooou!" they chorused, and I made my exit, waving and smiling. Walking back to my car, I discovered I felt the same way I did when I finished working a bar fight.

39

Godzilla Versus King Kong

"Be ready to skull him, Parker," my boss whispered urgently, watching the enormous drunk standing in front of him.

I was ready, my heavy five-cell flashlight gripped tightly in one hand. Ready, but not confident. The guy was well over six feet tall and probably weighed 250. He was so tall, I was going to have trouble applying my flashlight to his head if he made a truly hostile move toward the lieutenant. And he certainly seemed about to do just that.

Glaring at Lieutenant Swinney, he slowly dropped into a semblance of a karate stance, hands weaving back and forth. "Eeeeeooooooooooooooooaaaaaaaa!" he howled.

Swinney didn't budge. Standing like a rock, facing the guy, he clenched his big fists but kept his arms down, probably not wanting to antagonize his opponent any more than necessary. "Be ready to skull him," he whispered again.

"I'm ready," I said. Actually I felt like a midget next to two water buffaloes. Russ Swinney was just about as big as the oversized karate kid. If they did begin to fight, I wasn't at all sure that I and my puny flashlight would make much difference. It would be like King Kong against Godzilla.

The guy pulled one arm back, preparing to strike. "Sssssssssssssss," he hissed.

"Get ready, Parker."

"Eeeeeaaaaaaaaaaa!" he yowled, tensing.

Swinney raised his fists, and I leaned toward them, bringing the flashlight up. Any second now...

The call started out as a routine drunk disturbance at one of the bars. It was assigned to me, and as it happened, the lieutenant was the closest unit, so he volunteered to back me up. That didn't bother me in the slightest. I figured that between us we made a total of 440 pounds of deputy sheriffs. Of course, he accounted for almost two thirds of this total, but I didn't care. I liked going into a bar fight with a man who had to duck to get through the door.

We arrived at the same time, and the manager met us out front. "He left," he said, "but I think he's around back."

I asked what happened.

"Aw, he got drunk and started picking fights with the other customers." He smiled. "I talked him into leaving."

I knew for a fact this guy kept a sawed-off shotgun behind the bar. Although never loaded, it was certainly intimidating. I suspected this might have been the case tonight, but I didn't ask. I liked the manager, and I didn't really want to know too much. We headed around back.

"Be careful," he said as we drove off. "He's real big, and he says he's got a blackbelt in karate."

As I turned into the parking lot behind the bar, I saw a small group of people milling around next to the tall chain-link fence. They appeared to be arguing with a much larger guy. The blackbelt, no doubt. I parked and got out. Swinney was already ahead of me.

One of the men detached himself from the crowd and trotted over to us. "This crazy bastard is nuts," he said pointing at the big guy. "His friends are trying to get him to leave, but he won't listen. Someone is going to get hurt." He shook his head. "I think he's doped up."

This was not welcome news, but that's the way it goes

sometimes. Big, doped-up karate experts have a way of showing up when I'm on duty. Of course, I had my big, non-doped-up lieutenant with me, and I was fairly confident he could handle the guy. If not, I should have enough time to make my escape while he was turning my boss into hamburger.

The group fell back as Russ walked toward the man. "What's the problem, buddy?" he asked.

The big guy slowly turned. He stared at Swinney, and his eyes narrowed. A low moan came from his mouth. "Ooooooooooooooo," he said, rocking back and forth.

Swinney took a step toward the man. "Let's go, friend," he said firmly. "The show's over. Time to go home."

The man moved to the side until his left arm was touching the fence. Swinney moved to his right, following the guy step for step. Now he was up against the fence, too.

"Ooooooooooooooo!" The moaning was growing in volume, and he slowly raised his arms, elbows pointing out, fingers like claws. He started toward Swinney, who retreated a step, then stopped suddenly. The drunk stopped, too, and I was quite surprised to realize he was almost eye-to-eye with my boss. That was something I didn't see very often.

Russ looked concerned: his eyes were wide, his chest heaving, but he didn't give an inch. It was just like him. I had never known my boss to back down from a challenge, and it didn't surprise me in the slightest that he was staying nose-to-nose with this huge drunk. It was an impressive display of sheer guts.

Now we were at the crucial point in the confrontation. The guy was quivering, Swinney was ready to defend himself, and I had drawn my flashlight back for a home run swing. "Eeeeeeoooooo," the guy howled, "Eeeeeoooooo....errrp." The noise stopped abruptly, and the drunk grew noticeably pale. Suddenly, his eyes rolled back in his head, and he pitched forward, landing with a thud at Swinney's feet. "Ohhhhh," he moaned softly, then fell silent, out for the count, overcome by the alcohol.

154

Russ still hadn't moved. He was amazing! "Gee, that was great, Lieutenant," I gushed. "I thought for a minute that guy was going to have you for lunch, but you didn't move a muscle." I shook my head in admiration. "You've got guts."

"It wasn't guts, you idiot," he yelled. "I'm caught on this damn fence." He pointed. "It's hooked on my gunbelt, I can't budge."

It took some doing, but we finally got him free. I must say my admiration was diminished, but only slightly. I decided it took almost as much guts for Russ to face the guy knowing he couldn't move.

We let the drunk's friends load him up and take him home, since he hadn't caused any real damage. I completed my report and drove off but I kept wondering who would have won, Godzilla or King Kong.

40

The End Of The Rainbow

It was a quiet Saturday morning, and I decided to take a swing through the public campground in my district, to see who was there and to let them see me. Occasionally, I've caught runaway juveniles living in their cars, and once I recovered a stolen truck, stuck in the mud and abandoned by the thieves.

But there was nothing that dramatic going on today. In fact, there were only a handful of campers. There was a large motor home with Michigan plates parked close to the lake, and I headed toward it. An older man was wrestling with an awning on the side of the big camper. I pulled up beside him. "Want some help?"

He mopped his face, "I sure could use some."

I parked and got out. It was then I noticed an elderly woman on a lawn chair next to the picnic table. "Hi, how are you?"

She nodded. "Oh, pretty good."

It took us only a moment to unroll the balky awning, but it was definitely a two-person job. He stuck out his hand and introduced himself. "Thanks for your help. My wife is not feeling well, and I told her to rest a minute." We walked back to the table. "Would you care for some coffee?"

"Sure. I'm a cop."

He laughed. "I just made some fresh." He went inside and

returned with a pot of coffee and two cups. "You drink it black?"

"Of course," I said. "Doesn't everyone?"

"Well, the doctor says I'm not supposed to drink it at all, but what the hell. None of us is going to live forever, right?"

We sipped our coffee and it was quite pleasant, sitting there in the warm spring air. He told me he was a retired engineer and lived just outside Detroit. "I gave General Motors 30 years of my life, but I'm out now and glad of it."

"Did you design cars?"

"Not so you could tell it." He chuckled, "That's what I wanted to do when I got out of college, but I spent most of my time working on transmissions and drive trains." He stared into his coffee. "I headed up a group that worked on emission control devices for a while, but toward the end, I didn't really do much of anything." He looked at me. "How old do you think I am?"

The question caught me by surprise. I would have thought the middle 70's. "Well," I said, hedging, "I'm not very good with ages."

"Go on, take a guess."

I decided to wimp out and try for flattery. "Oh, about 69."

He snorted, "I'm 64."

I was stunned. If he had said 80, I would not have been surprised. It must have showed.

"That's okay, boy. I know I look like hell. I smoked like a chimney, drank like a fish, and ate steak five days a week all my life." He slapped his chest, "I've already had a quadruple by-pass, had my gall bladder taken out, a cataract removed, and every now and then, I pass a kidney stone." He pointed to his wife, dozing on the lawn chair. "Alice has diabetes, emphysema, and arthritis so bad she should have a hip replacement, but they don't want to operate until they build her up some." He took a swallow of coffee. "Course, we don't smoke anymore, but it's a little late now."

His wife stirred, and he helped her out of the chair. They walked to the motor home, and she had difficulty managing the two steps. He almost had to lift her inside.

He returned after a few minutes. "She's going to take a nap. She really shouldn't be here, but we're on our way to Orlando so she can see our new granddaughter. It might be her last chance to travel for a while."

The mood was rather somber, and I was thinking about leaving. This was not exactly my idea of a cheerful conversation. I started to get up, but he grabbed my arm, "You know, it wasn't the drinking or the smoking that did it."

"It wasn't?"

"No," he said, "it was the job."

"With General Motors?"

"Not just General Motors. It could have been Ford or Chrysler or American Motors." He shook his head. "But I'm not just talking about the car business. I mean the mind-set that keeps you doing the same thing for 30 years, hating it but afraid to quit. I grew up during the Depression. I know what it's like to go hungry. People of my generation wanted security above all else."

"Did you find it?"

"Sure, I found it. I made a ton of money, I'm financially secure for the rest of my life," he smiled bleakly, "what there is left of it. I've got plenty of insurance, our house is paid for, and I own this motor home free and clear." He slapped the table, "I can do anything I want to."

"Well, that's good," I said.

"There's only one problem."

"What's that?"

"I'm too damn old and too damn sick to do all the things I spent my life working for." He shook his head. "I always wanted to see the Grand Canyon, so Alice and I drove out there last year. All we could do was stand around the rim with the other tourists, because neither one of us can walk more than 50 yards without stopping to rest." He sighed, "We drove into Yellowstone, but we got caught in a traffic jam, and the engine conked out. Alice got sick from all the exhaust fumes, and we had to fly her back to Detroit.''

We sat in silence for a while, and I was again thinking of a graceful way to make my exit. A few more minutes and he was probably going to...

"You like your job, boy?" he asked, suddenly.

"What?"

"Your job," he said impatiently, "You like being a cop?"

"Oh, yeah," I said enthusiastically, "I love it. I can't think of anything I'd rather do."

He smiled. "That's good. If you're happy with your work, you'll probably be happy with your life. You don't make much money, do you?"

"No, not really," I said, wondering what business it was of his. "I make enough to live on. Of course, my wife has to work, too."

"Believe me, money isn't everything." He sighed. "If I'd had the backbone, I would have quit 20 years ago."

"What would you have done?"

"Oh, hell, I don't know. Sailed around the world, opened a pizza stand, painted pictures, took up skydiving." He waved a hand, dismissing the thought. "It doesn't matter. The point is, I shouldn't have stayed in a job that was eating my guts out." He looked off into the distance. "But I had responsibilities. I had bills to pay. People depended on me. I convinced myself I couldn't leave. So I stayed." He turned back to me. "I hated it, but I stayed."

"Well, what else could you do?"

His fist came crashing down on the table so hard I jumped. "That's just it. I could have done anything! I was young, like you. I had my health, I had energy and optimism, but I didn't have courage. It was a different world back then. You didn't make waves. If you had a bad job, you made the best of it." He was silent, remembering. "You know what?"

I shook my head.

159

"I wish I had made some waves, but now it's too late."

I was really getting uncomfortable. I stood up. "Well, hey, it's been nice talking to you."

He laughed, "Bullshit! Listening to an old man rave about how he wasted his life is certainly no fun, but I do appreciate your letting me spout off a little. Seems like we can only really speak our minds to strangers."

"Well," I said, "I think you made some good points."

He smiled, "You're too young to fully understand what I meant by not hesitating to make waves, but you'll figure it out as you grow older. The most important thing is to know what you want and to go after it. You'll never know how far you can go unless you start walking."

"I'll try to keep that in mind." I had no idea what he was talking about.

I got back in my car, and he leaned in the window. "You're a bright young man and a good listener. You'll do well."

We shook hands. "Good luck on your trip," I said.

I started the car, and he straightened up. "Remember," he said, "sometimes you have to make waves." I nodded and smiled and got the hell out of there.

That conversation took place in 1973, and while I never heard from the retired engineer again, his words have certainly stayed with me. He was right about several things. I learned the importance of goal setting early on, and that has been of immense help to me. I did have to do some growing before I really grasped what he meant about making waves, but as the years passed, I saw, ever more clearly, what he was getting at. I think it really had to do with fear of change.

Fear of change is natural. We all have a need for stability, but I think fear of change is also fear of risk and fear of new challenges, and if we let it take control, after awhile we just focus on the fear. Some of the saddest people I have ever met were those who said, "Sure, I hate my job, but I can't quit now. I've got too many years in."

160

I wish those people could have been with me on that spring morning, talking to the retired engineer. He wanted to be a wave-maker, but he waited too long. By the time he made up his mind to start splashing, it was time to get out of the pool.

41

Over The Bounding Main

When the thefts of outboard motors started to get out of hand on Pensacola Beach, the Florida Marine Patrol agreed to assign one of their officers to assist us for a week. We were asked to supply a deputy to ride in the boat, and the lieutenant selected me. "How come Parker gets to go?" Leamon Reaves whined.

"Probably because he washes the lieutenant's car for him when we're off," Hightower said.

"Nah, you guys got it wrong." All eyes shifted to Suarez. "You know we're short of personnel, and the lieutenant had to pick someone whose absence wouldn't degrade the efficiency of the shift."

"That means we're better off without you," the ever-helpful Wasdin explained.

I turned and raised my hand for silence. "Thank you all. However, I choose to believe the lieutenant is merely exercising his prerogative as our leader to pick the best man for the task at hand, and I think he has done a marvelous job in that regard." I turned back to the front, ignoring the uproar which greeted my little rebuttal.

When the commotion died down, the lieutenant said, "This isn't exactly going to be a cruise on the Island Princess, Parker. You're supposed to be out there working, so try and do some good."

I saluted. "Yes, sir, *mon capitain,* you can count on me. I'll do my usual efficient job."

He nodded grimly. "That's what I'm afraid of."

I was excited about the idea. Not only would it be a welcome change from our usual diet of family fights, drunk drivers, and shoplifters, it should be great fun riding around in a boat in the balmy night air, enjoying the gentle sea breezes, far from the hoards of mosquitoes.

I met the marine patrolman at a boat ramp about an hour after dark. His name was Bill, and I knew him slightly. I had always considered him a friendly, outgoing kind of guy, and I looked forward to working with him. We shook hands. "You ready to be a water cop?"

I laughed, "Yeah, sounds like fun." I stepped into the boat, trying to look jaunty and seaman-like. The effect was spoiled somewhat when my leather-soled shoes skidded on the slick fiberglass deck and I almost ended up in the drink.

"I meant to tell you to wear sneakers," Bill said.

"My fault. I should have known better." I was embarrassed at my clumsiness because I was certainly no stranger to the water. Growing up along Florida's gulf coast, I had done my share of water skiing and fishing. I had also spent two years in the Navy, cruising the Atlantic, Mediterranean, and Caribbean. With this maritime background, I always felt I would have made an excellent marine patrolman myself.

We knew the thieves were coming in off the water. Only the week before, an irate homeowner had watched helplessly as they removed his outboard motor from his anchored boat, loaded it into their own, and disappeared into the darkness. The whole time he was on the phone, trying to tell one of our dispatchers to send a boat to intercept the thieves. Unfortunately, we didn't have a boat to send, hence the request for assistance from the marine patrol.

Not surprisingly, many of the victims were also quite

influential, since it took a substantial income to afford waterfront property. After half-a-dozen thefts, they got together, contacted the sheriff, and raised influential hell. He promised immediate action, and this was the result of that promise.

After discussing it, we decided to patrol close to shore, hoping to spot the thieves before, or even after, they had stolen another motor. There were a few weak points with this strategy, however. For one thing, they had been hitting in a random pattern, sometimes once a week, sometimes three times, sometimes skipping an entire month. For another, there was about 20 miles of coastline, and we were only one boat, alone in the darkness. We would certainly have our work cut out for us.

Once out in the open water, Bill said, "Let me show you what this baby can do." The boat surged forward. "We're doing over 40 right now," he yelled in my ear. It felt like 100, but the ride was exhilarating. I admired the easy way he handled the big boat. After 15 minutes he shut off the engine. "Now we drift," he said.

For the next few hours Bill regaled me with tales from his career, which I thoroughly enjoyed because he was a good story teller. But, as time passed, the heat and humidity settled around us like a damp blanket. After a while, I noticed the boat was moving in an unusual way. It was a kind of a corkscrewing motion. Waves passed under the stern which lifted, then fell off to one side, causing the boat to heel slowly as the bow rose. I don't know why I hadn't been conscious of it before. Up, sideways, roll, down. Up, sideways, roll, down. Up, sideways....I began to lose interest in the conversation.

My partner was telling an interminable story about how the politics in his job had hindered his promotional opportunities, primarily because he refused to suck up to the right people. His voice had an irritating, high-pitched, whiny sound I hadn't been aware of previously, and it was giving me a headache. The smell of the gasoline in the fuel tanks wasn't helping, either. It seemed to be bothering my stomach, which was making strange sloshing sounds as the boat pitched and rolled.

We were supposed to stay in place for at least six hours, which at the beginning of the night seemed all too short. Now it seemed like several lifetimes. Quitting time finally arrived, and we headed for shore having seen no outboard motor thieves.

The ride back was thoroughly unpleasant, and Bill seemed determined to hit every large wave he could find. I found his piloting of the boat reckless in the extreme, and I was intensely relieved when, at last, we tied up at the dock.

I suppose I should have assisted him getting the heavy boat back on the trailer so he could haul it out of the water, but I wasn't feeling up to it. I made a flimsy excuse and left quickly. I had to drive back to the office to sign out, and the lieutenant was still there when I walked into the muster room. "Well, how'd it go?"

"Not too great," I muttered, "didn't see a thing."

He took a drag off his cigarette and blew a noxious cloud of smoke in my face. "How was the weather?"

"Fine, fine," I said through clenched teeth, fanning the smoke. I had never realized what a disgusting habit smoking was until then.

He looked at me strangely. "You feel okay, Don? You look sort of green."

"I'm fine," I mumbled. "I think I'm coming down with the flu or something."

"Do you want to go out again tomorrow night?"

My stomach jumped, "Can't you get someone else? I've done my time."

He laughed, "Sure, we'll spread the joy around. No reason for you to have all the fun. Right?"

"Yeah, right." I brushed by him and headed out the door, my stomach still doing flips.

42

Never Volunteer

The call was dispatched as a disturbance at a shopping center. Deputy Merle Cutts was assigned to that district but he was at the far end of his area, and I was right on top of the call, so I volunteered. I got to the store in question and found a young man shaking hands with the store manager. Hardly one's idea of a disturbance, but this guy had been shaking hands for 15 minutes and refused to let go. He was a short, muscular guy in his late 20's. The manager was close to 60 and obviously terrified. Sweat was pouring off him in little rivulets, and his eyes rolled wildly when he saw me come in. The younger man was mumbling and muttering, and I figured he was drugged or drunk or both.

I wasn't sure what to do. Forced hand-shaking wasn't something that was covered in rookie school, but I had to do something. The manager looked as though he was going to have a heart attack any minute. I decided to take direct action, so I stepped forward and pulled their hands apart. The manager scurried away, still bug-eyed with terror. I took the guy by the arm and escorted him out of the store. He went willingly enough but was obviously up in the ozone someplace. I got the door open on my cruiser and started to place him in the back seat. Things were going smoothly, and I was congratulating myself

166

on my expert handling of this potentially dangerous situation. Unfortunately, congratulations were a bit premature.

As he was getting into my car, he suddenly jerked away from me and went into a kungfu stance. Now, I am no expert in hand-to-hand combat. I have had no karate training, and I know very little about boxing. However, I have learned that when a suspect acts as though he wants to get serious about fighting, the best thing to do is overcome this resistance with sufficient force to end the fight before it begins. I so jumped on him. Instantly.

As I said, the lad was rather muscular, and it rapidly became apparent he was considerably stronger than I was. We rolled around on the ground, neither one of us able to gain the upper hand, and I realized I was in trouble. My strength was ebbing fast, but just when I was about to give out, I heard the welcome wail of approaching sirens.

Two other deputies arrived and joined the party. Believe it or not, even three of us could not handle this guy. It was like trying to compress a coiled spring. Just when I thought I had an arm pinned, he would jerk away, and I was left holding air.

Two civilians tried to help, but they were quickly put out of action. One caught an elbow in the nose, which broke with an audible crack, and the other guy got kicked against the curb, lacerating his head and knocking him silly. The battle continued, and suddenly our antagonist shook free, sprang to his feet and began running across the parking lot. Personally, I was happy to see him go. None of my companions made the slightest effort to stop him, so I suspect they felt the same.

Another screaming siren announced the arrival of reinforcements. The fleeing suspect turned around, ran directly at the still moving cruiser car and began pounding on the hood, evidently distressed by all the noise. Of course, there was nothing else for us to do but return to the fray. For one thing, we had attracted a large crowd, so we couldn't just lie there on the parking lot, although that would have been my choice.

More cops arrived, the parking lot was really getting crowded now. Finally, after great effort, we managed to get his hands cuffed, but it took five of us. We weren't taking any chances, so we cuffed his ankles, too. We then picked him up and slid him into my car.

Back at the jail, I charged him with disorderly conduct, resisting arrest with violence, five counts of assault on law enforcement officers, and two charges for the civilians. My uniform was a wreck, my body a mass of bruises, and my ribs so sore I could only breathe in little gulps. When I finally completed the paperwork, I hobbled over to the holding cell to check on the condition of my prisoner. He had removed all his clothes and was sitting quietly, crooning to a light bulb. As far as I could tell, he had suffered no injury.

It turned out he was high on PCP, or angel dust as it's called in the streets, a drug with the ability to anesthetize the entire body so the user doesn't feel any pain.

It was weeks before I could sleep on my side, months before I finished picking the bits of parking lot out of my hide, and years since that fight. But I haven't forgotten. I'm reminded of it every time I see someone shaking hands.

43

Safety First

The call was given to me as an armed disturbance at Coates Seafood, a combination fish market and grocery store, just a few blocks from the county jail. Male customers liked to stand around outside the establishment drinking beer and wine, and as might be expected, there was occasional trouble.

I arrived and contacted the store clerk. He informed me a patron had managed to shoot himself in the leg with a gun he was carrying in his pocket. "We tried to get the gun away from him," he said, "but he's too drunk."

Wonderful. "Where is he now?"

He pointed toward the rear of the building. "The last time I saw him he was wandering around out back."

I walked outside, wishing I had a backup, but it was a busy night and everyone was tied up. There was a crowd of drinkers standing around, and as soon as I stepped out the door, they started yelling: "He's over here, man."

"Watch that gun."

"You better call an ambulance he's bleeding."

I turned to the closest person, "Where is he?"

He pointed. "Around the corner."

I peered around the edge of the building. A whip-thin, grey-haired man, dressed in greasy work clothes was leaning against the wall, hand in pocket, a damp red stain on his right pants leg. I stepped quickly around the corner and grabbed that right arm.

"Hey, man, wha' you doin'?" he mumbled, trying to pull his hand out of the pocket.

"Just be cool, buddy," I said, keeping a firm grip on his arm, "I need to talk to you."

"I ain't did nothing," he said, trying to jerk away, "Leave me alone." As he struggled, his hand came partly out of the pocket, and I saw the butt of a small gun. I pinned him against the wall with one arm, and twisted the weapon out of his hand. It looked to be a .25 caliber, semi-automatic pistol. I dropped it in my pocket. "Hey, thass mine. Give it back!"

"Sorry, friend. You can't have it. You're under arrest for carrying a concealed firearm." I snapped the cuffs on his wrists and we started toward the car. Although he was limping noticeably and very drunk, I still had quite a time with him before I was able to get him in the back seat.

The county hospital was close by so we arrived within seconds. The man had indeed shot himself, the bullet lodging in the muscle of his right thigh. The doctor said unless there was an infection they would probably not even remove the tiny slug.

The only thing left to do was apply a dressing, give him a tetanus shot, and take him to jail. But things were jumping in the emergency room that night, and we had to wait for a nurse to get free. Meanwhile, my prisoner was becoming increasingly rambunctious. Twice I had to physically prevent him from getting off the examining table. The third time he caught me by surprise and rolled off the side. We wrestled around on the floor for several minutes before I was finally able to get him back on the table. During this little skirmish, his knee caught me a good one, driving the gun in my pocket into my leg, bruising it.

Eventually, his treatment was completed, and I half-dragged, half-carried, the still resisting prisoner to my car. When we got to the jail, several correction officers were kind enough to come outside and relieve me of my burden.

Later, back in my car again, I examined the little automatic. It was actually a good quality, American made weapon and I wondered if it had been stolen. I started to copy the serial number, when a chill went through me. I suddenly realized the gun was loaded. Not only loaded, but a round was in the chamber. It was ready to fire and had been, throughout the wrestling match behind the store, the struggle to get him in the car, and the battle in the emergency room. Ready to fire. In my pocket. The entire time.

I carefully unloaded the little gun and, with shaking hands, removed the live round from the chamber. It was a miracle I hadn't shot myself in the leg.

44

A Thin Line

The line between life and death can sometimes be a thin one. During my law enforcement career and my previous jobs as ambulance driver and hospital orderly, I have seen death come in ways the average person can hardly imagine. But, from these experiences, I have learned that, while life can sometimes be a fragile flame, easily extinguished, the reverse is also true, and the strength and resiliency of the human body is frequently amazing. There is also the will to survive, an instinct that probably transcends conscious thought.

I present five examples to illustrate how slender that line between life and death can be, and how, at least in one case, crossing the line was done only with the greatest reluctance.

Working a day shift one morning, I came upon what appeared to be a minor traffic accident. A carpenter, driving an ancient station wagon, rear-ended a pickup truck. The damage to the station wagon consisted of a dented front bumper, and we could find no damage to the truck. The driver, a burly man in his late forties, was not injured but asked me to call an ambulance for his helper, who had been knocked unconscious.

I did and then went to check on the extent of the injuries. The other carpenter was an elderly man, frail and tiny, who couldn't have weighed 90 pounds. He was sitting quietly, head back, eyes closed. I checked for a pulse, but there was none. He was quite dead, killed instantly when his head stuck the dashboard, breaking his neck.

In contrast, compare this incident with one which occurred on a freezing winter morning about 4 AM. A passing motorist on a desolate stretch of highway discovered a car wreck but had to drive 15 miles to the nearest phone to report it. I was an ambulance driver in those days, and we were called by the highway patrol to come and pick up the body.

We arrived at least two hours after the wreck happened. My first view of the scene was the sight of a 327 cubic inch engine sitting upright on the side of the road, about 25 yards from the remains of the car. It was placed so precisely I almost expected to see a "for sale" sign on it.

The car was a Corvette Stingray, and the driver must have been doing 80 when he left the road, cut down a telephone pole, and utterly demolished the vehicle. The trooper said there was a body in the wreckage, and he had been unable to detect any signs of life.

The main part of the car looked like a piece of paper someone had balled up and discarded. The driver was wedged under the dash, and I fumbled at his throat, going through the motions of trying to find a pulse. It was only a formality, of course. His skin was ice-cold, but I still had to make the effort.

I pressed my fingers into his neck and....he groaned. "Hey," I yelled, "this guy's alive!" We quickly untangled him from what was left of the car and placed him on the stretcher. All this moving around helped revive him.

"What happened?" he asked, groggily.

"You were in a wreck," I told him. "Just relax. We're taking you to a hospital."

That got his attention. "A wreck!" he shouted, sitting straight up. He stared at his once-beautiful automobile, and tears welled up in his eyes. "I broke my car," he sobbed, flopping back on the stretcher.

173

Except for a few cuts and bruises, he was unhurt. He was very lucky and also very drunk.

Some people seem to survive in spite of themselves. While I was in rookie school, a pathologist showed us pictures of a woman who tried to commit suicide. Despondent over a love affair gone bad, she took a revolver, placed it between her eyes, and pulled the trigger. She should have died instantly, but the ammunition was defective, and the slug didn't penetrate her skull. The base of the bullet was clearly visible in the pictures, and other than a bad headache and two beautiful shiners, the woman suffered only minor injuries.

Another time, when I was working as an orderly at the county hospital, one of my patients was a skinny car thief with a bullet wound in the shoulder, shot by a deputy when he bolted from his latest stolen vehicle. He was being guarded by a reserve officer who spent most his time in the nurses' station, sucking up coffee and flirting with the ladies.

This wasn't as careless as it sounded. The guard had a clear view of the prisoner's hospital room, and we were on the fourth floor, so escape was unlikely. But escape he did. When left alone for a few minutes, the kid climbed out the window, hung by his fingertips, then dropped 40 feet to the gravel roof below. His guardian angel must have been close by, because he only broke his foot. Crawling to the edge of the roof, he dropped off, thinking he was free.

Unfortunately, he chose the completely enclosed courtyard of the psychiatric ward and was soon located, lying in the shrubbery, moaning. In custody once again, he was put back in the same bed to recuperate from this latest injury.

Finally, a city policeman friend of mine told me of the time they were called to a disturbance at an unused pier on the waterfront. Around one in the morning, people reported shouts and curses followed by gunshots. The cops investigated and found several intoxicated winos who denied anything was wrong, although one was bleeding from cuts on his face. Investigating further, my friend was shining his flashlight along the edge of the pier when he discovered a hand extending above the water, clutching a pipe that was fastened to the pier.

The hand was attached to an arm connected to a body under the water. An autopsy revealed the man had been stabbed several times, shot twice, and his skull crushed with a brick. He was then tossed into the water. The immediate cause of death was drowning, although the pathologist said any one of the wounds would have been fatal.

In his last seconds, the guy managed to reach out and grab the pipe with what turned out to be a literal death-grip. In his other hand was a piece of fabric, torn from the shirt of one his murderers. Had he not made that last convulsive attempt to save himself, his body would not have been recovered for a week, and the crime would have probably gone unsolved.

45

Can't You Take a Joke?

Like members of most truly stressful professions, law enforcement officers are great practical jokers. Of course, cops are not noted for their sophistication, so the jokes tend to be of the whoopee cushion variety. But they do serve a useful purpose, because a little levity, no matter how crude, helps to ease the daily pressure.

How the term "practical joke" ever came into usage is a mystery to me. I never could figure out what was practical about pulling someone's chair out from under them, putting a stink bomb in their cruiser car, or giving them a hotfoot. But, when done right, some practical jokes become legends.

One of the best practical jokers I ever knew was a deputy, now retired, who was famous for tormenting new communications dispatchers. They were relatively easy targets. Being new, they didn't know the ropes, nor had they learned whom they could trust. He had several standard jokes, and one of his favorites was the "night shift rendezvous."

After signing in at the start of a midnight shift, he would go to the radio room and ask his intended victim to speak to him away from the other dispatchers. When a sufficient degree of privacy had been achieved, he would tell the wide-eyed rookie that he had arranged to meet later with a female admirer who had the greatest respect for law enforcement officers.

This particular woman was the lonely wife of a man who worked midnights, and it was necessary that their meeting be kept secret for two reasons: first, there was the husband to consider, and second, the deputy's job might be jeopardized if the wrong person, like the shift commander, for instance, found out about it. To keep everything super-secret, he was simply going to come on the radio around 3 A.M. and check out at the woman's phone number.

In order for the tryst to be successful, the right person had to be handling the dispatching duties on the patrol frequency. Needless to say, the gullible rookie was the one the prankster had in mind. Appropriately dazzled at being entrusted with such responsibility by a veteran, the rookie would quickly agree to be doing the dispatching at the appointed hour.

Sure enough, at the stroke of three, the deputy checked out at the supposed phone number of the love-starved wife. As the trusting dispatcher wrote the number down, something about it seemed familiar. Suddenly, he realized why: It was HIS phone number!

Usually the kid immediately called his wife, waking her from a sound sleep, demanding to know what was going on. Naturally, she would be completely mystified and not a little put out. By this time, the deputy had sneaked back inside the radio room so he could enjoy the reaction of his victim, having actually made the transmission from inside the building.

"When you think about it, I'm really performing a valuable service," he would say in his own defense. "If the marriage is in good shape, the husband isn't going to believe for one minute I'm banging his wife. If he doesn't trust her, better to get these feelings out in the open now."

"Besides," he'd smirk, "if he makes the call, I've got a hot prospect."

He had a variation on the old phone number trick that also worked well. He would find out what car the dispatcher drove and make a note of the tag number. Some hours later, he would come on the air and inform the dispatcher he had discovered what appeared to be a stolen and burned automobile. It was now only a smoldering shell, with the wheels, seats, engine and bumpers stripped off it.

He'd say he had found a license plate and ask for a registration check. The poor sap on the radio would dutifully enter the numbers in the computer and shortly discover, to his horror, that the tag was registered to him. Urgently, he would try and call the deputy on the radio but would get no response. If he was lucky, he might finally look around before he suffered a fatal seizure and discover the deputy laughing at him.

I'm happy to say this sadist did occasionally fall victim to jokes himself. One time he really did have to make a quick exit from a house when a husband came home early. In his haste, he left behind his uniform shirt which had his name tag on it. For the next several days, he refused to leave the building when he got off duty, convinced he might be shot by the jealous spouse.

Early one morning he was propped up in a chair, dozing, when one of his former victims sneaked up and burst an inflated paper bag beside his ear. In the concrete and tile interior of the office, it must have sounded like a cannon shot. It was said the poor deputy fell to the floor clutching his chest, bug-eyed with terror. When the shrieks of laughter finally convinced him he was not shot, he even managed to smile and agree shakily that the joke was definitely on him for a change.

Like I said, a little levity helps to relieve the stress.

46

Bells Are Ringing

The building had been a waterbed sales outlet but had gone belly up, the owners leaving town abruptly. There was a burglar alarm system, and a large bell had been installed on the side of the building about 15 feet off the ground. For some reason the power was still on. It must have been one of the few bills the company paid before abandoning the premises.

Around three in the morning a thunderstorm moved through the area, and a nearby lightning strike set the alarm off. I was dispatched and arrived to find an empty building and a noisy alarm. A very noisy alarm.

There were two emergency phone numbers posted on the glass door, but when the dispatchers called, they discovered both had been disconnected. I suggested the radio room call the power company and have them send someone to pull the meter. The dispatchers were informed it would be some time before a crew was available, as they were tied up dealing with power outages caused by the thunderstorm.

This was fine with me, and I made the necessary notations in my report, preparing to leave the area. It was, however, definitely not fine with the nearby residents who had called to report the alarm in the first place. With the passing of the storm, the air was cool and still, and the clanging bell could be heard for miles. A small crowd of irritated citizens had gathered, and they were not pleased with my handling of the situation.

"You fixin' to leave?" a large-bellied man with thick glasses asked.

I nodded, "There's nothing more I can do."

He jerked his thumb toward the raucous alarm. "What about that bell?"

I shrugged. "We'll just have to wait until the power company turns off the electricity."

His eyes narrowed. "You mean to tell me we gotta listen to that damn thing for the rest of the night?"

"Oh, I don't think it will be all night," I said. "They should be able to get a truck out here within an hour or two." A burst of grumbling from the crowd greeted this news. I didn't blame them for being upset. We were on the opposite side of the building, and it was still hard to talk because of the noise.

"It ain't right," the man said, his jaw muscles quivering. "You're the police. Do something."

I pointed toward the building. "I've had the dispatcher call the emergency numbers listed on the door, but they've been disconnected."

He glared at me. "That's it, then?"

I nodded. "I'm afraid so." The rumbles from the crowd were getting louder.

"Well, maybe we'll just take care of the problem ourselves," he said. Mutters of support indicated the rest of his neighbors were certainly on his side.

"Why don't you try calling the power company?" I suggested. "If they get flooded with phone calls, they might be more inclined to make it a higher priority."

He waved this idea off. "You just don't worry about it." He turned and walked back to the group; they talked for a few minutes, then dispersed, heading for their various homes with purposeful strides.

The hellish clatter from the bell was really getting on my

180

nerves, and it was a relief to drive off and leave the clamor behind. I hoped they could figure out a solution. I certainly would not have wanted to listen to that noise the rest of the night.

Twenty minutes later I was dispatched to the same area. Someone had called, reporting the sound of gunshots. It didn't take me long to get there, and the first thing I noticed was the absence of noise. The bell was no longer ringing. Maybe the power company had secured the electricity.

The next thing I saw was the bell, lying on the deserted parking lot. The paint was chipped and gouged, and several large dents were now visible, dents that hadn't been there when it was attached to the side of the building. Very strange.

I shined my spotlight at the building and saw a ragged hole through the siding where the bell had been mounted. There were several other splintered areas and another hole right through the overhang of the roof. I started to chuckle. Someone had used a shotgun to shoot the bell off the side of the building. While a somewhat radical solution, it certainly had solved the problem. I had a pretty good idea who might have done the shooting.

The Lieutenant pulled up beside me. ''What's up?''

I pointed at the bell. ''I think someone decided they had listened to that alarm long enough.'' A persistent buzzing had been going on this whole time, and I stepped closer to the building, concerned there might be an electrical short. I saw, dangling from some loosened wires, the bell clapper, still vibrating furiously but harmlessly, since there was no bell to strike against. It was such a ridiculous sight I started laughing.

My boss was not amused. As far as he was concerned, this was a case of criminal mischief. ''You have any idea who might have done the shooting?'' he asked.

I thought long and hard, but finally shook my head. ''Nope. No idea at all.''

He pointed toward the residential area behind us. ''You think it might have been one of the people who lives around here?''

I looked at the darkened houses, occupied for the most part

by decent, hard-working people, many of whom would be getting up in less than an hour to go to work. They had already lost several hours of sleep because of the ringing alarm. "No, it couldn't have been any of them," I told him.

He started his car. "If you get any information about it, be sure to pass it on to investigation."

"I sure will," I said as he drove off, leaving me standing in the parking lot, now silent except for the low buzzing of the mangled alarm.

47

There's One Born Every Minute

The heavy rains of the last few days had washed away his carefully planted flowers, and the homeowner was walking along, retrieving them from the ditch. About ten feet off the edge of the road, in a patch of weeds, he found two women's purses. They contained three rather curious packages. The size of small bricks, constructed of tan plastic and heavily sealed with duct tape, they didn't look like something you'd expect to find in a purse. He called the cops.

A deputy soon arrived and opened one of the packages. White powder spilled out. The packages were filled with cocaine. There were three kilos, or six-and-a-half pounds, of the stuff, with an estimated street value of close to $200,000. Narcotics was notified, and several officers were soon on the scene. After some discussion, it was decided to establish a stakeout in hopes someone would show up to try and retrieve the coke. Two narcs stayed with it until well after midnight, but there was no activity.

At that point the story could well have been over, since the chances of someone's appearing to reclaim the coke were pretty slim. They had the dope, and it would make a nice news story when the six pounds of cocaine were spread out on a table in front of the TV cameras. Yes, it could have ended there, but it didn't.

Around two in the morning, as the narcotics officers were about to give it up, one of them had, at least in his estimation, a brilliant idea.

He got a piece of paper and wrote: "I found your purses and the contents. Call me. Large reward expected." He listed one of the confidential phone numbers that bypassed the department's switchboard and rang directly in the narcotics office. He put the note on a stick where the purses had been and left.

The next morning they reported their efforts to the lieutenant. He was not pleased. "You did what?" he said when they told him about the note. When the word spread about their brilliant idea, the shrieks of laughter from their fellow narcotics officers increased their discomfort. For the rest of the day the hilarity mounted as more people heard about the note and joined in. The merriment continued until three o'clock that afternoon but then died abruptly.

Because we got a call.

One of the female agents answered the phone, and a male voice asked if she knew anything about any purses. Not one to let opportunity slip through her fingers, she told the guy she and her boyfriend had the dope and would return it for $10,000, cash. The man countered with an offer of $5,000. She offered to hang up and sell the dope herself, and the man hastily agreed to the price. After more discussion it was decided they would meet at a phone booth at a shopping center.

At first the lieutenant was inclined to treat the call as a practical joke, so convinced was he that one of his fun-loving narcs had made the call. It took some doing, but when finally persuaded the call might be legit, he authorized a stakeout of the phone booth.

Half a dozen deputies took up positions in the parking lot around the phone booth, and soon a car with three men pulled up. Clutching a paper bag, one man got out. The female agent and her "boyfriend" were waiting by the phone booth, holding the two purses. "You bring the money?" the male agent asked.

The guy nodded. "Yeah. You got my stuff?" The narc took the bag and handed over the purses. Before the guy could move, he was looking down the barrels of two guns. Seeing their companion was in trouble, the other two started to make a run for it but were a little late. The driver's attempt to start the car was interrupted by a gun barrel inserted into his left ear.

The final score was six pounds of cocaine, $10,000 in twenty dollar bills, three suspects arrested, one car confiscated, and two purses, one a Gucci, recovered. The story did indeed play well on the evening news, and the sight of all that money and cocaine made for wonderful television. It also made the department look great, and everyone concerned got a big laugh out of the whole thing.

Except, of course, the three idiots who tried to buy their cocaine back.

48

To Tell The Truth

One of the hardest things a cop must learn is that people will lie. Often they will lie for no good reason, when the truth would actually do them more good. This tendency to lie was something I had to get used to, but it took awhile. Many times I was ready to totally believe one side of a story, only to find the other side was closer to the truth. Notice I said, "closer to the truth." After 18 years in the biz, I'm not sure I'll ever hear "the whole truth and nothing but the truth." When I was young and idealistic, this used to bother me a great deal. Now, however, I am far more accepting of what seems to be a universal human trait. It's just the way we are.

Most cops have developed a protective shell to use in dealings with victims, witnesses, and perpetrators. This is frequently mistaken for callousness, but it's not. I call it "pragmatic optimism."

This means we hope for the best but are prepared for the worst. I think this quality helps the best cops to keep a certain perspective about their jobs, allowing them to rejoice in the good and not be dragged too far down by the bad.

Being able to determine the truth is a skill as difficult to master as becoming a good hitter in major league baseball. If a player can get a hit one out of three times at bat, he can probably write

186

his own contract. As a cop, I would have loved to have batted .333 in the truth department. Even with an average that low, I'd still be way ahead of most of my peers.

And the truth can be elusive. I remember taking a law enforcement class taught by a retired judge, who used a very effective visual aid to help us realize how our own judgments could affect our perceptions of the truth. He took a piece of plastic about 12 inches square from his briefcase and held it up. "What color is this?" he asked.

Since we were looking at a totally white surface, there was universal agreement the plastic was white. He flipped it over, and now we were looking at a totally black side. He smiled, "I thought you said it was white."

There were howls of protest from the audience, accusing him of trying to pull a fast one.

He waited for the commotion to die down. "I didn't prevent you from looking at the other side," he said. "You people decided the plastic was white." He looked around the room. "Do you want to change your answer in light of this new evidence?"

We certainly did, and all agreed the square was white on one side and black on the other. Just when we thought peace and tranquility would reign, he suddenly turned the plastic edge-on and we saw a half-inch wide blue stripe. Having been burned twice, we made him rotate the square so we could see all four edges. All were blue.

We finally agreed the plastic was actually black, white, and blue. He even wrote our answer on the board, and we were happy. But then he separated the white half from the black half, and now we had two squares with two additional colors, green and red.

Thankfully, he ended the exercise at this point and asked for our reactions. A tall, slow-talking state trooper raised his hand and said, "Hell fire, judge. It's damn near impossible to figure out what the truth is."

"Give that man a prize," the judge said enthusiastically,

187

"because that is exactly the point I'm trying to make. During my years on the bench, it was often very difficult for me to decide the truth, and I had all the facts right at my fingertips." He looked at us. "If it was hard for me, think how hard it will be for you, out there in the streets."

Well, the judge was right, but it took me a few years to realize just how right he was. The longer I was in law enforcement, the more cautious I became about the truth, never really sure if I was looking at only one side of the plastic. Of course, this caution born of experience didn't sit well with everyone, particularly someone who had an interest in a case but was not directly involved.

That someone could be a parent, a spouse, a friend, or, in one case, an earnest young Navy ensign.

I was told to contact this particular ensign, the weekend security officer at one of the naval bases in our area, at the main gate. He had called the sheriff's department to report a kidnaping of the infant son belonging to one of the enlisted men on the base. The original complaint was received, he said, from the man's wife, who was accusing the sailor of doing the kidnaping. The crime had supposedly occurred at their apartment located off-base, which, of course, placed it in our jurisdiction.

The couple had separated, and the woman was planning to file for divorce. She had turned up at the main gate an hour ago, screaming and crying, saying her estranged husband had made off with the kid. The ensign had located the young sailor aboard the base, brought him to the security office, and questioned him at length about the missing infant. "I'm convinced he had nothing to do with the disappearance of his son," the ensign told me. "He's really pretty shook up."

I nodded, "I'd like to talk to them both."

He was not pleased. "I don't see the point in that," he said. "I think the best thing you can do is notify the FBI immediately."

"Well, for one thing," I said, "the FBI won't get involved unless it's a kidnaping for ransom, and this sounds more like a marital dispute to me.''

"A marital dispute?'' He was clearly shocked. "How you can say that? I've got a young seaman in one office, crying his eyes out, and the mother of that baby in another office, almost out of her mind with fear. Meanwhile,'' he said, tight-lipped with anger, "you're wasting time while that baby could be on his way out of the state!''

His reaction didn't really bother me. As so often happens, he had made up his mind based on what I thought were insufficient facts. "Ensign,'' I said mildly, "you called us because this occurred off-base, and you need our help. I'm concerned about the baby, too, but I need to learn all the facts so I'll know what action to take.''

He calmed down a little and agreed I probably should talk to both parties. I started with the wife. When I walked through the door, she was all over me, begging me to do something. It took a few minutes before she was able to get herself under control enough to relate what had happened.

She and her husband had been separated for two weeks, she told me, and he had moved back on-base. He demanded she relinquish custody of their infant son, but she refused. She woke this morning to discover the baby gone and no signs of forced entry. Naturally, she suspected the estranged husband, since he still had his key.

As she talked, she became more and more upset, eventually working herself into a state of near hysteria, screaming that the drunken, potentially homicidal maniac she was temporarily married to would likely kill her helpless baby while I was piddling around, asking a bunch of stupid questions. I tried to reassure her I would do everything possible to locate the child, but I wasn't much comfort.

I went to the other office to interview the father and now accused kidnaper. He was a sullen young man with several fresh tattoos, trying very hard to act the old salt. He agreed that he and his wife had been having problems, admitted he demanded custody of the child, but stoutly denied he had anything to do with the disappearance. He, too, worked himself into a state of high agitation and, at one point, fell to his knees, imploring me to spare no effort to locate his missing son. He swore on his mother's grave that he was totally innocent of the charges made by his wife and concluded by tearfully offering to take a lie detector test if it would make me happy.

The ensign glared at me as he tried to comfort the weeping sailor. There was no doubt whom he believed.

I, however, was convinced the boy was lying through his teeth. There was nothing definite I could point to, but I had an advantage over the ensign: I had experience. I had worked hundreds of family fights, many of them involving custody disputes, and there was something about this one that didn't add up to a genuine kidnaping. For one thing, the sailor's reaction was much too dramatic to suit me. For another, he was the obvious suspect. Now all I had to do was prove it.

When the boy regained his composure, I began talking to him, explaining how difficult marriage is, discussing a father's love for his son, telling him I totally understood how a man could get himself into a mess like this, and I finished by asking him not to throw a bright future away simply because he was angry at his wife. I let him think it over for a few minutes, then quietly asked where the child was. He ducked his head and said he had stashed him at a friend's house.

In relatively short order, we had reunited mother and baby and solved the problem, at least temporarily. The security officer was embarrassed. "He was lying the whole time, wasn't he?"

I nodded.

"But why?" he asked, clearly puzzled. "The truth wouldn't have hurt him."

I shrugged. "I sure couldn't tell you, but I can tell you one thing."

"What's that?"

"If you stay in security work long enough, you'll get used to it."

190

49

How to Please
Some of the People

One of the problems with being a part of a high visibility profession like law enforcement is the high visibility itself. Driving distinctively marked cars and wearing gaudy uniforms attracts attention, which can get a little tiresome. The department constantly receives complaints from citizens, irritated because some cop didn't come to a full stop at a stop sign, or inadvertently let a piece of paper blow out the window of a cruiser car, or failed to write a ticket for an obvious traffic violation. One of the more common complaints occurs when a citizen sees two or three marked cruiser cars parked at a restaurant and automatically assumes the cops driving those cars are inside wasting time and tax dollars.

But some agencies, including mine, assign cars to deputies to drive back and forth to work. The deputy keeps his or her car 24 hours a day, and some of those marked cars seen at coffee shops actually belong to deputies on their way home. Part of the time I was in the patrol division, I had a wife who worked shift work herself. With no particular reason to hurry home after I got off, I would sometimes spend an hour or more in a restaurant, writing, talking with my buddies, or working on reports.

I would get occasional glares from righteous citizens who came in after I did, ate a full meal, and left, while I was still sitting there, evidently shirking my duties. Every so often, some of the braver ones would make an acid little comment like, "Boy, I wish I had a job like yours," or "Who's out there protecting the county?" or "I guess this place won't get robbed." All very amusing. Since none of them really wanted to hear my boring explanation about being off-duty, I rarely offered it, preferring to let them warm themselves with the heat of their anger.

But, after a while, I realized I was doing neither myself, nor the department any favors. It wasn't helping our image to have a bunch of irritated taxpayers going around putting the badmouth on us. So I devised a plan. I went to an office supply store and ordered a small plastic sign about five inches long and three inches high, solid black with white letters. It had the following message:

This Deputy is OFF DUTY
He is on his own time and not wasting
your hard-earned tax dollars.

It cost me a few bucks, but I thought it would be worth the expense. I made a little stand for the sign and placed it on the table beside me. If an indignant citizen approached, determined to give me a piece of his or her mind because of my slothful habits, I simply pointed to the sign. They'd read the message and usually chuckle, admitting they were concerned about the highest and best use of my time. It was a good way to avoid misunderstandings and probably improved our public relations. Of course, it didn't work with everyone.

One time an elderly gentleman came up to me, read the sign, glared at me, anyway and said, "Very funny, young fella, but if you want my opinion (I didn't), I think a sign like that is a waste of tax dollars." He stomped out of the restaurant muttering to himself.

50

You Can't Forget
The Little Things

"But how do you keep up with all the details?"

I glanced at my passenger, "What do you mean?"

The boy pointed toward the dashboard of my cruiser car. "I mean all these buttons and switches and radios. It looks like an airplane cockpit," he said. "And all the reports and the different procedures. You must have a different report for every situation." He shook his head. "And that doesn't even include all the laws and ordinances and traffic violations you have to remember. I could never do it."

I had to laugh at his distress. "It's not really all that complicated. Believe me, you don't need the brain of a nuclear physicist to be a cop."

"Well, it sure seems like it to me."

"It's like anything else," I told him. "You do it enough, you get good at it. I've been in the biz so long I can do this job blindfolded. If you want to be a cop, you have to learn to keep up with the small things; your life might depend on it some day."

My companion for the night was a young high school student, taking part in a special ride-along program started by the sheriff. All the participants had indicated an interest in law enforcement as a career, and now they had the chance to see what the job was really like. Jason had been assigned to me, and I was enjoying his company. It was kind of fun to play the grizzled veteran cop, showing the young kid how to do it.

His open admiration and eagerness to learn at the feet of the master was certainly an ego boost, too. I admit I might have done just a little showing off for his benefit but it was all educational. Could I help it if the kid had a hero-worship complex?

We stopped at my favorite Waffle House, and I was warmly greeted by Randi the waitress, Ralph the cook, and several patrons, all acquaintances of mine. I knew I would get a nice reception here, which was one reason I chose this place. "Boy, you must know everyone," Jason said as soon as we were seated.

I gave a careless wave, "Well, I don't know about that, but I do have a few friends here and there."

I put my radio on the table between us, the speaker spewing a steady babble of dispatch signals, radio codes, and car descriptions. Jason listened intently, then shook his head. "I can't even understand what they're saying."

"It's just a question of getting used to what you're hearing. After all these years, it's second nature to me now."

"Easy for you to say," he said.

While we ate our sandwiches, I shared a few of my better war stories with him, all of which just happened to feature me in the starring role. I concluded with an account of a successful recovery of a stolen car, which had resulted in a letter of commendation for me. It involved my recognizing that the vehicle identification number plate had been altered.

"But how did you know?" Jason asked.

"It was simple. The rivets they used weren't the kind that came with the car."

He shook his head admiringly, "That's amazing."

"No, it's just an eye for detail." I leaned back in the chair. "You have to remember the small stuff if you want to be a cop."

I paid the bill and headed out the door, pausing to speak to some of the customers as we went. Back in the car, I felt a sense of deep satisfaction at being able to act as a mentor to this youngster. Who knows, I might even be the reason he chose law enforcement as a career. I mentally envisioned the title of the story he would write for *Reader's Digest*, "The Greatest Cop I Ever Knew." Jason was staring at the restaurant as I backed out of the parking lot. "Hey, wait a minute, Don; someone's waving at us."

I looked toward the building. Randi was standing at the door, and she was indeed waving. I liked the attention but sometimes they overdid it. "I guess Randi is telling us goodbye."

Jason was rolling the window down. "No, she's saying something." He leaned out. "She wants us to come back."

I drove to the front door. "Maybe they have some trouble inside," I said grimly.

"She's got something in her hand," he said.

Laughing faces were looking at us from the window of the restaurant. Something was sure going on, but I couldn't figure out what. I stopped beside her, and she leaned down. "I thought you boys might need this." She handed Jason my radio. "Have a nice day, and don't work too hard."

I had left the damn radio on the table.

Jason looked puzzled. "Is this really your radio?"

Waves of heat were radiating from my burning cheeks as I plugged it into the dash unit. "Uh, yeah, I was just about to go back in and get it."

"Gosh," he said, his eyes shining, "you think of everything. I thought you had forgotten all about it."

I handed him my procedures manual. "Why don't you read for a while, Jason?"

51

A Matter of Respect

"Okay, that's about everything," Lieutenant Morgan said, glancing over his papers. "Oh, wait a minute; the sheriff has been getting complaints about a traffic problem." He scanned the memo for a moment, then looked at me. "It's in your district, Parker, so you get to take care of it."

I was immediately suspicious. "What kind of traffic problem?"

"People are running the stop sign at an intersection near Navy Point Elementary School," he said. "The parents are afraid they'll be scraping their kids off the street. Go down there for a few hours, write some tickets, and show them the sheriff is concerned."

I knew the location. It was a "T" intersection and wide open in all directions. "Lieutenant, I won't be able to write any tickets there," I whined. "You can see for a mile in each direction. There's no place to hide."

Actually, the question of concealment was a non-issue to me. I just didn't want to spend two hours sitting there like a lump, enforcing boring traffic laws. I was still young and eager. I wanted to be out there doing important stuff like catching armed robbers, breaking up drug rings, battling organized crime. I considered my time much too valuable to waste on such mundane duties.

196

Unfortunately, the lieutenant felt differently. "You won't have to worry about hiding. Just write some tickets and let the residents see they're getting some action."

"I'll do it," I grumbled, "but I doubt if I'll get to write any tickets."

When I was a rookie, I was convinced I knew it all. This thinking was, of course, seriously flawed, but I didn't know any better. Convinced my supervisors were spineless ninnies, I yearned for the day when I, too, would be a supervisor. Boy, things would be different then. But when that day finally came, I was amazed to discover I was just as spineless as the supervisors I had criticized so harshly. Having to shoulder responsibility tended to make one cautious. As I was promoted even further up the ladder, I found there was a direct correlation between caution and responsibility: the greater the responsibility, the greater the caution.

My human relations skills in those days were also rather rudimentary. I operated on the premise that, since my customers were usually wrong, I could treat them any way I pleased. Although constantly counseled by shift commanders to be careful of my mouth, I paid little attention. After all, I knew everything.

Ah, the sweet bliss of youthful ignorance. I figure the only reason the victims of my sarcasm did not feed me my badge was because they felt sorry for me.

I drove to the intersection, and it was as I remembered: open in every direction. The school playground was on one corner, a vacant lot on the other, and houses, set well back from the road, crossed the "T". I was still annoyed at having to be here at all, so I parked five feet from the stop sign, right on the edge of the road. We'd see how many tickets I would write now.

I had barely taken up my position when the first three cars to come up the street ran the stop sign, right in front of me. I was stunned. One of the drivers even gave me a jaunty little wave as he sailed through the intersection. They had been running that stop sign for so long it had become invisible to them.

197

I stopped the fourth car, and believe me, I was steaming. I stormed up to the vehicle to let the driver know exactly how I felt.

A short, rounded man in his early fifties, his thinning grey hair framed a placid face. He was wearing work clothes and heavy shoes. Dangling from his pocket was a photo ID card, and he had one of those plastic holders, crammed with pens and pencils. He was an employee of one of the large chemical plants in the area.

I started in on the guy immediately. "You know, I would have thought a grown man like you would have to be able to read to get a job, but obviously, you can't. Since you totally ignored that stop sign back there, I guess you must be illiterate."

I continued in this vein for a few minutes, really getting some zingers in. As I vented my anger, the driver remained silent, nodding occasionally, until I finally ran down, then he began speaking.

"Son," he said mildly, "I have the greatest respect for anyone who risks his life every day like you do, and I wouldn't do your job for a million dollars."

I have to admit, his comments took me by surprise. I expected him to defend himself or reply in kind to my scathing remarks. "You know," he continued, "I think I'm probably old enough to be your father, and my daddy always told me to treat people with respect. But, son, that's not a very respectful way to talk to a person." He stared at me. "Would you talk to your father like that?"

I squirmed in embarrassment, feeling the color rise in my cheeks. "Well, no, I guess I wouldn't."

He nodded. "You write me that ticket if you have to, because I sure ran that stop sign, but I don't think you should talk to me like I was dirt under your feet."

I didn't say anything, but his words had a profound effect on me. It was as if the sun had suddenly come from behind a cloud. Of course! I could treat people decently and still do my job. Why didn't I think of that myself? I should have thanked him for this blinding revelation, but my pride wouldn't let me. I was only 24 and still took myself very seriously indeed. I finished writing the ticket, which he signed without comment. He drove off, but I was a changed man. From that day forward, I made a conscious effort to treat people better, particularly when it was only a traffic violation. That man, whose name I have long since forgotten, helped me understand that everyone deserves to be treated with respect. I learned a basic lesson in humanity that day. I hope I'll always remember it.

52

Fender Benders and Bumper Thumpers

It is virtually impossible for a cop to drive a cruiser car without denting it occasionally. I have had more than my share of wrecks during my career, but most came in my early days when I was young and eager and drove like a maniac (some people still feel this is an accurate description of my driving, even today).

I find it interesting to consider the demographics of my traffic mishaps. For instance, I must have been quite fond of my fellow deputies, since three of my wrecks involved either my hitting another cop or being hit by one. I liked Cadillacs, too: I managed to collide with two of them. I also had a talent for wrecking unmarked cars: four in one year, two in one week. I obviously had it in for inanimate objects as well. I have run into a building, a fire hydrant, two trees, and a culvert.

But don't think for one moment the sheriff's office was pleased with my driving. Far from it. As the toll mounted, so did the level of official displeasure. After a particularly spectacular collision, I was warned the next wreck that was my fault was going to cost me several days off without pay.

This definitely got my attention, and I tried to drive with extra care for the next few days. Perhaps I was trying too hard, because less than a week later, while working a slow midnight shift, I caved in the right rear quarter panel when attacked by a tree in a dark parking lot. If I reported the wreck, I would be suspended for sure.

I stood by the side of the car for a long time, trying to think of some way to save my career and decided desperate measures were in order. I called a friend who owned a paint and body shop, waking him from a sound sleep. After much begging and pleading, he agreed to meet me at his shop to survey the damage.

He arrived in 20 minutes, not exactly overjoyed, but my pitiful whimpering must have softened him up a little. He walked around the car several times, examining it from all angles, while I waited in breathless silence. "Well, I think I can fix it," he said at last.

"Oh, thank God!" I fought the impulse to throw myself on the floor and start kissing his shoes.

"But you're gonna have to help," he said, reaching for his tools.

I was already unstrapping my gunbelt. "No problem. You just tell me what to do."

"You're lucky you didn't tear up anything but the quarter panel. We'll pull it off and try to pound it out." He looked at it with a critical eye. "I think we can smooth the rough places with body filler and repaint it." He laughed. "Course, it won't look all that great close up."

I was, of course, taking an enormous risk. If the lieutenant wanted to see me or if a really big call came in, I was finished. But I had no choice. I did have my portable radio, so I could communicate with the office; I just wouldn't have a car to drive.

We got the quarter panel off in short order, and he pounded out the damage and started sanding. The work went quickly, but not quickly enough. Just as he was about to start applying the body putty, I got a call. A fight in an after-hours bottle club, only a mile away.

I got there the same time as my backup, who was a little surprised to see me drive up in an orange wrecker. "Don't ask," I said as we headed into the club. We restored the peace, but it turned out I was going to have to arrest one of the fighters who had pulled a knife on the manager.

"Well, I guess you'd like me to take this arrest for you," my compassionate, considerate buddy said.

I smiled, grateful for his help. "Man, that would be great," I said, as we started out the door with the handcuffed prisoner. "Yes," my close friend agreed, "that would be great, and for the right offer, I might just do it."

My smile faded. "What kind of offer?"

He shrugged. "Oh, trade a few days off, buy a few meals, make a few house payments for me: that sort of thing."

"But that's blackmail. You know I've got my tail in a crack." I glared at him. "You're just trying to take advantage of a bad situation."

"Who, me?" He was shocked. "I'm only trying to do a little business here."

"Well, I won't do it."

"Fine," he said, pushing the arrestee at me. "Better put your prisoner in your wrecker."

The man looked at me and then at the brightly painted truck. "I ain't getting in that thing," he shouted.

"Will you keep your voice down;" I hissed, "I'm trying to work this out."

"You put me in a real police car," he demanded. "I know my rights."

My backup strolled toward his car. "Have a nice trip."

I gave up. "All right. You win. Let's talk this over." We came to an agreement involving the trading of several days off and my buying him breakfast for the rest of the shift, but I couldn't argue. I was just glad he let me off the hook for the house payments.

I headed back to the paint and body shop, trying to slouch down in the seat so passing motorists wouldn't see my uniform.

The body putty had been applied, and the drying process was being helped along with several lights. "When this thing is painted, it won't exactly match the rest of the paint job," he told me.

"Look, as long as it's the right color, I don't care." I glanced at my watch. It was almost four. "How much longer?"

"It should be ready to go in a few hours."

Luckily, I didn't get any more calls, and the lieutenant never tried to meet with me. After the body filler set, my friend sprayed it with paint, let it dry for awhile, then put the car back together.

And none too soon, either. It was almost time to change shifts. The repair looked good, at least at a distance. The quarter panel was a little dull because the body putty really soaked up the paint, but when I got back to the office, I parked that side next to the fence. Three weeks later the car was traded for a new one, and I never told a soul about that wreck...until now.

53

Burglary In Progress

"Aw, come on," I said. "It will be fun."

"I don't know, Don," my brother said, "I don't exactly fit in with deputy sheriffs."

"Okay. I agree your hair is kind of long, but this is a midnight shift. It's a lot less formal. Besides," I said, trying to work on his emotions, "this will be the last chance you have before you go back to San Francisco."

"Yeah, that's true." He was silent for a few seconds. "All right, I'll try it."

I was elated. "Great! I'll pick you up at Mom's right after muster."

Roger had said several times he wanted to see what it would be like to ride with a cop. Twice, on previous visits, I had made the necessary arrangements, and twice he had wimped out on me. True, his hair was on the shaggy side, but that's the way they wore it in San Francisco in the early seventies.

I was working one of the outlying districts tonight, and I didn't expect him to have much contact with the rest of the troops. If he shocked a few of the rednecks we met on calls, that wouldn't do any harm. I was really looking forward to spending the shift with him. During one of the nights he was supposed to ride, a wino decided to take a little snooze on the railroad tracks and was chopped into stew-meat by a passing train. Bloody fragments were scattered for a hundred yards, and I was really irritated Roger wasn't along to share that experience.

I pulled up in front of my mother's house, and he stepped out the door. Silhouetted by the lights behind him, his hair was longer than I'd realized. Also, his clothing was a little less than conservative, but the departmental dress regulations only specified coat and tie for participants in the ride-along program. The fact the coat was a double-breasted Edwardian, brocade print and the tie a pencil-thin canary yellow, wasn't exactly prohibited by the rules. He got in and closed the door. "I'm not used to riding in the front of one of these things." he said.

I laughed. "You can always try the back if it makes you feel more at home."

"No," he brushed his hair out of his face; it really was very long. "I'll sit up here for a change."

The night passed quickly, and Roger was quite interested in everything that happened. It was a steady shift with a good variety of calls. I made several traffic stops, investigated a few bar fights, and handled the usual mix of family fights, prowler calls, and loud parties common to midnight shifts. By 4 A.M. it had slowed noticeably. "Want to get some breakfast?" I asked.

He yawned. "Yeah, sounds good." Another yawn. "Isn't it hard to stay up all night?"

I pulled into an all-night restaurant. "It's not so bad once you get used to it."

The place was nearly deserted as we sat down, and our breakfast arrived quickly. I immediately started shoveling it in. Roger delicately cut a small slice of omelet, sprinkled it lightly with salt and placed it carefully in his mouth, chewing slowly.

I gobbled two large forkfuls of pancakes, and stuffed a whole link sausage in behind them. Roger's distaste for my dining style was obvious. "Do you always eat like a starving wolf?"

"Shuff. Epslly mf aye annto pffish efrroar taygive mmacal."

I shoved another sausage in my mouth and slurped half a cup

of coffee.

He shook his head. "I couldn't understand a word you said."

I raised a finger as I gulped the last of the pancakes, washing it down with the remaining coffee. "I said I always eat like this, especially if I want to finish before they give me a call."

He cut a second small piece of omelet. "I'm surprised you don't die of indigestion." He broke off a corner of toast. "What happens if you get so busy....." He stopped as I grabbed the radio.

"109," I said. "Go ahead."

"10-4, the city police have a burglary in progress at the Family Recreation Center. They're requesting assistance."

I was already heading for the door.

Roger hadn't moved, toast still in hand, halfway to his mouth. "Come on, Rog," I yelled, "we've got a call." Jolted into action he dropped the toast and followed me out the door.

"This place is right at the edge of the city limits," I said, as we shot through a red light. "This time of night, the city cops have only one guy working this area and I'm probably closer than his backup." Roger nodded, but he wasn't about to waste time talking; he was too busy watching the road and the speedometer.

We hit a long straightaway and the needle surged past eighty. "Dear God," he muttered as we slid into a turn. As I straightened out, the city unit pulled in behind me, blue lights flashing.

"This is great," I yelled at my wide-eyed passenger. "We'll both get there together."

"Yeah, great." he said, but he didn't seem all that thrilled. We shot through another intersection against the light, and Roger closed his eyes.

As we turned into the parking lot, I glanced at the front door, it was intact. I pulled around the corner and saw the back door, splintered and broken, hanging from one hinge.

"Wait by the car," I told my brother as I jumped out. The

206

city officer was already standing by the ruined door, waiting for me, gun in one hand, flashlight in the other. "You ready?" I asked." He nodded. "Go!"

He went through the door, and I followed him in. We were in the main room, rows of pool tables stretching away from us in the darkness. A quick sweep with our flashlights showed us we were alone. We started down opposite sides, hugging the walls, headed toward the office where the cash register was.

As we approached the front of the room, the office door suddenly began to swing open. Off went our flashlights as we took cover behind the pool tables. A shadowy form stepped into the room. Our flashlights blazed, blinding a heavyset man, who was holding a revolver. "POLICE!" we screamed in unison. "DROP THE GUN!"

The revolver tumbled to the floor. "Don't shoot!" he pleaded, hands shooting skyward. "I'm the owner, I'm the one who called." And so he was. Spending the night in the office he had been awakened by the sounds of the back door being smashed open. Hiding behind the desk, he got his gun and called the city police. When the burglar tried the door to the office, the man yelled he was armed. The next thing he heard was running footsteps, going out the door. He waited a few minutes, then stepped out to see if the guy was gone and almost got shot.

The burglar was probably still in the immediate area, so we ran back outside. Roger was standing next to the car. "Come on," I said, "we're going to start searching."

By this time city and county cruiser cars were converging on the recreation center, and the entire block was sealed off. Behind the building was a vacant lot, overgrown with weeds and shoulder-high shrubbery. We started working our way through the tangled growth. Two minutes later a cop shouted, "Hold it right there!" We stopped, trying to pinpoint the location. "BLAM!" The sound of a gunshot sent me to the ground, Roger right beside me.

There were shouts and yells from all around us. "Who fired

the shot?''

"Anyone hit?''

"Spread out, spread out.''

"I almost stepped on him," a voice yelled, "He ran south, and I shot into the ground.''

"Get some spotlights on the south side," the lieutenant shouted, "and don't shoot again unless you have to; I damn near pissed in my pants.''

Roger and I were stumbling through high weeds, seeds attaching themselves to his dark jacket. I laughed, "Boy, that shot sure got my attention; how about you?''

Roger could only nod, his eyes the size of pie plates.

"Anyone got a description?'' the lieutenant asked.

"Yeah," a new voice said from my left. "He's a white guy, about 5' 10", skinny, long brown hair, brown jacket.''

I chuckled, "Hey, that description fits you to a 'T', Rog.'' Silence.

"Don't you think that sounds like you?'' I said. No answer. I turned. He wasn't there. "Roger?'' I shined my light all around. I was alone. "Roger?'' Definitely alone. I started to turn around when I head the sound of running feet.

"There he goes!'' someone yelled.

Another voice chimed in, "You better stop, you little bastard!'' More running, shouts, yells, curses, the sounds of bodies thudding into the ground. Finally, "All right, we got him.'' I hurried toward the noise. Lying face down, under the interested stares of a dozen cops, was a skinny white guy with long brown hair, breathing hard, hands cuffed behind him.

I was relieved to see it wasn't Roger.

I walked back to the car and found my brother sitting in the front seat. "Boy, you had me worried for a minute there," I said. "I couldn't find you.''

"I had you worried?'' He shook his head. "I was the one who was worried.''

I was puzzled. "Why?''

208

"Are you kidding? Right after that gunshot, they describe someone who could have been my twin." He took a deep breath. "All these cops with guns, running around in the dark; that's when I knew it was time for me to go back to the car."

I laughed, "Aw, you would have been all right if you stayed close to me."

"I decided discretion was the better part of valor."

We finished up the night without further incident, and Roger returned to San Francisco. He eventually moved back to Pensacola, but I was never able to get him to ride with me again. He said one time was enough.

54

Seeing Is Believing

The barmaid was still shaking as she recounted her narrow escape. "So I told him that I was married, and even if I weren't, I don't date customers." She laughed shakily, "Besides, I would never go out with a slimeball like him."

"What did he do?" I asked.

"He got pissed!" she said. "He told me I must think it was made out of gold."

I could guess what "it" was. "What did you say?"

"I told him to get the hell out." She clenched and unclenched her fists. "I don't take that kind of crap from no one."

I was making notes as she talked. "Did he go?"

She shook her head. The man refused to leave and continued to curse her. Unfortunately, it was early afternoon and except for the cook in the back, they were the only people in the bar. "I finally told him I was calling the cops, and that's when he did it."

"Did what?"

She looked at me as though I were demented. "That's when he tried to hit me with the barstool," she said slowly.

I smiled. "I know that, but I have to hear it from you in your own words." I wrote for a moment. "But you weren't hurt?"

She shuddered. "No, but he sure tried," she said, pointing

at the handcuffed man across the room talking to Deputy Leamon Reaves. "I yelled for Bessie to come help me, but it was all over before she got out here."

"What did he do then?"

"Nothing," she said, gritting her teeth, "And that's what made me so mad. He just stood there laughing at me, telling me to go ahead and call the cops, that it was my word against his and I couldn't prove a thing." She gripped the edge of the bar, "Is that right? I've heard you have to have witnesses if a crime happens."

I chuckled, "Don't believe everything you hear."

"Are you going to arrest him?"

I closed my notebook. "You can count on it," I said. I walked across the scarred dance floor to talk to the other half of this dispute, a paunchy balding man, badly in need of a shave and a bath. He was wearing a dark blue work shirt with a patch over the pocket that read "Wayne."

He was swaying slightly, still very drunk. "You gonna listen to my side now?" he asked, smirking.

"Yeah, I'll listen," I said, "but not for long."

"She ain't got shit on me," he sneered. "I ain't done nothing."

"She says you tried to hit her with a barstool."

"Thass bullshit," he said, his sour beer-breath washing over me. I tried to lean to one side. "She tol' me I hadda pay fifty bucks to go to bed with her."

"What about the barstool?"

"There weren't no barstool," he chortled, "the bitch is jus' making that up."

One of the things I love about drunks is their ability to totally block out what they don't want to see, secure in their alcohol-drenched minds that reality will conform to their beliefs. The truth matters little, and their ability to lie when confronted with absolute facts is breathtaking. Such was certainly the case with this guy. I took him by the arm. "Let's go, pal, you're under arrest."

He jerked away. "Arrest?"

"That's right," I said, taking a tighter grip on his arm. Reaves grabbed the other arm.

"You can't arrest me. I ain't done nothing."

We headed toward the door. I would normally have ignored him, but decided to offer a further explanation to this particular drunk since this was really a special case. We stopped. "You are being charged with aggravated assault," I said. "Do you know what that is?"

He shook his head, "Hell, no, and you know what?" I didn't answer. "I don't give a shit."

I continued with my legal lesson for the day. "Aggravated assault is a third degree felony in this state," I told him, "punishable by up to five years in the state prison. You see, you didn't actually hit the lady with the barstool; otherwise I would have charged you with aggravated battery."

"I don't know what the hell you're talking about, and I think you're as full of shit as she is."

"*Au contraire,* my inebriated friend, we have a solid case against you."

"You ain't got no solid case," he sneered. "There weren't no witnesses."

"True, true," I said, "But aren't you forgetting about the evidence?"

"What evidence?"

I turned him until he was facing the scene of the crime. The bar itself was illuminated by fluorescent lights concealed behind a valance made of sheet rock. This valance extended about two feet from the ceiling. When the drunk swung the barstool, it never reached its intended victim, striking the valance instead, embedding itself in the soft sheet rock, coating the whole area with plaster dust. And there it hung, suspended over the bar. Still.

I pointed at the incontrovertible evidence. "The barstool!" I said dramatically.

The drunk squinted at this rather damning affirmation of his intentions toward the barmaid and was silent for long seconds. Finally he smiled. "Oh, that," he said airily. "That was here when I came in."

55

The Barking Woman

"What kind of assistance do they need, Headquarters?"

"Complainant reported her mother has fallen out of bed," the dispatcher said, "and she needs help getting her back in."

"10-4, I'm on my way." I put the microphone back in the dashboard holder. It was not unusual for elderly people to need this type of help. If the spouse or other care-giver was getting along in years, too, a simple thing like getting someone safely back in bed could be a real problem. Although this was not a true emergency, we were frequently called on to provide the necessary muscle power. No sense running up a two hundred dollar ambulance bill when the cops were free.

Over the years I had handled dozens of such episodes, but not all of them were easy. Once an enormous naked woman of at least 400 pounds fell off her commode and got wedged between wall and toilet. I thought for a while we were going to have to get a block and tackle, but we finally unscrewed the toilet from the floor, freeing her. She wasn't injured, which was fortunate. I don't know how we would have carried her to the ambulance.

I found the address and knocked on the door. A harassed middle-aged woman let me in. She certainly seemed fit enough to get an aged mother back in bed. I hoped this wasn't another commode pinning. "Did you call the sheriff's department?"

She brushed her hair back distractedly. "Yes, I did. It's my mother. She's fallen."

"Is she hurt?"

"No, she's drunk."

I started to say something when a slurred voice burst into song from the next room. "When Irish eyes are smiling, sure it's like a morn' in spring...."

The woman glared at the doorway, "Oh, Mother, will you shut up!"

The volume increased dramatically. "...IN THE LILT OF IRISH LAUGHTER, YOU CAN HEAR THE ANGELS SING." I followed the lady into the next room. Lying on the floor at the foot of stairs was a round little woman of about 70, wearing a pair of heavy flannel pajamas. She was smiling broadly and drunk as a skunk. She recoiled in mock terror when she saw me, "Don't shoot, ossifer, I give up." She threw both hands in the air and collapsed with laughter.

Her daughter was not amused. "No one thinks you're funny, Mother." Actually, I thought the old lady was very funny, but I didn't want to upset the daughter by laughing.

"What seems to be the trouble, ma'am?" I asked, squatting beside the still prone woman.

"Well, I'll tell you. I ain't been gettin' laid since my husband died, and I'm pretty horny."

"MOTHER!" her daughter cried, blushing. "Don't use that kind of language."

"How 'bout you, General," the old lady said, fumbling at my leg, "you want to do a good deed?" I removed her hand, trying not to smile but failing. "I think he likes me," she cackled, "Give him to me, Laura; I'll make a man out of him."

Laura was not amused. "Mother, he's here to help me get you back upstairs, not listen to your gutter talk." Her mother, she explained, was an alcoholic who went on frequent binges. She would get so drunk she couldn't walk. Usually her daughter could handle her alone, but tonight she had managed to slide down the stairs undetected, and she was too heavy for Laura to carry. She was also not cooperating much. "I do everything for her," she wailed, "I wait on her hand and foot, and this is how she treats me. Like a dog."

The woman regarded her daughter owlishly, "Arf, arf."

"That's not funny, Mother."

It was time to take charge here. "Ma'am, let's see if we can get you up."

The woman put her hands in front of her like a dog begging. "Arf-arf, arf-arf," she barked. I managed to lift her to a sitting position. She licked my sleeve and panted, tongue moving rhythmically. It was a very convincing imitation.

"Mother, that's totally disgusting. I wish you could see yourself."

The woman rolled her eyes. "Arrrooooooooooo!" she howled mournfully. I got her under the arms, her daughter took her legs, and we started the long climb up the stairs. The old lady was surprisingly heavy, and it took us some time, with frequent stops, to get to the top. Through it all she kept up the dog act, barking, howling, and panting.

We carried her to the bed, and I was relieved the job was done. "Well," I said, breathing heavily, "she should be all right now."

"Arf, arf," she barked, and turned suddenly, biting at one arm, attacking imaginary fleas. It was too much, and I burst out laughing. She patted the mattress and began begging again, panting and leering at me.

"All right, Mother, you've had your fun!" Laura shouted. "You've made a total fool out of yourself, now go to sleep." She attempted to pull the covers up.

"Rrrrrrowf," the old lady snarled, snapping at her hand. Laura barely snatched it out of the way in time.

It was time for me to go. "I think I'll be on my way."

Laura turned, "Thank you so much for your help. I could not have managed by myself."

"Ooooooooooooooooooo," her mother howled, expressing her

regret. I walked down the stairs, listening to Laura shouting at her mother, the sounds of barking and snarling following me out the door.

56

The Best Laid Plans

We just called him "Shorty," and he was, pure and simple, a hustler. As long as I had known him, almost 20 years, he was always working some sort of scheme, often on the wrong side of the law, so our paths crossed frequently. The fact that I had to deal with him professionally didn't bother him in the slightest. Like a lot of crooks, he had his own twisted sense of ethics. "Hey, it's just business, Don," he told me one time when I arrested him on a warrant for receiving stolen property. "You're just doing your job. I understand that."

The state attorney later dropped this charge, as they did with most of Shorty's cases, because the formerly rock-solid witnesses developed sudden memory lapses. While he was as slippery as they came, eventually his hustling caught up with him, and the IRS got him for evading taxes on several hundred thousand dollars. He's in prison now, but I'm sure he'll be out soon, hustling again.

This was not the only time he had some bad luck. I remember the "Great Taxicab Ripoff" scam that didn't end up exactly as planned. It seems Shorty had a friend who drove a cab. They were sitting around one afternoon, discussing the huge settlements awarded to people by insurance companies simply to avoid the cost and publicity of a trial. In the midst of this discussion, Shorty

218

came up with one of his brilliant ideas. He and his buddy would fake a wreck.

The plan was simplicity itself. Shorty would be riding in the cab, driven by his buddy, which would proceed to run a stop sign and crash into an old clunker driven by another crony. The collision would leave Shorty writhing on the ground, screaming about whiplash, the cabdriver clearly at fault. Shorty would graciously agree to allow the insurance company to settle out of court for $50,000 and divide the spoils with his friends. The one drawback was that the cabdriver would be instantly fired, but they figured $20,000 or so would more than comfort him for the loss of his job.

The big day arrived, and after an extended drinking session to bolster their courage, the two drivers positioned their vehicles, Shorty in the back seat of the cab. For obvious reasons, they had not had a dress rehearsal and, as a result, were not prepared for the split-second timing required for a broadside collision. The first try was almost a clean miss, although the cab did catch the rear bumper of the other car, spinning it around and knocking out the left headlight on the cab.

However, the damage was so slight they knew they could never get away with claiming serious injury. They decided to increase the speed on both vehicles. The next attempt was considerably more successful. Both cars were doing almost 40 when they hit, and the wreck was spectacular. Although neither driver was injured, Shorty was thrown out of the cab and was pretty banged up. He broke his collar bone, dislocated his shoulder, cracked four ribs, took most of the hide off one leg, and suffered a concussion when he hit the pavement.

The cops arrived, promptly arrested both drivers for DUI and called an ambulance for the injured mastermind. Shorty spent three weeks in the hospital and was more than a year recovering from his injuries. The insurance company paid his hospital bills but declined to come up with the expected 50 grand. When Shorty vowed to sue, they told him to have at it. Of course, he couldn't take the chance of having his shaky companions grilled by skilled attorneys on the witness stand, so he eventually gave up the idea.

We were reminiscing about the abortive taxicab ripoff one afternoon, and Shorty said, "You know where I went wrong?"

I assured him I did not.

"I should have worn my seat belt so I wouldn't have been thrown out of the cab." He sighed, "It's just not safe to be in a wreck without one."

57

It All Depends

I was enjoying the cocktail party. The annual bash of a local advertising agency, it was really done right. Elaborate hors d'oeuvres, ice sculptures, open bar, and flamboyant decorations. I had a mouthful of Swedish meatballs when I suddenly found myself involved in a conversation with a moderately inebriated, overweight insurance salesman I knew only slightly.

He walked up behind me, giving me a friendly slap on the back, causing my wine cooler to slosh on my hand. "So, Don. How ya doing?"

I gulped down the meatballs and shook the wine off my hand. "Oh, fine...uh, great party, huh?" I couldn't remember his name.

"Yeah, great party." He took a healthy swallow from his drink. "You catching a lot of crooks?"

"I try to catch my share," I said, impaling a boiled shrimp with a long toothpick. "I don't lack for things to do, if that's what you mean." What the hell was his name? "How's the insurance business?"

"It could be better." He drained the glass. "Let me ask you something."

"Shoot."

He stared at me in silence for a moment, then grinned, slowly raised a hand, index finger pointing at me, thumb extended. "Bang-bang." He chuckled, "Get it? You said shoot, so I did."

"Yeah, I get it."

"Bang-bang," he said again.

"Right, very funny," I forced a smile. "You wanted to ask me something?"

"Huh?" He lowered his hand, thinking. "Oh, yeah. Can I ask you something, man-to-man?"

I speared another shrimp. "Sure, go ahead."

"Man-to-man."

He was really getting on my nerves. "I think that's the only choice we have," I said, "unless there's something I don't know about you."

He did the staring bit again, slowly digesting my comment, the seconds ticking away. Finally, the smile. "You sombitch," he laughed, "that's good." He punched me on the arm, but I was ready this time and didn't spill a drop. "You're funny, you know that?"

"Thanks."

"Seriously," he said, "I want to ask you something."

I waited.

"I want to ask you about speeding."

"What about it?"

"Well, I'm on the road a lot, and sometimes them state troopers and me disagree." He pretended to be writing. "You know what I mean?"

"You get a ticket."

"Right. And that's the question."

"What's the question?"

"About the speeding," he said.

I sighed. Talking to drunks was like talking to someone who doesn't really understand English. "What about the speeding?"

"You know." He was starting to get a little irritated. "You're a cop. How fast can I go?"

I had an idea where he was headed with this non-conversation.

"Well, that depends on the speed limit."

"Naw, I don't mean that," he said chuckling. He draped a beefy arm across my shoulder, "I mean, how fast can I go? Come on, Don, man-to-man."

If he said "man-to-man" one more time, I was going to stab him with my toothpick. But I knew what he meant. Like many people, he believed cops allowed drivers to exceed the speed limit by a certain margin before we'd issue a ticket, and if he could just find out what this magic number was, he would never get a speeding ticket again.

Well, there is no magic number, of course. Theoretically you can get a ticket for being one mile over the speed limit, but no one is going to get a ticket for that. For that matter, you're reasonably safe at two, three, or four over.

But, when you exceed the speed limit by five miles an hour, the probability of getting a ticket begins to increase. When you get to ten miles over, you're definitely pushing your luck, because that's something of a psychological barrier to us. Break it, and you might get ticketed.

Of course, the farther above the speed limit, the greater your chances of getting a ticket, but a lot of it depends on your attitude. An abusive, belligerent driver may well get a ticket at six over, while a driver who is apologetic and courteous may slide, even if he's 20 over. Cops are human, too, and if we are having a bad day, we may be more sensitive to loudmouths.

Personally, I was always a soft touch when it came to writing tickets. If a driver had a really heart-rending excuse, one that would bring tears to my eyes, I frequently let him or her off with just a warning.

So, a lot of factors can affect your chances of getting a ticket, but the major factor is, of course, how fast you were going. Which brings us back to the magic number which held such a fascination for my drunken friend. "So you want to know how far above the speed limit you can drive without getting a ticket?"

"Yeah."

"Well, this is not something I would normally talk about, so you have to promise to keep it to yourself, okay?"

He nodded vigorously, "You got my word."

I put my hand on his shoulder, "Man-to-man?"

"Man-to-man, I swear it."

"All right." I looked around carefully to make sure no one could overhear us, then pulled him closer. "Actually, there is a way to avoid speeding tickets," I said quietly, "and if you use the method, I absolutely guarantee that you will never get another ticket again. Do you want to hear it?"

"Hell, yes!" He whispered.

"Like I said, we don't normally tell civilians, but you look like a guy I can trust. You're not going to tell anyone, are you?"

"Not a soul. This is strictly man-to-man, Don." He put his hand on his chest. "You can count on me."

"Okay. Here it is." I leaned close to his ear and whispered, "Don't speed."

"Huh?" He was confused.

"If the speed limit is 55, then drive 55. If it says 35, then do 35." I straightened up. "It works every time."

He stared at me. "That's it?"

I nodded, "Never fails."

His mouth was moving, but no sounds were coming out. He frowned, concentrating mightily, trying to make sense of what I had told him. Suddenly, it penetrated his alcohol-soaked brain cells. "You sombitch," he chortled. "That's pretty good. Boy, you really had me going there for a minute." He shook his head. "You're funny, you know that?"

"So you said."

"No, I mean it," he said. "You're a funny sombitch."

"Thanks." I never did remember his name.

58

Cocaine Blues - Part 1

I was sitting by myself in the coffee shop, working on a report, when I became aware someone was standing beside me. I looked up and saw a man with close-cropped grey hair, probably around 60. "Can I talk to you a minute?" he asked.

"Sure." I pointed to the vacant seat. "Sit down."

"Thanks." He slid into the booth. "My name's George Zimmer." We shook hands. He was wearing clean but faded work clothes and heavy shoes. From the coarse feel of his hand and his lined face, I had him pegged as someone who worked outside, perhaps as a mechanic. He ordered a cup of coffee and, when the waitress left, leaned across the table. "I hope you're the one who can help me," he said quietly, "everyone else just gives me the runaround."

"Well, I'll do what I can, Mr. Zimmer. What's the problem?"

His eyes darted nervously. "Do you think anyone can overhear us?"

No one was close. "I don't think so."

"Good." he lowered his voice still more, and I had to strain to catch the words. "I've invented a machine that can find oil in the ground."

"Oil?" I was puzzled. "What has that got to do with me?"

"I'm getting to that." He looked around again. "My machine

finds oil but, you know how the oil market is right now, don't you?"

"I've heard it's pretty bad."

He nodded vigorously, "It's plumb awful, so I can't sell the rights to my invention. No one wants it."

I still didn't get it. "So why are you coming to see me?"

"Cocaine," he whispered.

"I beg your pardon?"

He twisted his hands nervously. "Cocaine," he said again.

"You mean, like the drug?"

"Keep your voice down!" he hissed. The coffee arrived, and again he waited until we were alone. "Yes, I mean, like the drug."

"What has that got to do with your problem?"

For the first time, he smiled. "My machine can find it."

"Find what?"

"Cocaine."

This was getting very strange. "I thought your machine finds oil."

"It does find oil," he said patiently, "but I can't sell it because of the oil glut, so I changed it around some and now it finds cocaine."

"How does it do that?"

"Well," he said, "ain't cocaine an alkaloid?"

I nodded.

"My machine detects minerals, and an alkaloid is a mineral, so it finds it." He smiled again.

I didn't know if this was correct or not, but I wasn't going to argue the point. "How does your machine work?"

The smile disappeared. "You don't think I'm going to tell you the secret, do you?"

"I guess not." This guy was weird. "I know some Zimmers," I said. "Where are you from?"

"I'm from here."

"I mean, where do you live?"

226

He lowered his eyes. "I live at the mental health center, and that's part of the problem."

That was interesting. "What is?"

"They won't let me work on my invention. They think I'm crazy."

"Who does?"

"Them doctors," he said contemptuously.

I had the picture now. "Where is your machine?"

He tapped the side of his head, an appropriate gesture. "I got it all right here."

"So, what do you want from me?"

His eyes glittered. "I want you to get me some cocaine so I can test it out."

I shook my head. "I'm sorry, we don't do that. You'd have to get a court order."

"You mean you won't help me?"

"I'm afraid not," I said. "But I'll tell you what. You build your machine, and I promise we'll test it with some real cocaine."

His eyes narrowed. "I'll just bet you would," he said sarcastically. He stood up. "You're just like all the rest. You want to steal my invention. Well, it won't work!" He turned and strode angrily from the building.

After he left, I called a friend of mine at the mental health center. I told him a Mr. Zimmer wanted to borrow some cocaine. My buddy said the guy had only recently been released from the state mental hospital and still had a long way to go. He thanked me for talking to the man, and I hung up.

I left the restaurant feeling sorry for the guy, but there was a part of me that wondered if he really did have a machine that could find cocaine.

59

Cocaine Blues - Part 2

The dispatcher called my number, and I gave my location. "10-4, 109, contact a Mr. Ezell in the parking lot near the Winn-Dixie store," she said. "He'll be driving a red pickup."

"I'll be there in just a minute. You said this was an assistance call?"

"That's 10-4. He said it was confidential, and he had to talk to a deputy."

I found Mr. Ezell's pickup easily enough. A large, roly-poly man I presumed was Mr. Ezell was leaning against the front fender. He was wearing blue denim coveralls, and a lump of chewing tobacco bulged in one cheek. I pulled up beside him. "Did you call the sheriff's department?"

"Shore did," he said, pointing toward the store. "I used that pay phone to do it."

I smiled, "Well, here I am. What can I do to help you?"

He loosed a brown stream. "Name's Ezell," he said. "You reckon you can hep me?"

"I'll certainly try." I opened my notebook and pulled a pen from my pocket. "What do you need?"

He spit. "I need some of that there cocaine."

I put the pen down. "You need what?"

"Cocaine. Coke. Like them dope dealers sell." He spit. "You

228

know what it is?''

I laughed, ''Yes, sir, I know what it is, but why do you need some?''

He didn't smile. ''So I can hep you fellers stop it.''

''Stop cocaine?''

''Yep.'' He spit again.

I had no idea what Mr. Ezell was talking about. ''Do you want to act as an undercover informant?''

''Nope. I jes' want to show you fellers how to find it.''

''How do you intend to do that?'' I asked.

He spit. ''I got me a machine.''

''What kind of machine?''

''A coke machine.''

This had to be a joke. ''Say that again?''

''A coke machine.'' He spit, and a dribble of brown liquid ran down his chin. ''I invented it. It finds cocaine.'' He wiped the tobacco juice off with his right hand, and I made a mental note not to shake hands with him.

A strong feeling of *deja vu* washed over me. ''What do you want the cocaine for?'' As if I didn't know.

''I need it to test my machine out.'' He smiled slightly. '''Course I already know it works.''

''You do?''

''Oh, sure.'' He spit. ''You ever heered tell of a dowsin' rod?''

I nodded. ''It's a forked stick or something that finds water.''

''Right. Well, my machine works sorta like that. I know it will find cocaine.''

''How do you know?'' I asked.

He spit. ''I just do.''

''Have you built your machine yet?''

''No, not yet. I need the cocaine.''

Of course, he did. ''I'm sorry, Mr. Ezell. We don't give away cocaine, even for something like this.''

His face didn't change expression. ''Then you're missin' the boat. This could really hep' you fellers.''

229

"Have you made any plans of the machine?"

He shook his head. "Ain't got no plans. This kind of machine can't be wrote down." He spit. "I jes' know how it's supposed to look when it's done."

I nodded. "Okay. Here's what I'll do. You build the machine, bring it to the sheriff's department, and I personally guarantee we'll get some cocaine for a test."

He stared at me for a few moments, his jaw working the tobacco. "It may take a while."

"You take all the time you need." I started my car. "I'll be waiting to hear from you."

He got in the truck. "I'll call you," he said and spit. We didn't shake hands.

60

Cocaine Blues - Part 3

The wedding reception was nice, and I certainly hoped this marriage would work out better than my buddy's previous attempt. We were all quite surprised when he announced his engagement to a sweet Southern Baptist girl who didn't drink or smoke. A hard-drinking skirt chaser, Danny had certainly cleaned up his act since he met Mary Beth.

Holding the reception in the fellowship hall of the church meant it was a non-alcohol event, quite a change from the booze-soaked near-riot of his first wedding. I remembered when it came time for him to remove the bride's garter to toss to the waiting bachelors. About three sheets to the wind, he attempted to take it off with his teeth. Shrieking and screaming, his new wife tried to get away, and they fell to the floor, his head completely under her long dress. I thought for a minute he was going to consummate the marriage right there.

This reception was considerably more genteel. It was also rather boring, but that didn't seem so bad. Maybe I was getting old. I finished my fruit punch and walked over to get another cup. A tiny white-haired lady was serving. "Are you with the sheriff's department?" she asked, pouring the punch.

"Yes, I am." I pointed toward the groom. "I'm a friend of Danny's."

She shook her head. "You boys are so brave. I could never do that job."

I laughed. "Oh, it's not that bad. Sometimes it's really boring."

She shivered. "My goodness. With all that dope out there, you take your life in your hands every time you arrest someone."

"It can be dangerous," I agreed, taking a sip of punch. This lady obviously did not want to hear about the monotony of law enforcement.

"All that LSD, marijuana, cocaine, and heroin," she said. "You just don't know what those dope fiends might do."

"That's true."

She leaned closer. "Well, I've got some ideas how you all can get rid of some of that dope."

"You do?"

She nodded. "Yes, I do. I've spent a lot of time thinking about it and....oh, excuse me." Another woman was gesturing from the kitchen. "Would you mind serving the punch for just a moment? I'll be right back."

"I'd be glad to," I said. She hurried into the kitchen. I had a feeling she was going to start telling me about her marvelous machine that could detect cocaine. Or maybe this time it would be marijuana or heroin, maybe even LSD. Where did these people come from?

She was back in a moment, looking serious. "Can I tell you something?"

I sighed. "Sure, go ahead."

She looked around to be sure we were alone, then leaned close and whispered, "My coke machine doesn't work."

Why was I not surprised? These loonies must all come from the same bin. Oh, well, it certainly wouldn't do any harm to listen and would probably make the old lady feel better. "So your coke machine doesn't work," I repeated.

She looked alarmed. "Don't say it so loud. Someone might hear."

232

I smiled. "Let me try and guess what's wrong with it."

"We think it's out of gas," she said sadly.

This was a new one. A gas-operated cocaine machine. What would these wackos think of next? "Are you sure that's what it is?" I said teasingly.

"Well," she said, uncertainly, "it might be something else. I'm not very mechanical."

I almost laughed. "Are you sure you don't just need a little cocaine?"

"Pardon me?"

"Cocaine," I said, "for your machine. Wouldn't that do the trick?"

Her eyes widened. "You mean, like the drug?" she whispered.

This time I did laugh. "Come on, lady, I know what you want. Why don't you just ask for it and stop beating around the bush?"

She started backing up. "I don't know what you're talking about."

"Your cocaine machine," I said condescendingly, "Don't you want the sheriff's department to supply you with a few ounces of the white stuff to test your machine?"

"Cocaine?" She was still backing up. "I was talking about the Coca-Cola machine in the kitchen. It's not working. I think the tank's empty." She turned and fled out of the room.

I left quickly. I figured I could always see the pictures later.

233

61

First Time on TV

The conversation with the sheriff's secretary had been brief: "If you have some free time on Tuesday or Wednesday, the sheriff would like to talk with you."

A chill ran through me. Talking with the boss always made me nervous. "Did he say what it was about?"

"No," she said, "he just asked me to call and give you this message."

I hung up, pondering the call. If I was really in trouble, Carolyn would not have been so casual. In that case the "request" to meet with the sheriff would have come through my lieutenant, and we both would have attended. I was all too familiar with that scenario, having had to defend myself against complaints from outraged citizens on more than a few occasions. But sometimes the sheriff asked me to give a speech for him at a civic club or church when he had a scheduling conflict.

Tuesday morning I was sitting in his office, nervously waiting for him to tell me what was on his mind. He riffled through his phone messages, finally selecting one. "Don, this woman called me last week," he said, handing me the paper." She wants me to come on her television show and talk about consumer fraud." He chuckled, "I don't know anything about consumer fraud but I told her I had just the man for her, a real expert." He pointed at me. "You."

I stared at him. "Sheriff, I don't know anything about consumer fraud either."

"But you will. By the time the show comes around, you're going to be an expert." He stood up, "Call the lady and confirm you'll be on her show." We shook hands, and I left.

The woman worked for the Chamber of Commerce and had a weekly five-minute show about business which aired on Sunday afternoons. It was taped on Tuesday, which meant I had a week to prepare. She was pleased I would be on the show and asked me to come in uniform. "I've never been on television before," I told her.

"Oh, that's all right. You'll do fine," she said. "It's really quite easy, once you get used to the lights."

I was puzzled when she asked me to bring a list of ten questions for her to ask about consumer fraud. "You want me to bring you questions?"

She laughed, "Of course, I don't know anything about consumer fraud; you're the expert."

"Oh, yeah, sure. No problem. Do you want me to mail them to you?"

"No, just bring them with you to the station." She hung up.

That seemed strange as well. How was she going to research the topic sufficiently to know what she was talking about if I supplied the questions? Did she think her viewers would believe the questions she was asking came from her own store of knowledge?

She did indeed, and she was right. In my innocence, I naturally assumed that TV talk show hosts knew all about the subjects discussed on their shows. Not only is this rarely the case, but it is truly astounding how a glib host with only the skimpiest of preparation, can seem knowledgeable about the topic under discussion.

I spent the week researching consumer fraud, talking to the state attorney's office, calling agencies at the state capitol, and reading court decisions.

I thought it would be a simple task to come up with ten questions. It was not. I was still sweating out the last question on Tuesday morning and finally decided to go with, "Give us a brief summary of applicable Supreme Court decisions as they relate to consumer fraud." I had an armload of documents to back up all my statements.

The taping was set for two in the afternoon at WEAR TV, the local ABC affiliate, and I arrived a half-hour early. The receptionist told me to have a seat, so I put my documents on a low table and sat on the vinyl-covered couch in the lobby. I wasn't too comfortable because my polyester uniform pants kept sliding on the smooth vinyl, and soon I was almost prone. I must have hauled myself erect half a dozen times before I discovered I could lean on the handle of my gun, forcing the leather holster into the vinyl, and keep myself from sliding.

Ten minutes before the scheduled taping, the hostess arrived, slightly out of breath. I stood up. "Oh, Deputy Parker," she gushed, taking my hand, "it's so nice to meet you. Thank you so much for agreeing to come on the show."

"Well, actually, it was the Sheriff's idea."

She laughed, "Yes, I'm sure it was, but I know you'll do wonderfully well. Shall we sit and talk a moment?" We sat.

I was careful to lean on my gun to hold myself on the couch. "I've brought some material with me for reference," I said, indicating the 15 pounds of law books, magazines and notes.

Her eyes widened slightly. "My goodness, we certainly can't take all this on the set; there's no room."

A little flash of nervousness shot through me. "Well, I was going to use it in case you asked me something I couldn't answer," I said.

"I'm not going to ask you anything but the questions you prepared. You did bring them?"

"Oh, sure," I said, rummaging through the pile. I extracted the three closely spaced typewritten pages and handed them to her.

236

"Good gracious, I only asked for ten questions."

"There are only ten."

She scanned the first page. "Let's see..... discuss the legislative intent behind the act which led to the establishment of the Federal Trade Commission and summarize our own state laws which directly or indirectly protect consumers." She looked slightly alarmed. "Are all the questions that long?"

My nervousness was increasing steadily. "Actually, that's one of the shorter ones. You see, I thought it was important to give your viewers a broad view of the history of the pertinent legislation; then we could go into some of the specifics regarding the...."

"We only have five minutes, Deputy Parker."

"I know we only have five minutes, but I thought I should be prepared..."

"Actually, it's less than five minutes because I have to spend 15 seconds doing the open, about a minute reading a list of upcoming events, 15 seconds doing your introduction and 15 seconds to close. You'll only be on the air for a little over three minutes."

Sweat was beading on my upper lip. "Maybe I can..."

"FOUR MINUTES TO TAPING," a voice bellowed from behind me, making me jump. I turned as a bearded young man retreated through the door. My heart was beginning to race.

She was busily making notes on the back of my carefully prepared questions. "Well, don't worry. I'm sure we'll do just fine." The door opened again and the nightly weatherman along with the sports guy, came in and stopped at the receptionist's desk. I watched them as they chatted, envying their poise and easy manner. Perfectly groomed, they looked exactly like they did on television.

I leaned forward slightly, and as I did, my holster slid across the vinyl couch, making a noise like a rhinoceros breaking wind. All conversation ceased as every head snapped toward me. I was instantly and totally mortified. Blushing furiously, I could think of nothing to say and finally mumbled, ''Excuse me.''

''Well,'' said the hostess brightly, ''let's go into the studio, shall we?''

I only wanted to die, but I stumbled along after her, feeling like I was headed for my own execution. The studio was a cavernous room that looked like an unfinished construction project. Exposed girders in the ceiling were festooned with lights and wires, the floor had cables running in all directions, and two large cameras were being pushed around by men wearing headsets. There were several TV monitors positioned around the studio, currently showing a test pattern.

The only order in the middle of all this hi-tech chaos was the homey little set, decorated with several artificial plants, two chairs, a small table, and a beige carpet.

I saw the chairs were covered with the same vinyl as the couch in the lobby and I lowered myself gingerly, terrified my holster would sound off during the show. The studio lights were so bright that, looking out from the set, I could only see vague shadows moving around. I found myself squinting against the glare. The lights were also hot. Very hot. Drops of sweat were beginning to crawl down my back. I tried to move out of the direct glare and discovered the chair rocked and also swiveled from side to side.

I flinched as two hands came over my shoulders. A young guy with a ponytail and an earring was standing behind me holding a clip-on microphone. ''Take it easy, Sheriff'' he laughed. ''I'm just getting you wired for sound.''

''Oh, sure, no problem,'' I said weakly as he clipped the microphone to my tie. Sweat drops the size of marbles were running down my neck.

''Deputy Parker?'' I turned to the hostess. She pointed toward the monitor in front of us. ''Don't look at the monitor once we go on the air. It's very distracting to the viewers.'' I nodded and tried not to look at what I had been ignoring. Now that I was aware of the monitor, it seemed almost irresistible. I snuck a quick glance. Still the same test pattern.

"Listen, what happens if I...."

"STAND BY TO ROLL TAPE," someone shouted. I froze. The glowing eye of the monitor was drawing me like a magnet.

"FIVE-FOUR-THREE..." the voice intoned. Desperately, I tore my eyes from the monitor and looked at the hostess. She was staring at one of the cameras, a fixed smile on her face.

An arm flashed down, finger pointing at her. "Good afternoon," she said cheerfully, "and welcome to our show. Today we have a very special guest whom we are going to meet in just a moment, but first, let's hear what's going on this week at your chamber of commerce." She began to read the upcoming events off a sheet of paper.

Through all of this, I had been immobile, an absolute statue, too frightened even to blink. Rivers of sweat continued to pour off me and I was sure I must look like someone who had been wet down with a hose. "Don't look at the monitor!" I screamed silently to myself. But I couldn't help it. I took another quick glimpse and was tremendously relieved to see the screen was filled with a tight shot of the hostess, still reading her announcements. I relaxed slightly, rocking the chair a bit. It seemed to help.

"....and to tell us more about this important subject, I am pleased to introduce Deputy Sheriff Don Parker. Welcome, Deputy Parker."

I jumped a little, and the chair rocked. "Thanks very much, I'm glad to be here." My voice sounded about two octaves higher than normal. I had to relax.

"Tell me, Deputy Parker," she said, glancing down at her notes, "what recourse does a consumer have if they feel they have been defrauded by a merchant?"

I stared at her, chill wings of panic beginning to flutter through my chest. This was not one of the questions I had written. "Uh...well, let's see;" I said, stalling, "what do you mean by 'defrauded'?"

"I mean, if someone feels they have been cheated, perhaps with a bait-and-switch ad."

What the hell was a "Bait-and-switch ad"? Sweat was dripping off my nose. "Yes, well....that depends on the circumstances." I gulped, "Particularly if the law has been violated."

She was getting nowhere fast with this question. "Moving to another subject," she said hurriedly, "how serious is the problem of consumer fraud in our area?"

"In our area?" She nodded. "Oh, gee, well, I would say, here in our area, we do have some consumer fraud but not as much as in other areas."

"And what types of consumer fraud are the most common?"

This was a nightmare without end. "Gosh, that's difficult to be really specific about. Ah...let's see...probably uh, bait-and-switch, I guess." I was breathing hard.

She gave up. "Deputy Parker, do you have anything else you want to say before we close?"

"Uh....well....I suppose....I, uh, no. No, I don't."

Caught by surprise, she had to ad-lib for a few minutes to fill the remaining time, and finally, the show limped to an end. Mercifully, the lights flicked off, and the crew began bustling around, removing our microphones, breaking the set down, moving the cameras. The hostess was all smiles. "Deputy Parker, thanks so much for coming on the show; you did a fabulous job."

"Yeah, great job, Sheriff," the kid with the pony tail said mechanically as he unhooked the microphone. I stumbled out of the studio, knowing they were both lying.

When I saw the show the following Sunday, it was an exquisitely painful experience. The squinting, sweating, stammering creature I saw slouched in the constantly rocking chair looked and sounded like some sort of brain-damaged accident victim. I wanted to cry.

But some good did come from it. It made me realize how intimidating television can be, but I was determined to improve. Six years after that first catastrophic appearance, I would host my own hour-long weekly talk show on a cable station. For four years, "The Cop Show" would provide information and education about the law enforcement profession to the citizens of our county.

It was a live show, which meant we had our unexpected surprises and occasional problems, but in all the years I did that show, I never once had a guest that was as bad as I was during my first time on television.

62

At Least That's Perfectly Clear

All cops spend a great deal of time in court, and many of us become quite accomplished at testifying. The ability to give clear, concise, easily understood testimony is a quality that separates the true veteran from the inexperienced rookie.

The following testimony is taken, word for word, from an actual murder case. Notice how I respond to the defense attorney's question, every word carefully selected for maximum impact.

DEFENSE ATTORNEY: "Was it dark at that time of day, or was it daylight?"

PARKER: "It was light. It was beginning to get dark, I believe. I don't recall exactly. I believe it was either...it was either dark by then, or it was just about dark. It was, you know, late in the evening. This was in January, so...."

DEFENSE ATTORNEY: "No further questions."

63

Guilty As Charged

I have a confession to make. I hope this will not be too shocking a revelation, but I am not a day person. I don't leap out of bed each morning to greet the rising sun with a song on my lips and joy in my heart. For most of my life, I have left my bed barely conscious, staggering to the bathroom, not really waking up until five minutes into my shower. I am used to how I feel in the morning, and if that feeling occurred at any other time of the day, I would not hesitate to call an ambulance.

Needless to say, this reluctance to rise, much less shine, has caused me occasional problems, but I've generally gotten by. I survived two years of active duty in the Navy without once being placed on report for being late and during my years working a day shift as a deputy sheriff, I always managed to get myself to work. To be sure, I did suffer occasional lapses, but my boyish charm and the good nature of my supervisors usually let me slide through.

Until Lieutenant Odis Davis took over the shift.

A Marine Corps veteran, he was spit-and-polish all the way and a real stickler for the rules. Of course, we all knew his reputation, and I made an extra effort to get to work on time. I did well for several weeks, but then, the inevitable happened. I let myself go back to sleep after the alarm went off, and I was

20 minutes late. Lieutenant Davis discussed at length and in depth with me the importance of being on time. His tone was cordial but firm.

Two weeks later, I was late again. We had another discussion, but this time his tone was not so cordial. I apologized effusively and swore a solemn blood oath I would do better. He accepted the apology, and again explained my responsibility as a subordinate and his responsibility as a supervisor should I continue to be late.

A week later, it happened once more. This time the discussion was short and to the point: if I was ever late again, I should, to use his words: "Dig a hole and crawl in."

Badly rattled by the memory of his chill tone and expressionless eyes, I decided elaborate precautions were in order. As it happened, my wife was out of town, so I figured I could make a commotion without bothering anyone. That night I set my clock radio, I put an alarm clock in the bathroom, and I even set the timer on the stove. I was determined to get up.

The next morning all the alarm clocks functioned perfectly. I lurched from room to room, and by the time I got them turned off, I was well and truly awake. I was elated to see it was only 5:30 A.M. I didn't have to be at work until 6:45. The sheriff's department was only ten minutes away, so I had plenty of time. On the way out the door, I scooped up the morning paper, tossed it in the front seat, and at the first stop light, glanced at the headlines. A small box, outlined in red, caught my attention. "Spring Forward," it read, "Daylight Savings Time is Here Again." My heart stopped. It couldn't be.

I looked at the clock on a nearby bank and felt the blood drain from my face. It was 7:20. Daylight savings time. Spring forward, fall back. I had not changed my clocks. I was a dead man.

When I got to the muster room, Lieutenant Davis was still there, working on reports. He didn't look up as I entered, signed the attendance sheet, and sat beside his desk to await my execution. He finally raised his head, and I gave him my lame excuse about forgetting to set my clocks, my wife being out of town, thinking

I was arising early, etc. He continued to stare at me coldly for a long time before he finally spoke. "You know, Parker," he said, "I believe you. No one else would even dare try that one on me."

I assured him every word was god's honest truth.

"Normally, I would simply suspend you," he said. My heart sank. "But I'm not going to do that." He thought for a while. "Do you know what your punishment is?"

I said I did not.

"You are required to write 'I Will Not Be Late For Work' ten times on the chalkboard in the muster room. Sign it and leave it there for a week. Do you understand?"

I nodded, scarcely believing my ears.

He turned back to his paperwork. "Well, get on with it."

And that is how, at the age of 35, I came to write "I Will Not Be Late For Work," ten times on the chalkboard in the muster room of the sheriff's department. Since all the shifts used the same muster room, my handiwork was seen by the entire patrol division, which was exactly what Lieutenant Davis had in mind.

Naturally, I got to see the reactions, since I was in the muster room for most of that week. Deputies would come trooping in, laughing and talking, spot my chalk-written words, and grow quiet. Some of the slower ones would stand for long minutes, lips moving silently, heads turning slowly back and forth, reading the entire text. When they finally finished, they'd turn to me, obviously puzzled. "What the hell is that?" they'd ask.

Without smiling, I'd explain it was punishment for being late to work.

My serious demeanor and the strange penalty were too much for many of them. They'd shake their heads, take their seats, and mutter that the lieutenant was certainly weird.

Unusual though the punishment might have been, it did have the desired effect. For the rest of my time in the patrol division, I was never late again.

64

A Different Frame of Reference

I saw the car first. Nose pointed skyward at a forty-five degree angle, it was definitely going to take a wrecker to get it out of the ditch. Then I saw the fight. Two black guys were grappling beside the car. I spun the wheel of my cruiser and roared down the street, sliding to a stop beside them.

They hadn't really gotten to serious punching yet. "All right, calm down, calm down," I shouted, trying to get them separated. The bigger one let go reluctantly, and there was a good deal of snorting and cursing, but no more actual violence.

The shorter of the two, and he was by no means small, was certainly more agreeable about ending the fight than his companion. "Hey," he gasped, breathing hard, "I said I was sorry, man."

"I'll show you sorry," the big guy said, lunging at him. I put my shoulder into him, deflecting the charge. He turned, ready to give it another try. "That's enough," I said. He tensed, then thought better of it and relaxed.

It turned out the big guy had loaned his friend the car, which he had promptly backed into the ditch. Although there was no real damage, it was going to be expensive to hire a wrecker to get it out. The smaller one kept protesting that he would pay. "Where you gonna get any money, man?" the big guy said scathingly. "You ain't got nothing!"

I collected driver's licenses and ran warrant checks on everyone, but there was nothing outstanding. I decided the best thing to do was to keep them separated, so I told the smaller one to get in my car and I would drive him home.

We rode quietly for a few minutes, then he said, "Hell, I didn't mean to put the car in the ditch. I can drive."

"I'm sure you can."

"I just didn't see the ditch." He brooded for a while. "The man is my friend. He shouldn't get so mad."

"He was just a little excited, he'll be all right when he calms down."

He nodded, then said, "I owned a car once."

I was puzzled. What did he mean, "owned a car"? I had owned at least a half a dozen cars at that point in my life, and he was probably ten years older than me. "When did you own the car?" I asked.

He thought a moment. "About three years ago. I drove it all the time. The engine blew up, and I ain't been able to get it fixed. I still got it, though."

I was beginning to understand. "Is that the only car you've owned?"

"Yeah, but I might get another one."

I didn't say anything, but I was truly astonished. It was a type of culture shock I had never experienced before. While I certainly did not come from a wealthy family, we always had a car and I had bought my first one at the age of 19. Now I was face-to-face with the realization that this man, and probably many others like him, didn't even own a car. It was mind-boggling. How could he not own a car? How did he get around? How did he get to work? What happened if a family member got sick? How did he buy groceries?

I dropped him off at his house, and saw his "car", a faded, rusting clunker, sitting forlornly in the back yard, up on blocks, all four wheels off. He thanked me for the ride and for not arresting them, and I drove off, disturbed by this grim bit of reality that had penetrated the shell of my insulated, middle-class, white world.

65

A Little Bit Of Patience

Trained hostage negotiators and SWAT teams are a relatively recent development at most law enforcement agencies, mine included. In the old days, individual shift commanders had to handle such problems on their own, and some were better at it than others.

I remember a disturbance involving a homicidally-minded husband, who more or less caught his wife in a motel room with another man. He had spotted his wife's car parked at the motel but didn't know what room she was in. Unsuccessful in locating her, he stormed into the office, demanding the clerk tell him where she was. Not having the faintest idea what this maniac was yelling about, the clerk promptly called the sheriff's department. The enraged husband, displeased at this lack of cooperation, vented his frustration by throwing a typewriter at the now-terrified clerk.

I was not far away when the call came in and arrived at the motel to find the man gone and the typewriter in pieces on the floor. I got a good description of the guy and his vehicle, a Volkswagen van, and had the dispatcher broadcast it on all channels. Five minutes later, one of the investigators stopped the VW a few miles up the road. I was headed his way, and as I topped an overpass, I saw the vehicle make a U turn and head directly at the investigator, who jumped out of the way. The van turned on a side road, and I was right behind him, siren screaming, blue lights flashing. Then ensued what I would call a low-speed chase. The underpowered Volkswagen certainly wasn't going to outrun my powerful cruiser car, but he wouldn't stop, either. I was right on his bumper as we proceeded down the road at 45 miles per hour.

The man finally made a quick turn into a driveway, bailed out of the VW, and took off running. By the time I got stopped and out of my car, he had quite a jump on me. "Halt!" I bellowed, drawing my gun. The guy didn't slow. "I SAID 'STOP'!" I shouted. He jumped a fence. I aimed up in the air and pulled the trigger.

At the shot, the man seemed to leap off the ground as he accelerated, disappearing into the darkness. I followed as quickly as I could and finally caught a glimpse of him as he sprinted across a large field, ran inside a large mobile home, and slammed the door.

Now what?

My boss, Lieutenant Pete Morgan, and several other deputies arrived within minutes, and we surrounded the place. I was still pretty excited over the chase and was all for lobbing in the tear gas. Morgan listened to my disjointed account of what had occurred and recommended we wait for awhile.

"I say let's go in and get him out of there, Lieutenant."

He looked at me. "What happens if he has a rifle? You want to be the first one to charge?" The trailer was in the middle of the field, and there were 50 yards of open ground on every side.

I felt my enthusiasm ebb. "But we have to do something."

He nodded. "Yeah. We'll wait."

I was disappointed. This was definitely not the way Dirty Harry would have handled it. Still, the boss had a point. I glanced at the trailer and felt a chill along the back of my neck. The lights inside were going out one by one. I suddenly became aware that I was perfectly silhouetted by the street lights. I slipped behind a telephone pole, but it wasn't big enough. My nose stuck out one side and the back of my lap on the other. This wouldn't do at all. I took a chance and ran to a large tree. It was considerably more substantial and gave me good cover. I felt a lot safer.

A dispatcher got the guy on the phone and, for the next hour or so, negotiated with him, assuring the man no one would hurt him if he surrendered peacefully. He was having no part of this argument, convinced, he said, that if he came out, he would be shot.

"Headquarters, tell him no one is going to shoot him if he surrenders," the lieutenant said over the radio.

There was silence as the dispatcher relayed this information. "Lieutenant, he says he doesn't believe you. Someone has already shot at him."

I could hear the irritation in his voice as he said, "I've been here the whole time, and no one has.....stand by a minute. 109?"

I keyed my portable radio, feeling butterflies flapping in my belly. "Go ahead, Lieutenant."

"Switch over to channel 4." I turned the selector knob to the unused frequency. "You there, 109?"

"Uh, 10-4 Lieutenant."

"Did you take a shot at that guy?"

"Not me, boss." I was frantically reloading my gun and rubbing the powder stains off the frame. "He must be drunk."

Warning shots are strictly prohibited and can result in an automatic suspension, but no one else from the department had seen me pull the trigger, so I was safe. For now. I buried the empty shell casing beside the tree.

I stayed hidden as the negotiations continued, peeking out from time to time. Finally, the man agreed to give himself up if we promised not to shoot him. He came out of the trailer with his hands raised, and I cuffed him and placed him in the back of my cruiser.

No one had gotten hurt and I was glad the incident had ended quietly. Thinking it over afterwards, I had to admit, reluctantly, that maybe Lieutenant Morgan knew what he was doing, after all.

66

Reward!

A thin, nervous woman with exceptionally bad teeth opened the door to the motel room. "What do you want?"

"We're with the sheriff's department," I said, as if she couldn't see the three uniformed deputies standing outside. "We're looking for an escaped prisoner, and we want permission to search your room."

She licked her lips. "There's no one in here but me and my three kids."

"We'd like to look, anyway."

"Well...okay." She opened the door.

In this case, the term "escaped" was really a misnomer, because the guy we were after was not someone who had fled from a work gang or sawed his way out of a jail cell. The prisoner in question had simply walked away from the community correctional center, a halfway house where inmates in the state prison system were prepared for life outside the bars. Like the other residents, he worked a job out in the community during the day and spent his nights in the center. But he wasn't doing well. He had been disciplined for coming back to the center with the odor of alcohol on his breath, and one afternoon he didn't come back at all.

In due course, local law enforcement agencies were notified

of his ''escape'' and furnished with a description. Several days went by, and we began to pick up bits and pieces of information about the guy. He was believed to be in the company of his girlfriend, and they had been seen at a few of the local bars. This morning we got a tip he was at this motel, one of those seedy places which rent more rooms by the hour than by the night.

We stepped inside and were confronted by three wide-eyed, grimy faced children ranging in age from three to about eight. They were sitting in the middle of the double bed, watching our every move. I gave them a big smile, trying to relieve some of their anxiety. ''Hi, kids.'' No response. So much for my Deputy Friendly act. We started our search, and it didn't take long, since there was only the bathroom and a closet left to check. No escapee.

We questioned the woman about her activities over the past few days, and she gave evasive answers. ''Ma'am,'' I said, ''if we find out that you have been harboring a fugitive, you could very well end up in prison yourself.''

''And you can kiss your babies goodbye,'' one of the other deputies added, playing a little hardball. ''They'll be put in foster homes so fast it'll make your head spin.''

Her eyes widened. ''I don't know what you're talking about. I don't know nothing about no escaped prisoners.'' But, as she continued to proclaim her ignorance, she started pointing toward the bed, as though she wanted us to look under it. Of course, we had considered the bed, but there was only a three-inch clearance from the bottom of the frame to the floor. It didn't seem possible anyone could be under it. Still, it was the only place we hadn't looked.

''All right, everyone off,'' I said. When they were out of the way, we picked up the bed, and lo and behold, there was our man, looking somewhat the worse for wear, having endured the weight of the bed and the occupants for the past ten minutes. Evidently, the box springs were flexible enough to give a little as the bed was lowered, which gave the illusion it was sitting almost flush on the floor. He didn't give us any trouble, and as we were handcuffing him he turned to the woman. "Thanks, Ella. You did what you could."

She kissed him on the cheek. "Well, I tried, Harvey." None of us said anything. No sense in letting him know how it was we just happened to look under the bed.

On our way back to the jail, I had to ask him the question that had really been bugging me. "Why did you leave the correctional center? You only had three weeks to go."

His answer was probably indicative of the thinking that put him in prison in the first place. He shrugged, the cuffs clinking softly. "I just got tired of it."

Since I was assigned the call, I booked the guy and thought no more about it. Three months later I was amazed to receive a check for $25 from the State of Florida, along with a brief note explaining it was a reward for catching the escaped prisoner. It never occurred to me I could get a reward. I thought about splitting it with the two other guys, but I was afraid they would be deeply offended at being offered money for simply doing their jobs. Fortunately, I was not.

It was the only reward I ever earned.

67

The Real Thing

It was a blazing hot summer day, the temperature and humidity both in the high nineties. I was experiencing the heat firsthand because I was presently standing in an intersection, directing traffic beneath a malfunctioning light, my toes slowly parboiling inside my shoes.

When the traffic light died, I had the incredible misfortune to be just three blocks away. I had to give the dispatcher credit. She was careful to ask my location before giving me the call. If I had realized I was going to be spending the next two hours in a puddle of sweat, choking on exhaust fumes, I would have lied like a dog and told her I was just south of Point Barrow, Alaska. Instead I made a serious error; I told the truth.

So here I was, uniform shirt soaked with sweat, jaw aching from being clamped around the whistle, arm muscles screaming in protest from the constant waving. Traffic streamed by, children gawking at me. A city policeman passed, smiling, happy he was not in my place. I thought about shooting his tires out but decided against it. I didn't want to waste the bullets.

As the heat pressed in I became aware of a raging thirst. There were gas stations on three of the corners, but I was afraid to leave my post. Traffic was so heavy it could become dangerously snarled in seconds. The possibility of a serious accident occurring while I was standing on the sidelines, sipping a cold drink was not a pleasant thought.

For what seemed like the one millionth time, I raised my arms and stopped traffic with a long blast on my whistle, the shrill noise a perfect counterpoint to my vicious headache. As the cars came to a stop, I noticed a small boy standing at the curb.

Perhaps eight or nine, he was wearing a Spiderman T-shirt, a pair of blue shorts, and black high-tops. Eyes riveted on me, he was clutching a can of Coca-Cola. No doubt he wanted to get across. Well, I could help him accomplish that. When I was sure it was safe, I motioned to him. He scampered off the curb but stopped in front of me, extending the Coke. "My dad said to give you this," he said.

For a moment, I didn't understand what he meant. My heat-fogged brain was working slower than usual. But then, I got it. He had brought me something cold to drink. I accepted the proffered Coke, the cool drops of moisture beading the sides of the can a foretaste of the blessed relief that waited within.

But I was still a little confused. "Where is your dad?" I asked. The lad turned and pointed toward one of the service stations. A battered pickup, swarming with children of various sizes and genders, was parked at the side of the building near the vending machines. Standing at the front, looking as well-used as his vehicle, was a large-bellied man with several days' growth of beard on his jowly face. He was smiling and gave me a friendly wave. I waved back. I had no idea who he was.

The little delivery boy ran back across the street and climbed into the back of the pickup. A moment later the whole crew drove off in a cloud of oily smoke, the kids waving madly.

I drained the can of Coke right there in the middle of that boiling intersection and resumed my duties, considerably refreshed not only by the drink, but by a simple act of kindness from a stranger.

CAROLDON BOOKS
1075 Farmington Road
Pensacola, Florida 32504

(904) 474-1407